CAPTURE . . .

"Who's there?" she called out with a razor-thin voice.

He moved, quickly and silently loping to the pool, keeping his eyes fixed on her. At the ledge, he put his hand in the water and deliberately stirred it enough to make a soft rippling sound. At once her head jerked in the direction of the noise, and she sank farther into the water. He could sense her shivering. He could smell her fear.

"Who is it?" she called out, louder this time, her breath coming in short bursts.

He was under the water before the echoes faded into the night.

Arthur Combs. Silent shark. Ultimate hunter. . . .

Arthur paused for a moment, savoring the idea of how her wet skin would feel under his fingers. . . . She was holding on to the narrow spillway that ran around the pool and gasping for air.

Biding his time, he watched as she raised one knee to the shelf. The other. Before she could lift herself fully out of the water, he took a single stroke, glided until he was under her, and reached up with both hands. The right one brushed her side and closed tightly over her breast. At the same time his other hand covered her mouth.

"No need to be afraid," he said softly. "My name is Arthur. I'm your biggest fan."

BOOKS BY HAL FRIEDMAN

A Hunting We Will Go

Over the Edge*

Published by HarperCollins Publishers

*coming soon

A HUNTING

WE WILL GO

A HUNTING

WE WILL GO

Hal Friedman

HarperPaperbacks
A Division of HarperCollins*Publishers*

HarperPaperbacks
A Division of HarperCollins*Publishers*
10 East 53rd Street, New York, NY 10022-5299

This is a work of fiction. The characters, incidents, and dialogues are products of the author's imagination and are not to be construed as real. Any resemblance to actual events or persons, living or dead, is entirely coincidental.

ISBN 0-06-109590-7

HarperCollins®, ® , and HarperPaperbacks™ are trademarks of HarperCollins Publishers, Inc.

A hardcover edition of this book was published in 1998 by HarperCollins Publishers.

Cover illustration © 1998 by Alexa Garbarino

First printing: September 1998

Printed in the United States of America

Visit HarperPaperbacks on the World Wide Web at http://www.harpercollins.com

❖ 10 9 8 7 6 5 4 3 2 1

For Sophia, Jesse Lee, and Cory

Great perils have this beauty, that they bring to light the fraternity of strangers.

—Victor Hugo

ACKNOWLEDGMENTS

This work could not have happened without four very smart, very caring people: Irene Markocki, my angel of mercy–cum–mistress of horror; Carolyn Marino, an incredibly empathetic, skillful, and incisive story editor; Arthur Pine, who supported an idea with energy and belief; and J.P., who has always made me better by example.

A HUNTING

WE WILL GO

PROLOGUE

Arthur Combs stirred restlessly in his bed, unsure of whether he'd actually heard the voice or only imagined it in the darkness.

He could never be certain when it would come.

When the call pierced the night again, Arthur's body stiffened.

"Is that you, Bo?" he called softly, respectfully. "Are you here?"

"Yes, Arthur. There's something you have to do."

Hearing Bo's voice again was reassuring. It had been days since they had talked. He had begun to think something was wrong.

"Of course, Bo. Anything you want."

"I want you to visit someone."

Arthur felt a tingle of fear, then a shiver of pleasure.

"Is she very beautiful?"

"Very, very beautiful, Arthur. And very, very wicked."

"What else, Bo? Tell me everything."

"No questions, Arthur. Not this time."

Arthur could hear the subtle rebuke and fell silent.

"You're not afraid, are you, Arthur?"

"No, of course not. Never."

"There's nothing to worry about—as long as you listen carefully. I promise, you won't be disappointed."

Arthur believed Bo. He always believed Bo.

"Who is she?" Arthur asked. "How do I find her?"

"Her name is Anne. I know where she lives."

PART 1

HUNTING IN HOLLYWOOD

ONE

Arthur Combs entered the heavily wooded area at precisely ten o'clock. A proficient predator, he'd chosen a moonless night, the perfect cover. When he was done there would be no evidence of his passing.

After a short walk he arrived at the spot he'd chosen earlier under the tallest trees and put down his small black gym bag. In a few deft moves he stripped off all his clothing. The night air caressed his freshly shaven body, every part tingling in the breeze.

With practiced hands he retrieved a small glass bottle from the gym bag. The vial contained three ounces of undiluted civet, a musklike secretion from cats. The oil, a natural aphrodisiac, masked his scent and signaled the presence of a dangerous predator to any creature nearby.

He applied a thin coat to his skin and massaged it in. The ripe odor infused him with warmth and made him feel eternal. When he was finished he stuffed the vial and clothes into the bag and placed it under a pile of brush. Then he sprang from the ground and became part of the canopy.

As he climbed, Arthur felt a connection to all hunters since the beginning of time. Once in the treetops he savored the seductive, ocean-scented wind and the prickly feel of bark under his bare feet. His senses reeled from the intoxicating perfume of bougainvillea and laurel that rose from the ground. The natural world was always his greatest source of strength. And with each hunt he reveled more in the pleasure and confidence it gave him.

He was stronger now in his thirty-ninth year than he had ever been, even more than when, for two years, he purged his body of chemicals and trained in counter-insurgency with the military. He had learned the drills well and drawn on the training since—perfected it, until he had mastered the science of "zero presence." He had made his body harder since then, until it was as sturdy as bronze, and he was able to stand for hours in the trees—if he had to. This night's station had been selected for its complete view of the walled compound below, including a cabana with glass doors that opened onto a patio and pool.

His instructions from Bo had been precise, and he would execute them to the letter. Bo had not told him why this one had been singled out from the many, or why this time he was not to bring her back for a more unhurried discipline, as he had been instructed before on occasion. But he never questioned Bo—any more than leaves questioned the wind.

Invisible in the tallest bough, Arthur closed his eyes. He felt that he could fly. He was omnipotent. He reveled in the feeling and waited serenely, unmoving.

Still lost in his euphoria, he could nevertheless tell when something in the air changed. He smelled her scent before she stepped out into view on the patio. He raised his head. Inhaled deeply. Anne Marie Warren was alone, as he knew she would be, protected only by the thin beam of a security system which would soon be rendered useless by a single, catlike leap of brilliance. For a long while, he watched her from his high station. His vision was acute in the dark. He studied the way her body moved, every nuance of her motion, as she began to unfasten her robe and move unaware to the edge of the pool to test the water with her toes.

When she let the robe fall from her shoulders, her unexpected nudity sent a warm ripple of pleasure through his loins. He became as hard as granite. He had anticipated a minimal bathing costume, like the abbreviated white halter and small triangle of fabric she wore the last time he had observed her. He remembered how it had become transparent when wet, how the points of her breasts strained to push through.

But nothing had prepared him for the perfection of her completely exposed body. In the muted lights that rimmed the pool, her skin was luminescent. Shining up on her from below, the lights accentuated the sturdiness of her breasts, which stood high and away from her torso, the stiff dark nipples crowning their aureoles. Something pretty for Bo, he thought.

As he watched, she arched backward and her hips flared provocatively, funneling his vision to the thick pelt that wove her thighs together. Her scent was intoxicating. He felt his heart race, his hands sweat.

Arthur closed his eyes, steeling himself against the impulse to begin.

Savor the hunt. The hunt is everything.

No, not everything.

He felt cradled by the nightscape that surrounded him. The ancient forest was dense, separating Anne Marie's house from the nearest one by several acres. A curious stillness had seized the woods. Sensing the cat hunter, other creatures went silent and would remain so until they were certain the unpredictable predator had moved on.

Satisfied that the two of them were alone, Arthur slipped along a sturdy bough with perfect balance, his arms at his sides. There were only a few more tall trees between him and the backyard, and he glided through them effortlessly. Only once did a slight snapping of an unseen branch cause her to look up. But by the time she did, she saw nothing.

When he was past the wall Arthur crouched in the large tree and looked down. As he watched her almost directly below him, Anne Marie lowered herself into the pool and purred luxuriously. Arthur tried to imagine her face the moment she realized she wasn't alone, the look of terror when she would see his tall, sleek, naked body next to hers. The sound her throat would make.

He waited until her head slipped under the water. Quickly, like a spider in free fall attached to an invisible silk cord, he dropped from the limb and landed on his feet on the grass. He was beyond the sensor beams. The expensive security system never came into play.

He studied her for a time as she moved fluidly through the pool. The aquamarine liquid parted easily before her slow and deliberate strokes. Her arms were tanned and powerful, her long fingers and white, cupped palms pulling the water effortlessly past her. At the end of each stroke her buttocks rose and fell rhythmically, like some diaphanous nymph fornicating with the water. He touched himself and matched her stroke for stroke.

When she made her turn at the end of the pool, Arthur sprinted to his right, skirting the edge of the lighted area in a wide circle that led to the door of a utility room. Slipping inside, he went to a metal box that was the source of power to the house. It opened easily, with a small squeak. He pulled the lever and heard a faint human cry of alarm drift through the sudden darkness.

When his eyes adjusted he could see her in silhouette standing halfway across the pool, waist deep. She was afraid to move, an antelope frozen in its tracks, sensing a lion nearby.

"Who's there?" she called out with a razor-thin voice.

He moved, quickly and silently loping to the pool, keeping his eyes fixed on her. At the ledge, he put his hand in the water and deliberately stirred it enough to make a soft rippling sound. At once her head jerked in the direction of the noise, and she sank farther into the water. He could sense her shivering. He could smell her fear.

"Who is it?" she called out, louder this time, her breath coming in short bursts.

He was under the water before the echoes faded into the night.

Arthur Combs. Silent shark. Ultimate hunter.

In a few seconds he glided to a place where his fingertips sensed warmth and he rose to the surface with his eyes open. He could see her try-ing to move away, clumsily, but the water held her to a slow retreat. She was slowed further by the need to keep looking behind her, not believing what she saw. There was nothing graceful about the way she moved now. Nothing elegant in her manner. Ungainly panic, panting like an animal that had been running for miles.

Arthur paused for a moment, savoring the idea of how her wet skin was going to feel under his fingers. He thought about swimming under her, between her legs, and surfacing suddenly into her. She was holding on to the narrow spillway that ran around the pool and gasping for air.

Biding his time, he watched as she raised one knee to the shelf. The other. Before she could lift herself fully out of the water, he took a single stroke, glided until he was under her, and reached up with both hands. The right one brushed her side and closed tightly over one breast. At the same time his other hand covered her mouth.

"Hush now," he said softly. "No need to be afraid. My name is Arthur. I'm your biggest fan."

TWO

Jennifer Dureau awoke to absolute darkness, lying on her side. She had a trace memory of smooth, warm hands moving over her body, examining its parts, and removing her clothing, slowly, carefully. The strange smell of something animal in the air. It was still present, fainter now. She sat up and brought her knees to her chin protectively, wrapped her arms around them. Her head settled into the cleft between them, and she began to pray.

Dear God, not like this. This can't be how it ends.

Valiantly, she fought mental disintegration, making herself concentrate on her surroundings. Her hand went to the floor. It was wood, deeply rutted planks that had partially rotted. The smell of old lumber combined with cooking grease suggested she was in someone's house or that one was close by. Somewhere in the distance she could hear the drone of traffic on a highway. Street noises below, a few stories down.

At first she thought the low, hissing noise might be tires on pavement, even rain. But the sound was coming from directly behind her, only a few feet away. Someone breathing through his nose.

Don't say anything. Don't make it start.

The all-consuming dread had begun with a similar sound earlier that night, she remembered with a shudder. The photographers had flocked to her press party to shoot the model with the $10-million face. Afterward, she had gone home and quickly fallen asleep. That same hissing sound had awakened her from a deep, carefree slumber.

An inhuman figure at the foot of her bed had peered down at her through the dim light. His skin was glistening and there was no hair anywhere on his body. With her scream the creature leaped onto the bed and smothered her cry with something foul-smelling that he pressed over her nose and mouth. Her head filled with cotton, and she spiraled into an abyss. The same wet sound. The odor of decay.

Whoever it was, or whatever, it was creeping slowly around her now in the pitch blackness. Circling, like a large, invisible cat.

Worse than any nightmare. Ever.

Fighting a wave of nausea, she inched backward on her buttocks as noiselessly as she could. Small needles of wood penetrated her flesh, but she kept moving and did not cry out. Breathing was an effort.

"There's no place to run, Jen," a velvety male

voice said from the void. It came from the right side. "Honestly, I wouldn't lie to you."

Something in her belly suddenly burned like a red-hot coal, and she pivoted to face the voice.

It was a small idea, but all she could think of. *Make him get in front of you. Use your legs. Heels in his face.*

She brought her knees to her naked chest, coiled them. "Why are you doing this? What do you want?" she shouted, trying to sound defiant. But she could hear the fraud in her voice.

"I'm not crazy, Jen. If that's what you're thinking."

She pushed herself further away. Somewhere, there had to be a wall, an anchor. The musky scent was stronger—the unpleasant, dirty way a cat could smell when it had been away for a few days. Spraying. Fornicating.

"Please don't, Jen. It won't do you any good, you know."

"Why does it have to be so dark?" she said, coyly, without planning.

He didn't answer. She sensed him moving again.

"I can see you perfectly, you know. You're very beautiful."

His breathing had become faster, more labored. Turned on.

"I'll do whatever you want. Just let me go."

"What I want is for you not to move anymore, Jen. It's very important that you don't move."

The voice was supremely confident. Unafraid. He'd done this before. Bile rose into her throat and she gagged.

Nearer to her, now. Coming for her.

"I like the way you smell, Jen."

"Please don't," she managed to whisper.

"I smelled you while you were sleeping. Everywhere."

His first touch froze her with fear. Fingers like spikes in her hair from behind. No chance to kick. The fingers reached down to her scalp and tightened their grip, pulling her head back toward him powerfully, then turning her around, forcing her face down, until her mouth touched him.

Too weak to struggle, she had a remarkably detached thought: *Quickly. And without pain.*

"Who are you?" she said, before he filled her mouth and she could no longer speak.

"How rude of me, Jen," he answered, softly. "My name is Arthur. I'm a big fan."

THREE

Los Angeles Chief of Detectives Elliot Stryker leaned heavily on the lectern, as though he bore personal responsibility for the violent acts that were the topic of his press conference. His compact stature and heavy features reminded the assembled reporters of New York State's ex-governor, Mario Cuomo, with whom he shared a gift for oratory.

So far, he hadn't acknowledged the eager young reporter who had been raising her hand urgently to draw his attention.

"These aren't isolated murders, are they, chief?" she was finally forced to shout.

Stryker let the question reverberate in the chamber, then said, "I don't believe we've heard from you before, but we can certainly hear you now."

There was a sprinkling of laughter around the room as a few of the old-time reporters unwittingly became his allies against a new fellow journalist.

"Katlyn Rome, WMTC," she answered, her eyes flashing.

Stryker had known who she was the instant he saw her, the newly ordained channel 10 evening news anchor. It was part of his job to know. He was momentarily distracted by the steady gaze of the young woman. Her face was far more luminous than it was on television, he observed. Not just another news clone, he thought. There was something more dimensional about her.

"And what can we do for you, Ms. Rome?"

Katlyn waited a few seconds for her heart to stop pounding. She had been told that Stryker was a consummate politician. With a flicker of anxiety she wondered why she had ever agreed to come. This was the last place on earth she wanted to be, the last kind of story she wanted to cover.

"Isn't it true that there have been at least two other attacks on female celebrities prior to Warren, and now Dureau?" she said. It was a startling fact her research assistant uncovered only hours before the press conference.

Her revelation sent a shock wave around the room. Stryker remained stone-faced despite the fact that her knowledge of the earlier incidents was a disquieting surprise. He made a mental note to crucify someone for leaking privileged information.

"Isn't it true," Rome continued in the unaccustomed silence, "that on April twelfth a young actress named Emilia Turillo was sexually attacked in her home? And nine days later, there was a similar attack on another actress, Bonnie Gaynor?"

"I don't think it's useful to discuss anything that might compromise the case at hand," Stryker said challengingly. "We'll answer all questions when the time is appropriate."

He scanned a half dozen of the reporters' faces and could see their dissatisfaction with his answer. The damage was done.

"Actually, neither of these women was in the same category as the more recent victims," he added. "They weren't movie people. And no attempt was made on their lives."

His new admission caused a buzz among the eager gathering.

"I believe Turillo had appeared on a few afternoon talk shows. And Gaynor had a commercial running at the time," Katlyn responded. "Doesn't that make them celebrities in their own way? Television celebrities?"

"That seems like a reach, Ms. Rome. And right now we have as many theories as we need, thank you." Stryker pointed to another reporter and raised his head expectantly.

His sarcastic rebuke left Katlyn at a loss. A big neon sign lit up in her mind: *Crash and burn.*

"Of course, I could have been misinformed," she continued, overriding the next reporter's question, "but weren't some of the circumstances of the earlier attacks very similar to the new ones?"

She saw that Stryker had been taken off guard. She had him on the defensive and needed to keep it going.

"Each of the assaults occurred after midnight. There were no clues to the identity of the attacker. And both of the surviving women said they smelled an unusual odor—an animal scent, isn't that right?"

He allowed that it was true.

"Didn't the medical examiner also find an unusual odor on the bodies of Dureau and Warren?"

Stryker glared at the impertinent reporter and stiffened visibly. It had been a mistake to let her take the stage for so long; his face showed it.

"I'm sure we're all impressed with your homework, Ms. Rome. But what is your point?"

In the absence of a substantive response, he had opted for condescension. She felt her face burning.

"Isn't it likely that the two recent murders are related—that this is really about someone who is attacking female celebrities and whose crimes have suddenly escalated?"

Stryker remained silent. Her accusation had been an obvious rebuke to the integrity of his office as well as him personally. He was also being accused of withholding important information from the public, no matter what his reasons might be.

"I appreciate the anxiety that's out there, Ms. Rome. I assure you we're communicating everything we can that will not compromise our investigation."

"And I can tell you that the women of Los Angeles are absolutely terrified, no matter how you're conducting your investigation."

The word *women* appeared to resonate, Katlyn noticed, and with good reason. Women had elected all major officials in the city, including the mayor, who picked the top cops. Stryker had to know that. Also, her television audience was over 65 percent female, and that probably wasn't news to him, either.

"Of course we're sensitive to that. But the fact is, this isn't useful." He looked away again, trying to shut her down.

There was one last pressure point she could attack. After that, for better or worse, she was finished.

"Sir, I think what we're really talking about here is trust. People know the LAPD has made mistakes in the past. Now they're wondering if they can trust their police department. Whether or not they can have confidence in what they're being told."

The ball was back on Stryker's side of the net, and it wasn't a lob.

"I'm sure the citizens of Los Angeles have

every confidence in their police force, Ms. Rome—just as they trust the members of the media to remain responsible." He let the new thought settle and spread his palms on the podium, as though he'd achieved something. "Perhaps you might want to join the rest of us in a more positive approach."

His blatant sarcasm derailed her, and he turned to the front row of reporters. "Now, if there are any more questions—"

Katlyn shifted her weight uneasily. At the moment she devoutly wished she had been a properly trained broadcast journalist instead of an ex–associate professor of English literature from a small-town college. Her lack of experience was about to show. She was out of ideas and didn't have a clue about how to disengage gracefully.

"Could you at least give some advice to all the women in the city who might be afraid tonight? Tell them how they might protect themselves while they're waiting for a break in the case?"

"Yes, as a matter of fact, I can," Stryker answered, dissecting her with steel-blue eyes. "I caution them not to listen too closely to well-intentioned but ill-advised news people who are only helping generate an air of hysteria."

His castigation reverberated around the room. Intended or not, he had berated all the assembled reporters, and there was no way the conference could continue with business as usual.

After an uncomfortable interval, Stryker pushed back from the lectern. "Thank you, ladies and gentlemen," he said curtly, and trudged off the platform.

Katlyn stood rooted to the ground. Having come to the conference with legitimate new information she now felt stupid and humiliated. Maybe in her naive search for the truth she had opened the lid on something that actually *would* hurt his investigation, and the safety of other women.

And for what, she asked herself, with a rising sense of failure. A few tenths of a point more in her station's ratings war?

As the veteran reporters filed out, they gave her a wide berth. A small voice told her she had no reason for being there. That she would never have the stomach for reporting.

And that someday she would regret pushing the chief of detectives so far.

FOUR

At ten minutes after midnight, Pam Lonnigan snuggled into the supple leather of
the stretch limo and felt the tension of the day
drain from her body. The filming had gone on
until an absurdly late hour, and she had luxuri-
ated in every pleasurable minute of it, including
the Cuvee Dom Perignon served by the director
after they wrapped. Fame had such a wonder-
fully decadent taste, like Double Death by Chocolate with a frosting of cocaine.

Since leaving New York a year and a half earlier, the pace of her success had been hard to
believe. In that time she had scored two hit
movies and was working on the third. Already
she had a not-too-shabby guest shot on Letterman, and a financial adviser who was helping her
acquire a diversified portfolio. Her home at the
top of Laurel Canyon was a steal in the current
soft real estate market.

And then there were the men—beautiful,
beautiful men. It just didn't happen this way—
except in the movies.

Lost in her reverie, Pam finally noticed that the driver wasn't her regular one. Harry always sat low in the seat. This driver was tall and much thinner, his head almost touching the roof. Harry never wore a hat and never drove so fast in the heavy traffic. He was as safe as they came.

"I don't think we know each other," she called to the front of the limo.

"Good morning, Pam," a smooth, silky voice said through the single intercom speaker. "It's nice to see you." He turned his head in her direction and pressed the corner of his eye close to the glass, staring at her. "Especially so early in the morning."

The way he said it made her skin feel instantly clammy. The way he addressed her by her first name was impertinent. She would report him later, she decided.

"What happened to Harry?" she asked.

"Harry couldn't make it. My name is Arthur," the soft voice said. "By the way, I love your work."

Through the tinted glass that separated front and rear seats she saw him take off his hat. He was completely bald and his head glistened as though it had been oiled. He was searching for something by his door. She wished he would keep his eyes on the road.

In a few moments she heard an irrevocable-sounding *thunk,* the door locks engaging.

"What's going on?" Her hands flew to the lock to her left, the closest one, then to the other.

They were inoperative. So were the windows. She was locked in.

"Why did you do that?"

"You can never be too safe."

At once, the apprehension she had been feeling spiked. She shot a quick glance out the window. Maybe she could get some passerby's attention. But the window glass was tinted for privacy. No one would notice her, no matter what she did. Limousines were too commonplace in Los Angeles. She was invisible and isolated, right in the center of the most populous city in America.

"I want you to stop the car right now," she demanded loudly. "I don't know you." The scent that she had become vaguely aware of after the locks went down suddenly became suffocating. "What's that smell?"

He didn't respond.

"Let me out! I swear, you'll be sorry if you don't."

"Hush, Pam. All in due time," he said calmly.

The limo continued ahead, still much faster than it should have, but not fast enough to attract the police, she thought. She fell back against the seat, struggling for air. In a while she could see her driver's shoulders twist one way, then the other, the upper part of his body now rimmed with light from the headlights of an approaching car. He had to be taking off his jacket.

He began to wrestle with the fabric, his arm

caught up in it. Continuing to struggle, he took his eyes off the road, and as soon as he did the limo veered to the left and crossed the center line. The alarmed driver in the oncoming car leaned on his horn and tried to swerve out of the way. Her own driver braked. Without her seat belt on, Pam's body shot forward and hit the padded part of the partition wall below the glass. Her shoulder felt as if it had popped out of its socket, and she saw a flash of white lightning.

Still fighting for control, her driver cut his wheel sharply back to the right and hit the brakes again, avoiding a certain collision, but putting the limo into a full sideways skid before it screeched to a stop.

Upright, Pam heard another scream of metal on metal from a car behind them. A violent impact rocked the limo and lifted the wheels off the ground. For a moment the limo teetered, then rolled over, and came to rest on its side.

When the world came into focus again, a number of people were standing outside. One of them called to ask if she was all right and reached in for her. She offered him her wrists and he helped her lift herself out.

By that time her driver was gone.

FIVE

A minute before the Team Ten Six O'Clock News began, Katlyn tapped her foot nervously under the shell that passed for a desk on camera. She looked at herself on the closed-circuit monitor and saw the tension that tightened her expression. She had made it clear many times that she wanted no part of the lead story she was about to report. And here she was doing it anyway.

Focusing on her image in the monitor, Katlyn was as surprised now to find herself on the business end of the camera as she was when they first chose her for the top spot on the panel. She looked nothing like the typical anchorwoman, she knew. Her face was more round than classically oval, with soft, pouty lips that bulged a bit too much near the center. She had a high school wholesomeness that in another time could have served as a model for a 1940s candy striper propaganda poster, but now had already been recast with a more cynical aspect. Large, restless blue eyes, which others said were signposts to an almost maniacally questioning mind, dominated all other features. What had shocked her most was the fierce new look of determination that had begun to stare back at her within the past year.

At odds with the controlled and professional look that she strove for was an abundance of thick cinnamon-brown hair that refused to be tamed, and a figure too full of curves to be hidden even by the severe black Donna Karan jacket she was wearing—and which didn't help her journalistic credibility.

As a further anomaly, she was moderately dyslexic, which meant she could not rely on the TelePrompTers the way her fellow broadcasters could. She had tried her best to turn this disadvantage into something positive, and in her compensating efforts to either memorize or extemporize most of her program, she had inadvertently developed a spontaneous-sounding style. It was a major reason, program director Marty Conroy had told her, that her audience warmed to her from the start.

The signature music faded, and Ron Lockhart, the show's producer, cued her from the control booth. She began the broadcast in a firm voice.

"The Los Angeles celebrity stalker who has become known as Starman, because of his nighttime attacks on female actresses, has struck again. But this time his intended victim has survived, and police have their first description, although it is only a sketchy one.

"As you may remember, on May 13, the body of actress Anne Marie Warren was found in her Bel Air home, the day after she was murdered. Eleven days later the body of top fashion model Jennifer Dureau was discovered in a park near her home only hours after her press party. The medical examiners said that both victims had been sexually savaged before they died, and an undisclosed part of each of their bodies had been severed and taken from the scene."

In the control booth, Marty Conroy noted with slight alarm the distaste with which Katlyn delivered the last piece of information. She was really uncomfortable, fidgeting nervously. In addition to the gory information, she wasn't using the TelePrompTer at all, which may have explained her nervousness.

"Last night it was Pam Lonnigan's turn. The controversial young star of the afternoon soap opera *Land's End* told police she was picked up by limousine after the taping of her show and abducted by the driver, who she now believes was Starman. Fortunately for Lonnigan, the limo was involved in a traffic accident, and she escaped with a bruised shoulder.

"Lonnigan said the man who held her captive for only a short time was tall and spidery, spoke softly, and was probably in his mid to late thirties. He was bald, or completely shaven, with shiny, greasy-looking skin. She also reported that his body gave off a vile smell. This description also coincides with that given by two other women who have just come to the attention of police. Both survived attacks earlier by someone who it now appears might have been Starman.

"However," Katlyn said, turning to the B camera with a sterner countenance, "police are advising the public not to make any assumptions as to the accuracy of Lonnigan's description, nor of its connection to the Starman. They cautioned that she was only able to view the driver through a tinted-glass partition, and that she had drunk several glasses of champagne before the ride."

Abruptly, Katlyn paused, without looking up. A few long seconds passed. Lockhart threw a worried glance at Marty, who could see she was wrestling with something. He had a bad feeling.

"C'mon, c'mon," he muttered at the control booth monitor. "Don't lose it now when you're done. Pass it off."

Katlyn put down her papers, looked up, and fixed the camera in a steady stare. Marty's stomach knotted. The expression on her face always made him nervous. A five-foot-five, 127-pound loose cannon.

"However," she continued with sudden assurance, "speaking for myself and the many women in Los Angeles who continue to live in fear, this official response is very disappointing."

Conroy was on his feet, his blood pressure

skyrocketing. Outside in the newsroom, the staff stopped what they were doing as Katlyn departed from the script. Lockhart was wiping his face with his whole hand. He had given up trying to get his news anchor's attention.

"I believe that rather than casting suspicion on intended victims, we would all be better served by an increased police effort to apprehend this vicious murderer. It's a fact of life that justice doesn't always come swiftly, but while we're waiting there is simply no reason for victims to catch the brunt of police frustration. It seems to me that in Pam Lonnigan's case, she has certainly paid enough of a price already."

When she finished, Katlyn cast an apprehensive glance at the producer's booth and saw Lockhart glaring back at her. He looked as if he were about to have an embolism. Somewhat deflated, she turned to the camera again.

"Of course, that was my own opinion, and doesn't necessarily reflect the views of this station."

With that, Katlyn turned to her co-anchor, her defiant expression of a few moments earlier completely vanished. "Doug?" she said calmly to the astonished Team Ten member.

The camera caught Doug Driscoll a split second before he could close his mouth. He recovered quickly and launched into the next story.

Once the camera was off her, Katlyn felt exhausted. Although it seemed as if it needed to be said at the time, with reflection she knew all too well that her impromptu speech was a cardinal breach of journalistic objectivity. Now she would have to deal with the consequences.

She could see Marty storming toward her, fire and brimstone in his eyes.

By the time she got off the set, he was waiting with his arms locked across his chest.

"Sorry, Marty," she said deferentially. "It just sort of . . . came out."

Marty stood rooted to the stage, his bulldog-like head swaying slowly back and forth. He projected an air of extreme calm, one of the worst possible signs.

Katlyn lowered her head and waited for the ax.

SIX

*B*o continued to stare at the television screen long after the closing credits ended. It was fascinating to realize how close the pretty young anchorwoman had come to putting in a perfect performance, at least for her adoring viewers. Katlyn Rome had been well coached, trained to appear spirited and ingenuous. But in reality, when one looked closely, her performance was deeply flawed.

If one had watched closely, it was easy to see the self-serving zealousness under the surface, a trait that was undoubtedly the reason she had risen so quickly in her profession. Clearly, it was her ambition that had driven her to uncover the scope of Starman's recent activities, and not her feigned concern for the welfare of her audience. Although she operated in a different world from the actresses, it was plain to see that she was as evil as the rest of them. And, for Starman, much more dangerous.

Like the actresses, however, she was afraid. The makeup artists had done their job well, but they hadn't been able to hide the corner of her mouth that curled slightly as she spoke, the full, painted lips that trembled slightly at the mention of Starman's most recent atrocities. Her eyes appeared to gaze out at the invisible audience in benevolent innocence, glittering *like fine-cut ocean-green emeralds. But there was an anxiousness behind them that wasn't stage fright.*

With Katlyn Rome, nothing was as it seemed. And for all her affected confidence, Starman had put a deep crack in her armor.

Seeing how much she dreaded the celebrity killer had been an exhilarating discovery.

In time, her boldness would be redressed and her own fear would become his ally. Soon, the exquisite moment would arrive when that unctuous smile would abruptly change to a mask of terror.

SEVEN

The stillness of the new house in Brentwood was something Katlyn had never gotten used to. It was four months since they had moved to the large stone Tudor residence, and she was still like their cat, Monty, who had to re-explore every nook and cranny each day before he felt safe.

The upstairs hallway was an endless brooding space, and at night the half-furnished downstairs was equally forbidding. Outside, an extensive lawn bordered by dense hedges separated their house from its neighbors and made her feel isolated. Only to the right was a house visible, the Hoffman estate, whose property was divided from her own by a broken-down fence. She was a long distance from her small, blue-collar hometown in southwestern Oregon, where houses and neighbors were closer in every sense.

In all her time in Brentwood she had come to know only a few local women, and they could not be considered friends. June Foxx lived and worked in the house on the corner, a real estate broker and mother of two, a balance that in many ways seemed ideal. Katlyn often wondered if she herself could find the energy to do both demanding jobs well—a question she asked herself more frequently, now that a similar path awaited her.

The Hartes were directly across the street, an outgoing, sincere couple with an immaculate Queen Anne Victorian house that sparkled in an area of opulent homes. They had spoken several times about getting together for dinner, but no invitation had followed.

Rachel Prescott was a plain-looking but pleasant enough young woman who had recently moved next door and occupied the gardener's cottage. She cared for the Hoffmans' estate while they summered in the Italian countryside. Rachel was close to Katlyn's age, and they had talked on several occasions. Katlyn had hoped for a kindred spirit, but so far she had found little common ground with the other woman. Rachel was friendly but preoccupied with her gardens, and shy to the point of discomfort. Not someone to spend an empty or even an idle evening with.

Tonight, Katlyn had been sleeping fitfully due to a succession of vivid and disquieting dreams, and an astonishing piece of news. Dr. Murray Alter had called earlier to ceremoniously announce that fertilization had been achieved in their attempt at in-vitro conception. She had immediately called her husband, Matthew, at the music studio. He had been deliriously happy and promised to come home as soon as he could finish up.

Two hours later, when he still hadn't arrived, Katlyn's body was still vibrating with the small miracle. Lately, in addition to fulfilling the dream of starting a family, she had also prayed that their baby would be the answer to a conflict that had begun to tear at the heart and soul of their marriage. Now they were one step closer.

It had taken until two in the morning for her to finally drift off to sleep. The last thing she remembered was a song playing on a tape that Matthew had compiled for her. Billie Holiday crooning something about having her man.

When an unaccustomed sound from downstairs woke her, the Sony digital clock read 2:03. Katlyn's first reaction was to reach for Matthew, but the space next to her was still cold. She assumed he was making the noise, bumping into something in the dark.

"Matthew?" she called. "It's okay, I'm awake."

There was no answer. The sound stopped as soon as she spoke. "Matt? Is that you?"

The silence continued. Suddenly apprehensive, she lay back in bed and drew the thin cover around her neck, wishing it was a thick comforter. Even if it wasn't Matthew, there was no cause for alarm, she calmed herself. Possibly she had dreamed that she heard something. The spookiness of the house had been on her mind before she fell asleep. Or, the noise could have come from outside. There were dogs in the neighborhood who got loose now and then. Maybe raccoons rooting in the trash. She didn't want to address the fleeting, nightmarish thought that came next.

The noise came again, this time a series of thumps that seemed to come from the library. *Definitely inside the house.*

For reassurance, Katlyn looked up at the keypad on the wall above the headboard. The security system display read INSTANT NIGHT, and glowed a dim green, as it should when the system was properly set. She breathed a sigh of relief. Just to be sure, she pressed the key marked STATUS, and as soon as she did a new message traveled from left to right on the display. *EXTERIOR . . . EXTERIOR . . . EXTERIOR.* Her heart raced when she saw it. The only explanation for the warning was that she had set the main alarm but forgotten the interiors. That meant someone could have gotten into the house before she set the alarm. This time she could not put away the terrifying thought she had had earlier. *What if it were Starman?* Her heart hammered in her chest.

The noise came from below again, more regular, not like an animal. She was afraid to call Matt's name again. If someone else were down there she would only be alerting him that she was awake.

In panic, she reached for the phone, and

drew the receiver to her ear under the cover. A short time later, a 911 operator answered, and, as calmly as she could, she reported her situation. The operator told her to lock the bedroom door and wait until help arrived.

Her breath was coming in short bursts as she slipped noiselessly out of bed, but her mind quickly seized on a new thought and she stopped in her tracks. Matthew could walk in at any time and confront the invader. That was the way people got killed. She had to do something more than wait for the police.

With a shudder of anxiety she remembered that there was a pistol in the night table drawer. Against her objections, Matthew had brought it home after she had gone on TV, and he insisted on keeping it loaded. Going to her knees she opened the drawer, slowly, so it wouldn't squeak. In a moment she gripped the cold stock of the SIG Sauer, drew it out slowly, and went to the door.

She could still hear a disturbance below, but it was less regular, careless sounding. Definitely from the library, books crashing to the floor. *Please don't let it be Starman.*

Katlyn covered her mouth with her hand and frantically tried to recall the drill Matthew had taught her with the pistol. Cock the trigger, aim at the center of the target, hold your breath, squeeze. She commanded herself to stay calm. She had the advantage of surprise, she reasoned.

She had the weapon. She reached the door without making a sound, and crept onto the landing at the top of the stairs.

As soon as she did the thumping from below stopped. Maybe he had heard her. *Or seen her!* He could be waiting for her to come down. Or possibly the intruder had found what he wanted and simply left, she prayed.

Something else Matthew had said about the gun flashed through her mind. She shouldn't take it unless she knew she could use it. And if she fired, shoot to kill. At the time it had sounded tremendously callous. Not now.

Crouching on the landing she scanned the empty space on both sides of her, searching for a flaw in the smooth plane of darkness. She was invisible, too, she comforted herself. But if he were already upstairs with her she probably wouldn't be able to see him until he was on top of her.

You will shoot. You will not hesitate.

The slight squeak of a drawer opening in the library rooted her to the floor. She couldn't breathe. There was no longer any doubt that someone was in the house. But at least he was staying downstairs. If it was Starman, why would he be staying down there? Why would he announce his presence so clumsily—*unless it was deliberate.*

She considered a loud warning, letting him know she had a gun. But that might force him to act, and he might have his own weapon. He might be on drugs and irrational.

Getting down on her hands and knees, she crawled to the edge of the landing. Carefully, she moved her finger off the trigger guard to the trigger itself, not having any idea how much pressure it would take to activate it.

As she peered down the stairway a narrow, dark shape suddenly appeared at the bottom of the stairs, and her heart stopped. In a moment the shape traveled a short distance farther on the tiled entrance floor, and halted. A shadow.

The man's profile was thin and elongated. The head looked too long and narrow in proportion to the torso, even more than could be accounted for by the distant light source.

She remembered Lonnigan's description of the limo driver. *Spidery.*

She looked at the edge of the shadow closely and saw no evidence of clothing. Either he wore something that was skin tight—or he was naked.

Stiffened by fear, she was leaning forward when the silhouette suddenly darted forward. The abrupt movement caught her by surprise, and her finger jerked back on the trigger. The room exploded. The recoil from the gun turned her body over and away from the top of the landing. It all happened so quickly, it took a while to realize she was no longer holding the pistol.

When she tried to get up her muscles didn't respond. Her ears were ringing so loudly she knew she wouldn't be able to hear the intruder if he came up the stairs. And if he came, he might find the gun, and Matt's prediction would come true.

She lay there for what seemed like an eternity, her entire body shaking. Eventually she realized that the piercing sound she heard was the security system alarm. A cool current washed over her skin. A breeze was coming up the stairs. It smelled like topsoil. The gardeners had put some around the shrubs the day before.

She pushed herself to the top step and looked down.

The front door was wide open.

The intruder had fled the house.

EIGHT

The alarm was still ringing loudly as she cautiously made her way down the stairs. At the bottom she turned on the hallway light and searched quickly in every direction. Satisfied that no one was there, she focused on the library and her eye went immediately to the large leaded-glass window behind the desk. A section of the glass had been cut away, large enough for a man to crawl through. It was the weak link in the security system, she remembered, an area impossible to wire without ruining the appearance of the colorful old art work. They had depended on the interior sensors to pick up a breach there.

The library looked as if it had been dismantled piece by piece. The thief's attention had been on the bookcase. All of the books had been removed and put in several piles on the floor. A large portion of the ransacking must have gone on before she woke, she realized with a shiver. It was hard to believe that so much disorder could have been created in so little time.

The built-in drawers beneath the shelves had been opened. There had been an assortment of personal articles in them, some valuable: a Hummel statue in need of repair and a Wedgwood serving plate she only took out for the holidays. A stack of old jazz records that were collector's items. They were now on the carpet next to a chestnut box that contained her mother's silver. She opened it, saw it was full, and breathed a sigh of relief.

Her handbag lay open on the other side of the room near a wastepaper basket, but it had been emptied, and she had to search for what was in it. She found her wallet on the bottom bookcase shelf. All of its contents, including nearly a hundred dollars and all of her credit cards, were laid out, eerily neat.

The discovery chilled her. *If he hadn't come for money, then what?*

When she opened the wallet, her pictures were no longer in their sleeves. Of all her possessions, they were the only irreplaceable items.

Her photos were in albums in the bottom drawers. There had been three of them, and some loose pictures in another box. One contained shots of her early life, including a blackand-white of her mother, a haunting shot taken just before she died when Katlyn was in high school. A grandmother she never met. They were the only remaining record of her original family.

The second album spanned the years from childhood through college, shots of friends lost along the way. The most recent one held her entire life with Matthew, including an irreplaceable shot of him winning a Grammy. The drawers were open and all of the albums missing.

Why would anyone want her pictures?

In alarm, she flashed on other photographs that were on a table in the living room. She raced to the room and saw the empty surface.

The hallway that led upstairs had displayed her only other photos. She and Matthew had hung them together. The wall was empty. It was as if part of her life had been stolen. He hadn't just taken her photos, he had taken her history.

While her back was to the door she was suddenly aware of a presence behind her, standing in the open doorway. In a blind fury she spun to face it, her hand raising the gun and pointing it directly at the intruder's chest, her finger closing on the trigger.

Matthew stared back at her in amazement, his mouth wide open. Gazing at him in terror, Katlyn gasped and slowly lowered the pistol. Distantly, she heard the sound of sirens.

NINE

Arthur could feel the familiar presence even before it spoke to him. It was as though one minute he was alone, and the next Bo was there. Sometimes Arthur didn't know who Bo was at all.

"Do you remember the one in Bar Harbor?" the voice that was patient this time said from a place that seemed very close.

Bo was testing him. Lately, everything had become so serious.

"The very first one, Arthur. Can you remember?"

"The dancer," he answered after a moment of deep reflection. "The one who took her clothes off and kept looking at me," he added with a mixture of delight and embarrassment.

He could tell right away that Bo was irritated.

"Not that one, Arthur. Not the one in Old Orchard Beach. You're confused. The drugs are doing things to your mind."

"You promised we wouldn't talk about the early ones anymore," Arthur said in an unaccustomed burst of irritation. He stopped there, careful not to invite a direct confrontation. Sometimes the arguments ended with a headache that could last a day or even two. Then, the pain was unbearable. None of the drugs could help.

"Tell me what you remember."

Arthur closed his eyes and went down his old list of names. There had been so many it was getting hard to separate them all. So many faces that now seemed to be the same face, and the reasons for visiting them as unclear as they always were. Bo's reasons.

"Sandra?" he announced finally and with great relief. "The one I met at the high school."

"Yes, Arthur. That one. Remember how much you enjoyed your little tête-à-tête?"

Arthur thought back. It seemed like a distant memory. A face came back, phantomlike, half woman, half girl. All the more beautiful in terror. She had chocolate-brown hair that smelled like rosemary, fragrant butter-soft skin. He remembered most the woods where he had taken her. He had made her strip and set her loose to try to hide. Then he tracked her by scent alone for one whole delicious afternoon. When he found her shivering by a stream he made it last a long time.

"I see I've stirred a pleasant memory," Bo said salaciously.

Arthur was lost in Sandra's breasts, her perfectly round buttocks. He remembered how she squeaked when he took the first of the souvenirs for Bo. She'd surprised him and was still alive at the time.

"Do you want to masturbate, Arthur? It's all right. I can help if you want."

The invasion into his most private thought

tore him rudely from his reverie. It was amazing the way Bo always knew how to get to him, using the knowledge of his secret thoughts to humiliate him. And it was confusing. Bo loved him more than anyone ever had.

"I've found another Sandra, Arthur. Even better. Her name is Victoria."

"Is she pretty, Bo?" Arthur said. "Tell me how pretty she is."

"See for yourself. I promise you won't be disappointed."

Arthur knew that it must be true. Bo never lied. He was grateful and tried to think of a way to show it.

"Would you like me to bring you something?" he offered after some reflection.

"Yes, that would be nice, if it's not too much trouble."

"Of course not, Bo."

"Something different this time. Pink and pretty. Surprise me."

TEN

Katlyn Rome walked with conviction to the news director's office but stopped abruptly before rapping on the door. She had been up all night making a painful decision and now found it hard to take the last step.

In the lull before the storm, she recalled the day she met Marty Conroy. She was an assistant professor of English literature at Claremount, a small upstate college that he was visiting for a conference on communications. After attending her lecture on contemporary maverick authors, he arranged a meeting that turned out to be a job interview.

By the time that semester ended, three years after she had first come to Claremount, she was dismayed by the politics of higher education. She had hoped for an opportunity to share her passion for literature in a community of common interest, but had been distracted since she got there by the continuous need to assuage egos, spend entire evenings debating the meaning of a single line of Homer, and, in general, be part of the insular and self-righteous world of academe.

On impulse she called Marty Conroy to see if

the job was still open, and it was. She shocked everyone—including herself—by taking it.

She knocked on his door and he summoned her inside. "You're not going to like it," she said. She was putting it mildly.

"Why do we do it, Katlyn, why?" he said, suddenly stopping her momentum before she built up any.

His mock philosophical gambit threw her off stride, a prelude to something *he* wanted.

"Not now, Marty. This isn't the time," she answered stiffly.

She tried to look him in the eye but couldn't. When they had started working together in Los Angeles she found Marty to be a staunch disciplinarian but with an honest and sympathetic nature, a gentle giant. He had a generous smile set in a rubbery face atop a six-foot-four frame and the kindest brown eyes ever—at least where she was concerned. Their chemistry had been extraordinary. What she had to tell him now was going to wound him personally and professionally. It was one of the hardest things she'd ever had to do.

"Perhaps it's my relentless need to pass along wisdom to the next torchbearer," he went on.

Headline, she said, deflating again. *Story to follow.*

Conroy raised his chin and gestured toward the softest couch at the station. That plush seat and his huge Federal desk were the only furniture that broke with the chilly neo-broadcast decoration.

She remained standing.

"Starman's been at it again," he continued. "Day before yesterday, with Victoria Della Cruz, the porn star. They just found her body."

"I know. I heard it on the radio when I got up. That's one of the reasons I want to talk to you. I think it's time that Doug handled the story."

"The creep dressed her up in the costume from her movie, for God's sake. Must have turned him on. He *took* something, too, a body part, like he's been doing. They're not saying which."

Another missing body part. Katlyn was repulsed beyond comment—but that wasn't the point of her visit, she remembered. Marty had thrown her off track.

"You can ignore me all you want to, but I'm not doing Starman anymore," she insisted. "I've made my decision. I said I'd try it, but our experiment has failed."

Conroy handed her a page of scribbled notes without changing expression. It was an outline of the report she had just declined to do. He wasn't listening at all, not even pretending to.

"I'm not kidding, Marty, I mean it. The story isn't me. It makes my skin crawl."

"Welcome to the club. But what's that got to do with it?" He looked at her more closely, as if studying a rare bird. "What's it been now since you got here? A year and a half? Less?"

"More. Almost two years."

"And, on the whole, a relatively good two years," he said with sudden firmness. "You came here with the qualities I thought I first saw in you, honesty, integrity, plus an unusual personal touch—something that can't be learned. And now you've begun to develop reportorial skills you unleash like smart bombs when you have to. Like at the press conference."

He was trying to confuse her with praise. It wasn't going to work.

"Did I tell you how Ron Lockhart describes you?" he continued. "He says you're the secret love child of Mary Poppins and Alan Dershowitz. An attack dog with a heart of gold."

"Look, I don't want to disappoint you, but putting me on the Starman story is miscasting. You know it, and so do I. It isn't me."

"It isn't anyone, Kate," he said, more fatherly. "We're talking about a homicidal maniac who likes to torture pretty young women—of which you happen to be one."

"I've been thinking about my newscasting career in general, not just this story. It's turned out that I'm either reporting about people who get raped or shot or mutilated, or I'm trying to trap some public official in a lie to get an exclusive for the station. This isn't what I thought it was all about."

For a moment Marty seemed to be injured by her accusations, but he shrugged it off. "To answer you point by point, yes, you deal in the lowest form of human behavior, but I thought we agreed earlier that people have a right to know what's happening to their friends and neighbors. And yes, you have to go after those who govern our lives—because many of them do it so badly."

She remembered the look on the chief of detectives' face at the end of the press conference. "Stryker hates my guts."

"Sometimes it's the only way you know you're doing your job."

He stonewalled her for another few seconds, then sat back in his large leather swivel chair and put his hands behind his neck.

"You know, I was just thinking about a certain picture I once saw. It's still on the wall in your office, I believe. A young girl in a go-cart beating a tough bunch of hotshot boys to the finish line."

"I was just a kid, and that was a long time ago," she said quickly, sensing his intent. The picture had been one of her favorites. Now it was being used to derail her. "It doesn't relate."

"You said it taught you one of life's great lessons."

"I don't remember."

"That if you didn't fight to get to the head of the pack you'd be forced to the rear. It was one or the other." He leaned over the desk conspiratorially. "That's how it is now, Kate. Trust me, all those other reporters want you out of the race. And our station, too. That's how it works."

She thought about it for only a split second, then said, "Well, I guess that's the difference between us, Marty. I no longer have to win every race I'm in. In fact, there are some I don't even want to enter."

He stared at her, but didn't seem worried. Like a lion, he knew that sooner or later his lunch would have to come to the watering hole.

"This is your first real trip to the plate," he said, launching into one of his accustomed sports frames of reference. "A lot of people are waiting to see if you score."

There was no way to know whether he sympathized with her or not. No matter what, he had to think about the station first.

"My house was broken into last night, Marty," she announced all of a sudden. "I didn't want to use it as a reason."

Conroy's face registered genuine concern. For a large man he came to his feet quickly. "Jesus, Kate, why didn't you tell me?"

"Whoever it was only took personal things, so I don't think it was an ordinary burglar. He took all my pictures, Marty!"

Marty didn't seem to know what to make of the disclosure, but he was alarmed. He grabbed her hand and pulled her down gently on the couch next to him.

"He took *all* of my pictures, Marty—my albums,

the ones that we had framed and hanging up. Even from my wallet."

"It's strange, I admit. I'm sorry for that, really I am. But what does this have to do with you quitting—and the Starman story?"

She wondered why he didn't grasp the significance of what she was telling him. He was usually so perceptive.

"I've had the feeling something like this would happen ever since I starting reporting on him—like I was opening some old cellar door and disturbing some creepy things down there. Matthew warned me. We've been fighting about it all the time."

"Everyone in our business feels that way the first few times. Trust me, it passes. Matthew will calm down about it when nothing happens."

Katlyn glared at him, suddenly angered. "You don't seem to get it Marty. Something has happened. I saw a shadow on the wall—like a creature from a science fiction movie. And I smelled something weird. It could have been the odor reported on Starman."

Conroy looked her closely, as if he sensed something in her that was short of absolute conviction.

"Okay, so I'm not sure about the smell," she admitted. "It could have come from the garden."

"What did the police say? I presume you called them?"

"They were very attentive, once they knew

who I was. But I could tell that they thought I was paranoid. One of them suggested that I'd had Starman on my mind too much. That it was only natural to worry about him attacking me."

"Not so farfetched a theory."

"Jesus, Marty. I know what I saw. I was hoping at least that you'd believe me."

He held up his hand and backed off. "Katie, I have a great deal of faith in your powers of observation. But you were frightened, and I'd bet anything that this was probably just a routine break-in. Or maybe an overeager fan who wanted a souvenir."

"*All* of my pictures are more than a little souvenir. It's crazy. Why would someone want my pictures?"

"I don't know, Kate. But as much as they mean to you, they're only pictures, after all."

"No. They're a lot more than that."

"What did Matthew do? What's he saying?"

"He was working when it happened. He got home after it was over, and I almost shot him when he came inside."

Conroy's mouth fell open. "What the hell were you doing with a gun?"

"It was Matthew's idea, ironically. The truth is, I'm glad I had it."

"Did any of the neighbors have anything to say? Did they see anyone in the area?"

"Not likely. No one even showed enough interest to come over and find out what happened. Hell, in four months I haven't even met the couple who live next door to me. What kind of town is this, anyway? I don't understand how people live around here."

"But the fact is, you're all right," Marty said. "Whoever it was didn't try to come after you, right?"

"Who knows what he was planning to do? I saw him at the foot of the stairs. Maybe he was on his way up when I got there. I only scared him off because I accidentally fired the pistol."

Marty stood and walked back to his desk, then turned to face her and leaned against the desk with his arms folded. "I know what it must have been like. It must have terrorized you. But let's be blunt. I think we can rule out Starman, if only for the fact that, if it was him, you probably wouldn't be here to talk about it, gun or no gun."

"Not true," Katlyn shot back. "His pattern includes attacks other than murder."

"His early pattern, maybe. But not recently. Isn't that what you told Stryker at the press conference?"

She could see the matter was settled in his mind. She could also tell by the way he was standing that he was ready to resume his role as boss. At the moment she wanted to be consoled, not lectured.

"And that's the real reason you want off the story?"

"No, not just that, it's everything. The kind of

story this is, the circus we're making it into just to make money. Anyway, it doesn't have to be me. Doug's the real pro at this kind of stuff."

"Doug's a good reporter, but the piece calls for someone with . . . more compassion."

She understood immediately. "You mean a woman, don't you?"

"Of which you happen to be the best at the station. Any station."

"And what about our deal? You said you didn't want me to come here and be like the others. I thought we agreed on that."

Conroy sucked in enough air to fully inflate his chest, then let a good part of it out. "Okay, so maybe I was a bit too optimistic—about our reality here. But most of the time I give you as much rope as I can. This just isn't one of those times. This story is too big and too important."

"Then this isn't the kind of place I thought I joined!"

"You know our most important reality is our audience. As in, if we don't have one we don't stay on the air long enough to do the warm and fuzzy stuff—not to mention collect a paycheck. Actually, I had a discussion on just that topic yesterday, with you know who."

As usual, the issue had degenerated into a discussion of financial concerns, Katlyn surmised.

"When's the last time anyone got a Pulitzer for making a station a lot of money?"

As soon as she said it she was sorry. She wasn't totally naive about the business of broadcasting. Evidently he had talked to Jude Sermac, the station manager. Their fearless leader's only mission in life was to wring every cent he could out of the news segment. Marty had probably been outvoted again on an issue of principle. He had a wife and three pre–college age kids. He had been forced to cave.

"I don't have to tell you that some people around here were very nervous when I recommended you for anchor, and for just this reason. Frankly, they see this as a test."

"Why, to see if I've grown up? Or copped out?"

"They're not always mutually exclusive."

"I've noticed."

"I'm sorry, Kate. I need you on this until it's over. Then we'll see what happens. I'm sorry about last night, but you've got to get past it."

She shifted her weight uneasily and couldn't look at him.

"Listen, I won't bullshit you. This Starman thing probably isn't going to end any time soon. But I promise, in the long run it'll be worth it." He leaned closer to her again and put a huge, fatherly hand on her shoulder and squeezed it. "Welcome to television news. Time to grow up, kid."

She felt the warmth of his hand soothe her nerves slightly, and wished it hadn't. But she had to admit it was the same speech she would have made to him if their roles had been reversed. Maybe her skin *was* too thin. Maybe the intruder *was* just some weirdo fan, and the whole experience was part of her seasoning.

She could feel her resolve of a moment ago draining. She knew the real reason. In the end, as scared as she was, as tough as it was going to be when she got home, she just couldn't disappoint Marty. Not yet, at least.

"I don't believe this," she said, shaking her head.

Marty smiled. The great big basset hound leaned over and kissed her on the forehead, and it was over.

Back in her own office, Katlyn scanned the notes he had given her when she left his office. They were complete and in order. But she couldn't concentrate. The prospect of doing the Della Cruz piece that evening triggered another attack of nerves. She felt as if she was in grade school again, about to do an oral book report in front of the class—except now she was twenty-nine and her classmates were two million viewers. She wished she could just read the TelePrompTer as the others did and divorce herself from the content of what she was saying. But her dyslexia was going to make her internalize it again, feel it.

She forced herself to think positively. In a few hours she would be leading the charge on the year's biggest story and playing to the largest news audience in Los Angeles. In truth, it *was* a great opportunity for her. And as a woman she *would* bring an empathy to the story that Doug Driscoll couldn't even approach.

Just one more try, she said to herself as she picked up the notes and started reading.

But not again.

Not even for Marty.

ELEVEN

O n Friday evening, a half hour after Team Ten was off the air, Katlyn was escorted to the elevator by a special security guard hired at Marty Conroy's suggestion after the robbery at her house. Outside the building, neither the bodyguard nor Katlyn was prepared when a tall, sturdy man in his mid-thirties sprang from a car that had screeched to a halt behind the waiting sedan. As soon as the guard spotted the man, he pushed Katlyn roughly to one side, dropped to one knee, and drew his revolver.

"For God's sake, don't shoot," the intruder yelled after flinging himself to the ground.

"It's all right," Katlyn shouted the instant she realized what was happening. "He's my husband!"

The panic was over. Matthew had called to say he was going to pick her up at work and get an early start on their weekend. But with so much on her mind, Katlyn had neglected to check her voice mail messages. The terrifying incident was evidence that, even in their normal rituals of living, all the rules were changing. It was also the second time in three days that Matthew had almost been shot.

An hour later, the mountains rose to welcome them, and the natural world began to work its regenerative magic, as would their destination, a rustic retreat in Hunter's Pass that was the antithesis of their house in Brentwood.

The remote log shanty overlooked a striking gorge filled with giant boulders and, in the melting season, cascading water, but it lay on a rocky escarpment which sustained no life other than red ants and poison ivy. The shocked real estate agent from whom they bought it took their money almost apologetically.

By the time they pulled into the driveway the netherworld of Los Angeles felt a thousand miles away, and they opened the car windows and gulped in the sweet, high-country air.

"That's better," Matthew said, letting his shoulders slump against the seat.

"Anything's better," Katlyn said.

Unwinding behind the wheel, he looked out the window and examined the grounds. His eyes came to rest on a dwindling woodpile stacked neatly a few yards from the cabin, not near enough to the wood-frame dwelling to invite termites. In the morning, he would chop enough of it to last the weekend, and feel every inch a mountain man doing it. His estranged father would have been surprised if he could see him then, Matt reflected, the disappointing son who looked like a football star but used his large hands to play the piano instead.

"Can you stand a little good news for a change?" Matthew said out of nowhere.

Katlyn studied him for a clue. His face was a mask of anger most of the time lately, but now and then she could still glimpse the gentle, almost boyish man she had met when she first came to L.A. almost two years earlier. He reminded her of the way men were in another time, Gregory Peck in *To Kill a Mockingbird,* or a folksy frontier cowboy. A Lyle Lovett kind of rugged good looks, rich in character. At the moment, his elongated face reminded her of an Irish setter, attentive, with big brown eyes, waiting to be stroked. Full of need.

"Someone you know intimately has just sold a title theme to Trio Pictures for their new movie."

"You're kidding!" Katlyn howled. She kissed him squarely on his mouth, then hugged him tightly. "Why didn't you say something before this?"

"I don't know. For some reason it felt better to tell you here, when we were away." For an all-too-brief moment, her happiness filled him with pride, but his mood was compromised by another, harsher reality. "I just wish it hadn't happened now—with everything that's on our minds."

"Hey," she scolded, "don't you dare let this moment go, do you hear me? Jesus, Matt, this is what it's all about for you."

"Thanks," he beamed, reminding her of a schoolboy who had just showed mom a good report card. He kissed her more softly than before, then nuzzled her neck and rested there.

With his sudden display of affection, Katlyn recalled that it had been like that much of the time when they met. How much more of a team they were then, rooting for each other's achievements. He was a successful commercial composer who had just won a Grammy for coproducing a top forty hit song. As long as he had his success in music, and she was apprenticing at the station, he seemed content. Then, when he couldn't follow up his first success with another, he crashed. Insecurities she had never seen before surfaced, and there was even a brief bout with cocaine. When she finally vaulted to the anchorwoman spot at the station, and they began to rely on her income, he got much worse.

Katlyn put her hand on his shoulder. "I'm so proud of you. I know how much this must mean to you."

"To us," he corrected her. He looked at her tellingly.

They decided to take a walk through a stand of silver birch to a clearing above the gorge. The night was unusually warm, and a half-moon was the centerpiece of a spectacular celestial offering. Below them the water was peaceful after an unseasonal light rain and was making playful, gurgling sounds.

"This could be the beginning of a new time for us," Matthew said. "I've been thinking a lot about it—especially after what happened at the house."

Katlyn heard an intent that went well beyond his words. "Thinking about what?"

"Well, given what's been happening with your work, you have to admit things have changed for us—and not for the better. Now that it looks like I'm getting something going again, well—I thought it might be time for us to reexamine things. Like what you want to do."

Katlyn looked at him with open disappointment. It came as no big surprise that the topic was her job, again, the topic they'd begun to discuss almost daily. "I don't really want to talk about this now, Matt. It's been a hard week."

Matthew took both her hands in his and faced her, very attentive. "See, that's exactly what I mean. Look what your job is doing. You're angry all the time at how the station is using you, about how you hate being on the Starman story. And now there's the robbery, which probably happened because you were on TV. Everything that's negative for you—for us—goes back to the job. And now you won't even talk about it."

Katlyn fell silent. For someone who was supposed to be good with words, she never knew how to answer him about this. Maybe because she suspected his real motive lay in his own insecurity, the intrinsic need to dominate the relationship, emotionally and financially, that most men had. But God knows she also harbored her own doubts about her job, and his objections played right into them.

"I don't know," she said finally. "I guess I'm not ready to throw it all away yet."

Her answer had silenced him for the time being.

Matthew walked ahead of her on the path that led to the gorge until they reached the level piece of stone on which they'd once made love in the late afternoon sunshine and dubbed, appropriately, *Bedrock*. The stone was still there, but it was another time in their life now.

They lay on their backs and stared up into a shimmering sky. Matthew could feel Katlyn's intensity was somewhat diminished and said, "I know we promised each other not to talk about it, but I can't help thinking about the baby."

"Neither can I. Lately, it's become my refuge." She turned to him. "Even though I know that it's a dangerous thought. We're putting so much faith in something that may never happen."

He knew what she meant. It was dangerous because there was no baby yet, and tremendous odds against a successful in-vitro, even at their stage in the process. He also knew how much they needed a baby to draw them closer together, to become a family. He was certain that once the baby was there, she'd make the right choice about her job.

"I have a good feeling about it. I really do."

Somewhere nearby, a small animal dashed into the brush, underscoring the new sense of danger Katlyn felt, on many levels.

"It was the dark side that was really breaking into our house, not just someone after our pictures," she said at length. "It's not supposed to be as good as we have it. That's why it's happening, isn't it?"

"It can be perfect for us. So easily."

Matthew made a move to take her in his arms, but she found herself bracing when they touched. She felt more distant than she dared to show him, especially in his hour of triumph.

"Just say you'll think about the job, will you?" he pressed. "Not just for me, for us. Promise me you'll think about it."

"I think about it all the time, Matt. And I'll think about it some more."

Before long the air became chilly, and she started shivering. Even the safe isolation of the mountain retreat now had a sinister presence. The break-in was taking its toll, she thought, slowly enveloping her, covering them like a dark vapor seeping out of the woods.

Back at the cabin, Matthew told her to go ahead in while he got the bags from the car. He was reaching over the front seat to grab them from the back when a cassette sitting on the console caught his eye. He was sure it hadn't been there on the way up, although it was possible that in his preoccupation over the Trio job he had overlooked it. He often brought along CDs and cassettes for the long trip.

The sky was nearly dark, so it was hard to see, but Katlyn had already put on the front door light and he held the cassette up to it. The tape didn't have a label, which was strange. He always labeled their tapes, just as he did at the studio, a habit from his advertising days when, by the time you got done, there were so many versions of every theme you needed to mark all of them. It must have been something Katlyn brought, he assumed.

Out of curiosity he found the keys and turned on the ignition. The tape went into the player smoothly.

The short two-line message repeated over and over, as though it were on a loop.

> *A hunnnting weee will go, a hunnnting weee*
> *   will go,*
> *Hi-ho, the derry-o, a hunnnting weee will go.*

TWELVE

At 5:48 Monday morning, the mirrored elevator doors opened onto a long, unadorned marble corridor and the sinister ambiance of an empty office building. Katlyn's uneasiness increased when she turned the corner and saw that Marty Conroy's office was still dark.

That was unusual. Marty lived in the suburbs, an hour farther away than she, but he was always there by the time she arrived.

As was their standing arrangement, the night editor had left the most important news on her desk. He did this so she could begin memorizing key facts and not rely on the TelePrompTers later.

The story on top of the pile brought her up short. There had been another horrifying killing, the acerbic talk-show host Shannon Conner. Like the others, she was found nude and had been sexually brutalized before being strangled. Her husband was out of town on business at the time and her body was discovered by the housekeeper.

This time the police had released one additional and gory piece of information. Before leaving, the killer had removed one of Conner's earlobes and had evidently taken it with him.

There were few other facts about the attack,

but one in particular made Katlyn's heart race. Police records showed that Conner's home had been broken into six days earlier and unspecified personal articles had been taken. Although the break-in wasn't attributed to Starman, the parallel to her own case spooked her.

As she sat down to her computer a squeaking sound in the hallway made her snap to attention. Rubber soles or sneakers on the marble tiles, much too early in the morning for the regular staff. Someone was coming in her direction, and not slowly.

She quickly realized that she'd left her office door unlocked, a careless habit that could have just become a terrible mistake.

Bolting from her desk, she lunged for the door and twisted the insubstantial metal lock until it clicked. The mechanism jiggled when she tried it and gave little assurance it would hold if someone tried to force it. The glass door put her on display, like a parakeet in a cage with a nasty cat on the prowl. No place to run, no place to hide.

If Starman had come for her, there would be no one to hear her scream.

THIRTEEN

The solitary figure that finally broke the plane of the wall was a worn but reasonable facsimile of Claire Fava, arriving earlier than usual. She did not see her boss, Katlyn Rome, go limp in her desk chair from relief.

Fava, as she was called at the station, stifled a yawn and headed toward Katlyn's office. On the way she hit the key that turned on her Mac computer. This single act of efficiency would save the sixty-five seconds it took for the computer to boot its programs, time that would be a lot more important later.

"What in the world are you doing here at this hour?" Katlyn shouted, when she unlocked the door for her assistant.

"Okay, okay. You don't look so hot yourself." Fava could easily see how unnerved her boss was. "I didn't mean to scare you."

"I thought you might have been someone else. Sorry, guess I'm a little on edge."

"Gee, that's hard to understand. You have a job that's enough for three normal people, some fruitcake breaks into your house and freaks the crap out of you, and for good measure you throw in an in vitro to think about on your down time. Doesn't take much to upset you, does it, girl?"

Fava unshouldered an enormous leather carryall and let it drop to the floor. Her left hand reached deep down into it and came up with a brown paper bag, soggy on the bottom. Somewhere, she'd found coffee for them both at that early hour.

"And what course of action are we charting for the destruction of our career today?" Fava asked. Her large, nearly round brown eyes had charcoal circles under them, but she affected a cheery look.

Katlyn nodded. "I know. I really messed up on that Lonnigan story, didn't I? Marty is still pissed, even though he says he's not anymore. Everybody is."

"No, not everybody. I was here last night when the ratings came in. By the time the program ended Team Ten was *numero uno*. Trust me, our ever-greedy Mr. Sermac will give you a few more years to cut that out."

"I didn't do it to get higher ratings, Fava. I really thought that it would help."

"I know it, honey. I just hope you never need any favors from the Los Angeles Police Department."

Katlyn nodded ruefully. "Yeah, just when I had Stryker eating out of my hand, too."

"How's your tolerance for pain this morning?" Fava said, in a more somber mood.

"Hey, I'm bulletproof, remember? At least that's what Marty tells me I have to become." But she looked at Fava tensely and tried to judge the severity of what was to come from her features. Even Fava's pretty round face and tawny Mediterranean complexion couldn't conceal what was a more haggard than usual look. And her darting eyes had gone quiet under thick, bushy eyebrows that drooped a bit where they almost met. Still, she struggled to maintain her impish smile.

Fava went into her bag and came out with a small tape recorder, the kind used for personal dictation. She rested it on the desk prophetically. "This is from that all-night talk radio show, *Lynch at Large*. You know, cranks, calls from Jesus freaks, homophobes, Jew haters—something for the whole family?"

Katlyn sighed.

"I missed some of the beginning," she said, her voice lower by an octave. "It hurts me to do this, after what's just happened to you, but the call was very, well . . . personal. I don't think it's going to be very easy to listen to."

"Can't be any worse than the build-up," Katlyn said. But she feared the worst. Larry Lynch was the king of overnight sleaze radio and had gotten there by baiting and ridiculing his callers, the time-honored formula for success in contemporary shock radio. His callers ranked among the nation's sickest.

Fava's finger moved to the PLAY button. In a

moment Lynch launched a few insults at someone, then another voice in the small speaker made Katlyn's skin crawl. It was macabre, something from a fevered dream.

"Everybuuudy luuuvs you Kaaateee, that's why iii'm in luuuv with youuuu, pretty Kaaateee. . . ."

"My God, Fava," Katlyn said. "It's him! The same voice that was on the tape at the cabin this weekend. I think he was there, watching us."

"What do you mean?" Fava stopped the player. "Who was there?"

"Someone put a tape in our car after we got out. The message on it said I was being hunted—and it sounded a lot like that. We left for home right away."

Fava was shaken by the news. "Are you sure the tape wasn't there before you took off?"

"We would have noticed it on the way up."

"Are you positive?"

Katlyn hesitated. "No. But it doesn't really matter how it got there, does it? Especially now."

Fava nodded reluctantly. "You want to hear more?"

Katlyn closed her eyes.

"Here's a big surprise," Larry Lynch shouted. "A genuine, bona fide nut case. Go on, Caruso. Sing your heart out for all those lonely people out there."

"Pretty Kaaateee, pretty Kaaateee."

"What is this, an audition for *Star Search?* Get a life. At least get a voice."

"The lovely Kaaateee, the one on teeeveee," the basey voice said in a monotone. It was followed by a hoarse, diabolical laugh.

"Katie Ceeee, the one on teeeveee," Lynch mimicked sarcastically.

His attempt at derision was more falsetto than the eerie tremolo of the male caller.

"I wonder how he does that, folks?" Lynch chimed in.

"I luvved your prettteee pictuuures, Kaaateeee," the voice intoned.

"He knows about the pictures," Katlyn whispered. "There's only one way he could."

The break-in wasn't a one-time thing, after all. As she had suspected, her tormentor wasn't going away. She closed her eyes and was back in her bed the night of the robbery when he had been so close. If he had come upstairs instead of being scared off . . .

Lynch groaned and dialed his volume control louder to override the caller. "How does this happen, folks?" he said with a mock lament. "How do they find me?"

"You want to stop now?" Fava asked.

Katlyn shook her head.

"I don't know how much longer I can do this, people. I tell ya, it's getting to be too much. I gotta pack it in."

"A hunnnting weee will go, a hunnnting weee will go."

Fava saw the numbness settle over Katlyn's

body. She was holding it together, but just barely. And the worst part was still coming.

"Youuuu broooke myyyy heaarrrt, Kaaateee. Youuuu brooooooke myyyyy heaarrrrrrt."

The song had become the voice of a madman spiraling out of control.

"I think we've had just about enough of you," Lynch barked. "Good-night, you schmuck."

The caller responded with raucous laughter, which was underscored in a moment by thumping. Lynch was pounding his desk, loving every sick moment of it.

After a few more seconds, Lynch punched in the melody from the end of the Looney Tunes cartoons, the traditional "Lynch at Large" insult. But the voice at the other end wasn't through.

". . . nevvverrrr let her get awaaaaay," the caller crooned, overriding the zany theme.

Katlyn was reeling. Outside, a man was coming hurriedly to the door. She spun around breathlessly and saw Rudy Gallico, the guy in charge of her wardrobe. When Fava saw him she punched the STOP button and held up her hand to keep him out—but he entered anyway.

"Now don't freak out, okay?" Rudy said nervously.

He held out a large manila business envelope and her Team Ten blazer. Two large holes had been cut into the blazer, chest high.

They were much too ragged to have been made with scissors.

FOURTEEN

"He was sending me a signal, wasn't he?" Katlyn said in a hushed voice when she had examined the jacket.

The two holes in the fabric were rough circles, cut on either side of the jacket, high up, where her breasts would be.

Fava remembered the reports of victims' missing body parts and shuddered. That was what Katlyn meant.

She reached for the envelope that Rudy had left for her, unwound the string ties and emptied its contents. Two of her hairbrushes, a mother-of-pearl makeup compact, and several pairs of conservative earrings were among the litter.

"Why did he take my makeup?" she said. "What the hell is going on, Fava? Now he's following me to work."

"I don't know. It's not making any sense at all."

Katlyn plucked one good pair of earrings from the pile. "These were from Matthew. I thought I'd lost them. They were a present when we were dating."

"What about the other things?"

Katlyn sorted through the items. "Some of it's mine, some not."

Fava spotted a small multicolored envelope just before Katlyn picked it up. It looked like an old-fashioned Valentine. The outside was decorated with lace and romantic motifs. Katlyn slouched in her chair when she saw the name *Katie* written on it in lipstick, her favorite shade. The lipstick smudged when she touched it.

"How long does it take lipstick to dry?" Fava asked.

Katlyn shrugged. She held the envelope up to the light and saw a piece of paper the size of an index card inside. With shaking hands she pried it out, and electricity surged through her body.

"Oh my God. It *was* him!" She gave it to Fava and turned away.

It was a photo, a picture of a newborn, torn on one side.

Fava had seen it before, too. At Katlyn's house—at the front of her album of baby pictures. The infant Katlyn Rome.

FIFTEEN

*A*rthur listened intently to every minute of the TV program, but there was no specific mention of the incidents that had appeared in the tabloid newspapers about Katlyn Rome's stalker. It was all very puzzling.

For one thing, Arthur could not recall making either of the visits that were reported in the papers, not to her house or the television station. And he certainly hadn't made the call to the radio station— at least, not as far as he could remember.

Of course, there was always the possibility that it had been Bo.

Whether it was or not, the evidence of Rome's distress had become more and more evident in her recent broadcasts.

The most pronounced sign were some nervous habits that she had developed: a tic in her left eye, a slight stammer that occasionally slipped into her speech, especially when she was reporting on Starman. Her concentration seemed to be slipping, too, and she was trying with difficulty to read a TelePrompTer, which he had never seen her do before. For some curious reason, she had also begun to reverse some words every now and then.

Katlyn Rome had turned out to be much more skittish than at first, like a fawn easily spooked by sounds somewhere in the underbrush.

Her fearfulness had done something else to her, something quite unexpected. It had smoothed away the few remaining hard edges, taken away a last screen. Underneath, the softer, vulnerable part now came shining through.

And there was no doubt about it. To Arthur, what was underneath was very fetching, very pretty indeed.

Like a magnet.

SIXTEEN

Chief of Detectives Elliot Stryker arrived at Katlyn's office at precisely 10:45 A.M., six days after the break-in at the house, only ten minutes after he said he was coming. He was there to personally address the escalation of events, but was obviously dressed for the cameras, right down to his shining, slicked-back hair, silk suit, and colorful Armani tie. His forced politeness and conciliatory manner toward her were the ultimate expression of police public relations procedure.

He was accompanied by a plainclothes officer introduced as Dan Jarrett, a completely opposite type, who was just as seriously un–put-together. A comfortable old sports jacket and slacks that almost matched, a clean but frayed shirt collar under which lurked a T-shirt of an undefinable bluish-green color. Jarrett was younger than his boss by a decade, a few inches taller, and had a rock hard build, like a middleweight prizefighter. Several faded scars on his face indicated the kind of exercise that might have kept him that way.

There was also something gentle and subdued in his manner which was at odds with his fighting-cock physique. And something about his name rang a bell with Katlyn.

Shortly after the meeting started, Matthew arrived. He had come quickly after Katlyn had called, had not even combed his hair. He looked as if he had a chip on his shoulder, but for the moment said nothing. He stepped protectively to his wife's side.

"We just heard the radio tape," Jarrett informed him after introductions. He pointed to the recorder on Katlyn's desk.

"Evidently that's only part of what's been going on here," Matthew snapped back.

"I understand that," Stryker responded. "We'll get to everything, don't worry about that."

His tone was overly accommodating, which only wound Matthew tighter. "All I want to know is what you're going to do about it," he said.

"We're doing all that we can at this point," Stryker responded civilly. "I had hoped that my presence here would speak to that."

Stryker looked at Katlyn closely enough to make her uncomfortable. The shoe was on the other foot now, she knew. She needed his help. But for some reason his reassurance bothered her. She wondered if he would be there at all if she weren't a member of the media with the power to publicly hound him.

"We've also been trying to figure out how any individual could get into the back offices here without being noticed," Jarrett said.

His manner was outwardly placid, but Katlyn noticed his eyes were alert. She caught him studying her a little too closely, and he dropped his gaze abruptly.

"I've talked to Rudy Gallico, the man in charge of wardrobe," she said, "but he didn't notice anyone unusual in his area. If he had he would have been the first to scream bloody murder. He's very . . . territorial."

"We interviewed him before we came in here," Jarrett said, underscoring who was in charge.

Suddenly Katlyn remembered where she'd heard Dan Jarrett's name before. She had come across his file while researching a story on the L.A. drug culture. He had been Capt. Dan Jarrett then, but lost his rank over his controversial killing of an especially sadistic gang leader who enjoyed butchering his victims—and their families. Jarrett had fired five slugs into the gang-leader's face and chest and one into his back. There was some question of which shot had come first. Thus the issue of a by-the-book warning had been raised.

In the end he was a hero in the deceased's neighborhood, but earned a black eye from his superiors, who punished him with a demotion—nothing new for the tough street cop. By the time he was thirty, he held the record for being busted the most times. And for being the most effective detective on the force.

"What about visitors, messengers, studio tours—that sort of thing?" Jarrett asked. "Any disreputable types you haven't seen around here before?" He looked at his creased jacket lapel and brushed something off it.

"They wouldn't be able to get in here. Everyone has to go through a security check to get on the special elevators. Even long-time employees."

"What about the inner stairway?"

"I don't know. I never think about the stairs," said Katlyn.

"Is there anyone here who might have a grudge against you?" Jarrett asked. "Professional rivalry? I understand that's common in your business."

He was living up to his billing, his questions unexpectedly direct. Even Stryker seemed to brace whenever he spoke, Katlyn thought.

"No more than in *your* business, lieutenant," she shot back.

Jarrett acknowledged the rejoinder with an impressed look and a nod. Stryker was not pleased.

For a moment, however, Katlyn did think about Doug and what bumping him out of the lead spot must have meant to him. He wasn't the type to turn it into a personal vendetta, though. And he still made more money than she did, even though she technically outranked him as lead anchor.

"I know everyone here, and I trust them."

"Mr. Gallico swears he was in the wardrobe

area all day, except for a rest room break. Claims he eats lunch at his desk."

"If that's what he said, that's what he did." Katlyn shifted her attention to Stryker. "I talked to everyone here who was in yesterday, and no one saw anyone unusual."

Stryker's eyes narrowed. "I know it's a lot to ask of a reporter, but in this case I'd prefer that you let us talk to your people. I'm sure you can appreciate why."

The more Stryker postured for power, the more easily she could see his imperfections. For one thing, his ego seemed much too uncontrolled and close to the surface. For another, he was a sarcastic SOB, but incredibly skillful at it. You never quite knew if you were being put off or put down.

On the other hand, Jarrett was straightforward to the point of pain. In his own rough way, he had a hell of a lot more class.

"When's the last time you saw your costumes?" Jarrett said.

"I made a change yesterday afternoon before the broadcast, around four-thirty. Everything was normal."

It dawned on her that they were really checking on Rudy's story. In any case, she was tiring of the question-and-answer format.

So was Matthew. "This is going nowhere," he barked. "What are you doing to catch the person who broke into our house? And what about the tape we found in our car?"

"We're dealing with things one at a time, as they happen, Mr. Demarco," Stryker said. "Right now we're trying to understand the call to the Larry Lynch show. The caller's reference to your wife seems to have been very direct."

Matthew glared at Katlyn in surprise—which soon turned to anger. "I don't know anything about this."

"I didn't have a chance to tell you everything over the phone," Katlyn said low enough for only him to hear. "It all happened at the same time."

"The call came in last night," Jarrett said. "The voice was disguised. He seemed to be threatening your wife, although we're not positive of that."

"Did Starman ever call a radio station before he attacked the other women?" Matthew demanded.

"Who?" Stryker asked with true alarm.

"Starman. That's who we're talking about, isn't it?" Katlyn joined in.

"No, it isn't," Stryker shouted, color rushing to his face. "No we're not. Look, I understand your concerns with what's been happening, but it's too soon to make any leap to Starman."

"But just to answer your question," Jarrett said on the heels of his boss, "there's no record that any of Starman's victims were ever threatened beforehand."

Stryker shot him an evil glance. "Given how he operates, it isn't likely that the caller was

Starman. That's what the lieutenant was trying to say."

Jarrett answered by remaining silent.

"Then who do you think it was?" Katlyn fired back.

Stryker's hand traveled to a bald spot on the back of his head and pressed down a few errant hairs, a nervous gesture. "Probably just some sick fan of yours."

"And what about the picture he left after ripping up my wardrobe? How do you explain that?"

Matthew looked surprised again.

"There was so much happening," she said to hold him off until later. She took the photo off the top of the desk and held it out. "It came in a Valentine addressed to me. Written in my lipstick."

Stryker edged closer to Katlyn's desk, but Matthew took it from her as he reached for it. "Jesus, Kate. It's from your album." He looked up at Stryker with a challenging expression.

"Have you been handling it like that, too?" Stryker said without missing a beat.

His admonishment embarrassed Matthew, and he put it back on the desk.

"I never thought about fingerprints," Katlyn said. "Sorry."

Stryker leaned down to examine the shot and looked up again. It was just another baby picture to him.

"This is one of your stolen pictures?"

She nodded apprehensively.

He looked disappointed. "I guess we're not just dealing with a random series of events, then."

"No shit," Matthew said. He turned his wrist over in a smart, military move to check his watch. "I'd appreciate it if you'd tell me what you plan to do about all this. I have to be somewhere."

Jarrett noticed Katlyn's crestfallen expression at her husband's show of impatience. And priorities. Something was going on between them, he guessed. He filed away the thought.

"For the time being we're treating your situation as a stalking incident. Which is why Lieutenant Jarrett is here."

Katlyn couldn't believe it, not after all that had happened. "A stalking? Is that all?" She turned to Jarrett. "Why aren't you taking this seriously?"

"We take stalking very seriously," Stryker said for him. "Someone is clearly menacing you and we will find out who."

"What about Starman? I thought you agreed that the attacks on me weren't random."

Jarrett started to answer but Stryker waved him off. "That doesn't mean it has to be Starman. If I thought it was him I'd be the first to worry. But so far there's no evidence that it is. We get dozens of stalking incidents every week, and we just can't assume it's the same person."

"But I know what I saw at the house—from the top of the stairs. What I told your men."

"I read your report, Ms. Rome, and to be fair, you only saw a shadow. Shadows exaggerate a shape. And you were frightened—so much so that you accidentally fired a pistol."

What he said was true. And she had been preoccupied with Starman, as the other officers had pointed out. But it seemed as real as could be. "I know what I felt. There was something primitive about the man, something that made my hair stand on end. That never happened to me before."

"I sympathize with what you went through, but the main thing is that the intruder never even tried to get to you, correct?"

She felt drained of energy, as if she'd run a hundred miles. "Don't you see what you're really saying to me? That I have to wait until he kills me before you'll believe me."

When Stryker didn't answer, Katlyn saw their suspicion of her. Matt was uncomfortable and preoccupied, probably with his work. He had an important music session in a few hours. In a way, she couldn't blame him. This part of his morning was going nowhere, and the same was true for her.

"I think it might help you to know that Lieutenant Jarrett isn't assigned to the regular force," Stryker said. "He's part of the special Threat Management Unit, which is the division that handles high-profile stalking cases."

Katlyn nodded but found little reassurance in his explanation. The police were writing off Starman as a possible suspect. She noticed that Jarrett looked defensive when Stryker described his role. She imagined that his previous indiscretions were the reason he was now in Threat Management, and she wondered how committed he was to his new job.

"That means we're officially considering all the incidents as part of the same pattern," Stryker said. "Your celebrity status is why we're channeling your case to the unit. Trust me, they're well-trained to deal with it."

Katlyn's gaze darted to Jarrett again. She also questioned whether he shared Stryker's confidence in the TMU.

"That's not enough," Matthew said abruptly. "From what I've heard the TMU is a tiny group compared to the thousands on the regular force."

"Small in size, yes, Mr. Demarco, but very effective. Since its inception, the unit has handled close to three hundred cases without serious injury to anyone targeted by stalkers."

A well-rehearsed remark, Katlyn thought. A sound byte or part of a campaign speech. "I keep telling you, this isn't a stalking. Your statistics don't apply here."

Before he could answer she saw Fava waving to her from the newsroom. She had a sheet of paper in her hand and a telephone to her ear.

Katlyn turned to the two officers. "I don't think there's any point in continuing with this."

Stryker seemed annoyed. "Lieutenant Jarrett will be here for a while to talk to the staff," he said. "We'll be in touch."

"Your call," she said curtly. She turned to Matt. "You might as well get to your session. I'll talk to you later." She took a few steps toward the door, then stopped and turned back to the chief of detectives.

"This special stalking force you've been talking about?" she asked. "Just how many people *are* there in it?"

"Nine men and women, all trained specifically for celebrity cases."

"Let me ask you something. In all those cases they've worked on, you said there was never anyone injured?"

"It's a matter of record."

"And of all these cases, just how many of the stalkers have you actually captured?"

Her question caught Stryker off guard. His hand went for his bald spot again.

"I don't have the exact figures," he mumbled. "I'll have to get back to you on that."

SEVENTEEN

Matthew listened to the entire tape before saying anything, then slammed Fava's small player down on the kitchen table. The freakish call confirmed his worst suspicions.

"I can't believe after everything that's happened you're still not ready to do anything about it," he said accusingly.

"It's all coming so fast. I haven't had time to think it through."

She had been relying on Matthew's support, she realized. More than that, she had assumed it. The last thing she expected was enmity and even more pressure.

"I want you out of there, now. Not one more day at the station."

She looked at him in total disbelief. His attempt to dominate her was repugnant, a side of him she had seen only recently—ever since the burglary.

"I hope you said that because you're so worried about me. Because if it was for any other reason—"

He thought better of whatever he was going to say. "What the hell did the radio station do about it? Did they at least trace the call?"

"What do you think? They're treating it like it was a crank call."

"But it was a specific threat. The caller used the name *Katie*. He mentioned taking your pictures."

"The station had no way of knowing what it meant, not that they'd probably care. Even Stryker thinks it could have been a reference to other kinds of pictures, like my television image. Or advertising shots of me on billboards."

"And what if it really *was* Starman on the other end?" Matthew shouted.

"To them, everybody sounds like Starman at four in the morning. That's what they want from their callers."

"Maybe Lynch could bait the person who called, get him to call in again and trace it."

"Even if Lynch would do it, I doubt Starman would be dumb enough to fall for it."

Matthew looked fit to be tied. She was afraid of him when he was this way. She seriously wondered whether he could become violent if pushed far enough. She studied her hands and saw a long crack in the polish on one of her nails. It was symbolic of her life lately. At work, and now at home. Things were splitting apart.

"What about the picture from the album that they found at work?" he asked more constructively.

"There's no doubt about what that meant, not even to Stryker."

Matthew pushed himself away from the table and went to the liquor cabinet. The bottle of Dewar's had been there unopened for months. Now, in a matter of a few days, he had gone to it a dozen times. He poured some in a water glass and took two deep swallows.

"Kate, I just don't know what to do to make you listen. Or what it's going to take for you to get some sense. But I'll tell you this. What's happened so far is only the beginning. You know that, don't you?"

She shook her head slowly, a half-hearted protest. "I keep telling myself, maybe it won't happen to me. That I'm different somehow from the other women he went after."

"Even if it's not Starman, it'll be someone else, sooner or later, attracted by your face on TV. We both know that, don't we?" He leaned over the table toward her, supported by his hands. "And if it *is* Starman doing all this, do you really think he's going to stop at cutting up your blazer?"

Katlyn was shaken by the calculated horror of his reference. It was a deliberate attempt to play on her fear, to persuade her to leave her job. His jealous attack wounded her deeply. And, separate from his own motives, the truth of what he said made it even worse.

"I don't know what to tell you, Kate. I just don't know."

"That makes two of us," she said, trying to

submerge her sudden anger. "Just give me some more time." She eased herself off the chair, then turned back and looked him squarely in the eye. "And do me a favor, will you?"

Matthew waited, his expression still petulant.

"Just make damn sure of your reasons for scaring the hell out of me like this. Make damn sure it isn't because of what *you're* afraid of." She grabbed the bottle of scotch brusquely from his hand and took a glass from a cabinet. "Something that has nothing at all to do with Starman," she snapped, walking away.

She left the kitchen in a flurry and headed toward the bedroom. She desperately needed a hot bath, a safe place to hide from the world— away from Matthew.

Later when she lay in the tub, she could feel the liquor spreading its warmth. Without wanting to, her mind fled back to the night they arrived at the cabin only to find the tape and then leave, quickly. She felt the same tingle now that had crept up her spine when Matthew played the tape.

She could still hear the simple and seemingly innocent children's song—*A hunting we will go, a hunting we will go*—and the malevolent intent behind it.

EIGHTEEN

With over eight hundred feet of space to choose from, Willy "Guano" Dunellen, the chief forensic criminologist for the City of Los Angeles, sat as close to cross-legged as his stubby little limbs allowed on the floor of his spotless laboratory. Years earlier, Jarrett had remarked that Dunellen could find fly shit in a cave full of guano, and his nickname was born.

The short, corpulent expert had a perfectly round bald spot covered with little beads of sweat. He looked like a rotund Trappist monk in a starched blue denim work shirt. Dunellen's reputation for detail was legendary, but lately, as an administrator, his personal visits to crime scenes were a rare occurrence. Jarrett had persuaded him to follow up on the investigations of the Katlyn Rome stalking incidents himself.

"Please, don't get up," Jarrett announced from the doorway as soon as Guano turned around.

"Well if it isn't the late great Danny Boy Jarrett," Guano said. "I didn't think they still let you out on the street."

"I try not to give them a choice."

Guano put down a tray he'd been peering

into. His hands were encased in thin latex gloves and his lab coat looked as if it had been starched. "No shit, Danny, how you doin' with all this damsel-in-distress TMU bullshit? I still can't get over the way they chewed your ass after you blew that scumbag away. Should've given you a congressional."

"Yeah, well, I get an assignment and I do it— just like always. Nothing ever changes all that much."

Jarrett's own words stirred up a memory. A picture of his father came vividly to mind. Thomas Jarrett had talked about change too. His father was a by-the-book man who, in a very different way, had tried to protect the innocents of his time. His chosen weapon was words, not guns, fingerprint powder, and ballistics like Guano used. As a social services lawyer he had learned to bust slumlords, negligent parents, and con men of every description with the law, not their heads with his hands. Jarrett often wondered what his father would have thought about the way he did the business of justice.

"I still think what they did to you sucked the big one," Dunellen chimed in. He stared at Jarrett for a few more seconds, then went back to his work.

Jarrett moved to a chair that looked like a barstool and lifted his butt onto it, still standing. All around him there was apparatus of every description, all immaculate and neatly arranged on gleaming stainless steel countertops. The whole place was sterile, not just in the way prescribed by his profession—in the way an obsessive-compulsive would do it.

"Your guys turn up anything at Rome's house yet? Or her office?"

Guano grunted disdainfully. He was fascinated by some object not bigger than the point of a pencil. "What do you think? There was bigtime pressure from the top, so we gave it the full treatment. Even though they were technically only break-ins."

"And?"

He turned the small thing over. His eyes never left it. "The problem on something like this is that we get too much shit, and don't even know what we're looking for."

He looked up and pointed to one of the cabinets. The door was open. There were a number of trays lined with plastic containers of every size and description, some of the stuff inside maybe connected to the Rome incidents.

"In the old days it was hunt and peck. These days I use a vacuum that saves anything it sucks up. Whatever the maid has missed for the last twenty years. And whatever the vacuum misses I get with the tape lift transfer. Shit, I got paint chips from Rome's house in colors that haven't been seen there for years. I got lint and dandruff and human hairs and pet hairs and carpet fuzz and fish food. I got organic and nonorganic, animal, vegetable, and mineral trace elements. And every now and then some shit that even the mighty Dunellen can't analyze."

"I didn't think they made anything like that—according to you."

"And that's just what we got from Rome's house. Plus enough shit from the wardrobe room at the station to connect it to a thousand people on the outside." He looked up at Jarrett. "Now, what was it you wanted again? Oh, yeah. You wanted to know if I *found* anything." He arched his head back. "O ye of little faith."

Jarrett eased himself off the stool, but Guano held his hand up before he got far, and shifted his weight back and forth until he was able to get to his own feet.

Jarrett stared at Dunellen quizzically.

The round little man ambled to a closed cabinet, opened it, and took out a small plastic bag. He threw it on the counter like a high roller throwing a blackjack dealer a ten spot. "Take a look. No extra charge."

Jarrett lifted it up to a ceiling light. He didn't see anything inside until he brought it closer to his face and squinted at an almost microscopic sliver of something that was sickly yellow. "A section of fingernail?" he guessed.

"Very impressive," Guano said. "But why not a toenail?"

"If you're interested in it it's because you found it at the crime scene. Most people don't commit crimes with their shoes off, or stop to cut their toenails. So it's a fingernail." He examined it again. "Any nail polish or lacquer? Skin cells you could run a DNA on?"

"Negative, unfortunately."

"Blood?"

"Uh-uh."

"So what can you tell from it?"

"Female, Caucasian."

"Which rules out the Starman theory. Did anyone ask Rome if she remembered tearing her nail?"

"Yeah, and she didn't. But it was a small piece and could have been already loose. She could easily have done it and not even felt it."

Jarrett thought about it. "What about age?"

"Beats the shit out of me."

"So that's it?"

"Hey, not too shabby for something I found sticking into a bookcase drawer. Gotta admit, it could have been interesting."

"You didn't find anything here that fits with evidence found at other Starman scenes?"

Dunellen quieted uncharacteristically. The question seemed to disturb him. After all the grisly things that he must have seen there wasn't much that did, Jarrett thought.

"We didn't find squat at the murder scenes."

"I thought there was always evidence, if you knew where to look."

Dunellen exhaled deeply, then sauntered

back to his futon and sat down with a sigh. "Yeah, there's even an axiom about it. Called Locard's principle. Locard's law says that everyone leaves a trace of their presence—always. And it's true. The only question is whether it can be trans- ferred to a single suspect."

"So how come you keep coming up empty with Starman? You're as techy as they come."

Dunellen looked genuinely hurt. "Okay, peckerhead, it works like this. Let's say we know someone was cut or shot—or, in Starman's case, had some body part separated with a knife—we know there had to be blood, right? But there's none we can see. That used to be the end of the line. Now I just whip out my trusty can of Luminol. Cutting-edge shit. I spray the place where the blood probably was, like around the body, or near where the murder could have hap- pened. Then I turn the lights off, and wherever there was blood, is now glowing blue. So I scrape up everything in the area and analyze it for traces of the blood."

"Sounds logical."

"Only in Starman's case, there's blue but never any evidence. Any blood or any anything. He never leaves Dick Tracy." He drilled Jarrett with a defiant glance. "Am I going too fast for you, rookie?"

"No, I actually think I've got it. Correct me if I'm wrong, but what you got from Rome so far is evidence that there once was evidence—but there isn't anymore. And despite this incredible forensic *tour de force*, you still collect a paycheck every Friday."

Guano digested the accusation for another moment, then adjusted his neck in a collar that used to fit. "Yeah," he said. "I think that about covers it."

NINETEEN

The gene that programmed Claire Fava to sit in the same position for hours at a time was the same one that sent lemmings over the cliff every few years, she figured. Usually the pain was only on the right side of her lower back, where it sat on a low flame until something brought it to a boil. Now she could feel it on both sides. And there was a long night of work ahead of her.

Pushing back in her chair, the research assistant who worked exclusively for the news anchor stared at her latest findings on the computer screen and typed a heading: Victim Traits. The file was a summary of similarities shared by past stalking victims that might lead to theories about what attracted Starman to them. If she could figure that out, she had a chance to discover his possible attraction to Katlyn—if it was Starman who had been stalking her. To date, other than the fact that he attacked female celebrities, no one knew for sure what got Starman's rocks off. Or how he selected the few from the many.

To help find out Fava decided to enlist the help of a battery of computer software. WMTC's management, meaning Sermac, had spent a sizable amount on potent new computers. Certainly not because he was a big spender. Given the intense competition among broadcasters, anything that shortened the interval between a news event and the time it could be reported was simply an investment in survival. And profit.

Fava's favorite tool was a Power Mac 8100i combined with an optical scanner that could input printed matter from any outside source. She was also grateful for a service called Lexis-Nexis, a database that gave researchers access to virtually all newspaper and magazine stories published during the past two decades. The service had become requisite for broadcast journalism, and in the wee small hours Fava had it all to herself.

A second valuable feature of Lexis-Nexis was its ability to select only what was wanted from volumes of information by using customized keywords. The more precise the word cue, the more specific the data. A general keyword like *water*, for instance, would select thousands of articles on any topic relating to it. Adding *sea* and *wave* would reduce the information retrieved to articles that satisfied all of those criteria, like pieces on tidal waves or hurricanes.

In Starman's case, the obvious limitation was that his victims formed only a small sample. Nothing other than their youthfulness, sex, and celebrity had surfaced thus far to link them. But she hoped that by using a much larger sample of similar cases over a longer period, a clearer pattern would emerge. Without Lexis-Nexis the project would have taken several weeks.

The first keywords she typed in were *stalking, celebrity,* and an arbitrary start date, *January 1980.* Minutes later, one of three high-speed printers clustered in the center of the newsroom produced a deck of pages two inches thick. When she examined it, almost all of the subjects were the famous celebrity cases everyone had read about, led, not surprisingly, by the attacks on Ronald Reagan and John Lennon. Other well-publicized cases involved the murdered TV star Rebecca Schaeffer, Sharon Tate, Jodie Foster, Johnny Carson, and, more recently, David Letterman. Unlike the way the LAPD and Threat Management Unit had discriminated between them, violent and nonviolent cases were all grouped together.

Soon, when duplicate reports were taken into consideration, the cases were reduced to a few dozen. Curiously, there were more men than women, the opposite of the statistics for the population as a whole.

On the next sort, she expanded the time frame to the full capability of Lexis-Nexis and sorted for violent attacks only. The new pile was much smaller—the murders by Starman already a decent percent of them. Katlyn had beaten incredible odds just to have been selected by him.

The next pass was an attempt to find similarities in the backgrounds of victims who'd actually been attacked. The sample wasn't large enough to be statistically reliable, but she was optimistic that what she might find would spark an intuitive leap. She'd guessed correctly on other topics, with even less to go on.

Working, then, from the general to the specific, she typed in criteria for age, race, birthplace, education, and sex. When she finished, the printer spit out list after list of different celebrity groupings based on the common characteristics of the people in those groups.

For some reason, the name *Katlyn Rome* was on none of them. When it came to shared characteristics, Katlyn was evidently a one of a kind.

TWENTY

On Thursday, at 10:00 P.M., the Music Factory was more active than it was during the day. Matthew took his place behind an immense digital mixing board, stuffed two slices of Big Red gum in his mouth, and wished it was a joint, or at least a cigarette. For the first time all day, he stopped thinking about how much Katlyn's job was imperiling their marriage.

Forty minutes later, the cheer that finally rose from the recording booth announced the arrival of Rob Marsala, the superstar singer chosen for lead. Without ceremony the younger man went directly into the inner sanctum, and took his place next to the two women and the man who already had their earphones on. The three walls on Matthew's side were insulated with sections of soundproofing material that had the texture of giant shredded wheat squares. The fourth was a thick soundproofed Plexiglas barrier in front of the recording area that separated those who produced music from those who performed it.

"Let him hear the band," Matt said to the sound engineer, Peter DeJong.

DeJong punched a half-dozen numbers into

his computer, and a giant reel, which held the master tape, started to spin.

Hearing the track played back even in a rough mix gave Matthew a surge of adrenaline. Although conceived as a traditional love ballad, his evocative orchestration included elements of gospel. The strings soared, the horns made it sexy, and the percussion brought it to a boil. When the band had finished performing their part, all it needed was Rob Marsala, the Pavarotti of rhythm and blues.

The big man put his earphones on and scanned the score. Halfway through the first chorus, Marsala began to play with the melody, coloring it with his own interpretation, making it his own. When the tape ran down, Matthew reached for the TALKBACK button that broadcast his voice into the soundproof room. "Not bad," he said with deliberate understatement. But what he was thinking was, *You crazy fucking genius, you've got it already!* "Let's put one down."

On the next pass, the voice that issued from the small but potent Bose speakers filled the room with a new vocabulary of expression. The spell Rob cast was infectious, and the other singers began to belt on their own. On the third try all of them went full-out, with a consummate exhibition by Marsala, who had found the heart and soul of the music and was singing with his eyes closed.

As the song built toward its climax a crowd

began to gather from other places around the studio. Anyone who'd heard that Marsala was singing or had picked up on sound bytes that leaked out of the control room and into the halls came running. They came like the searchers for the lost mountain in *Close Encounters of The Third Kind* and stood motionless, afraid to break the spell.

The singers' voices flowed in and out of one another's, as in a great flirtatious bacchanal. When the crescendo came, the entire studio reverberated with the truth and majesty of the career-making performance that Matthew De-marco had first heard only in his mind.

When the last of the notes faded, DeJong punched a button on the tape machine with a dramatic flourish and there was total silence. Then, as if a signal had been given, the assemblage let loose with a cheer. In the soundproof chamber, the backup singers hugged Marsala and each other, then shifted their attention to Matthew, who was allowing himself to savor the sweet taste of triumph.

In the midst of the jubilation, Marsala made his way to the front room and put his hand up as he approached. Matthew responded, and Marsala caught his hand in midair and held it.

"Welcome back, brother," he said simply and sincerely.

DeJong's part in the celebration was cut short by a blinking light on one of the phone lines. He pressed the button, picked up the receiver, and signaled Matthew.

Matthew moved away from the crowd. He hoped it was Katlyn. She had chosen the perfect moment.

The urgent voice on the other end belonged to Murray Alter. The doctor in charge of their incubating fetus had never called him personally. As far as Matthew knew, Alter didn't have his number at the studio—unless Kate had given it to him.

The call was brief. As the revelers continued to celebrate, DeJong watched Matthew out of the corner of his eye. He noticed that he wasn't talking, just staring unfocused at the dials on the console. Moments later he let the receiver fall onto the console without saying anything and covered his face with his hands.

TWENTY-ONE

D r. Murray Alter, M.D., F.A.C., Ob. Gyn., had rearranged his busy schedule so that he could meet with Katlyn and Matthew at eleven. It had taken an extreme act of resolve for them to come at all.

Alter was a world-class specialist in human fertility. People from all over the country went to him when their attempts at conception were not successful. They were the kind of people who did their homework on geneticists. His waiting list for an in-vitro procedure was so long that by his own estimate one couple out of three got pregnant or adopted before he saw them.

In his brief phone call to the studio the night before, he had told Matthew the worst possible news. Someone had gone to the hospital lab and violently ended their latest hope for a baby. He thought it would be better for Matthew to tell Katlyn.

They waited for him in a small anteroom—paneled walls waxed to a high gloss, wainscoting on the bottom, a delicate Pierre Deux design above it. It was more like the parlor of a Victorian home than a doctor's reception area, but the soothing environment did nothing to alleviate their mood of total devastation.

After an uncharacteristically long wait, Alter walked out of his office. A burly man of indeterminate age with bushy shocks of orange-red hair for sideburns, he looked very different from the last time they had seen him. His face was etched with deep concern, and Katlyn and Matthew rose heavily from their separate places in the room.

"I'm sorry I couldn't do this sooner. I imagine you can understand why." He took Katlyn's hand in both of his. "We'll get through this, I promise."

In contrast to the waiting room, his own office was austere. Two entire walls were lined with framed photos of families. No diplomas were visible. The children in the pictures were the only credentials he needed.

Alter's fingers toyed absently with an oversized paper clip as he floundered for a way to start.

"I've lost children before for reasons which have always been in God's hands," he said finally, "never in such a senseless way. I don't know what to say to you."

It was obvious he took the loss personally, and it brought Katlyn near tears. "We're just empty, that's all," she said.

"I'd be surprised if you weren't. Of course, this isn't the end of things."

He looked intently at Katlyn when he said it. The comment was a probe.

"We need to know more about what happened," Matthew interrupted. "Do they have any idea who it was?"

"Or should we take a good guess?" Katlyn said acerbically, turning to stare at Alter.

"The police haven't learned anything other than what they told me originally. Someone got past the hospital guard and completely destroyed the lab."

"Was it that easy to do?" Katlyn said.

"Evidently it was. The idea of security in a hospital lab is mostly about the threat of contamination. We never considered that anyone would go there to destroy human life." He leaned back in his chair and folded his hands in his lap. "But times have changed, I guess. For what it's worth, we've already taken steps so that it can't happen again."

"How much was destroyed?" Katlyn asked. "Everything? Or were we singled out?"

Alter knew what had been happening to her and that a lot was riding on his answer.

"The destruction was systematic and complete. We had sixteen embryos incubating, and all were removed from their atmospheres and smashed on the floor. Seven belonged to my patients," he added sadly, putting his hand on a pile of green folders and touching them as if they were the lives he was talking about. "I have to talk to the other parents today."

"I don't envy you," Katlyn offered.

"I don't envy me, either."

As tragic as the news was for the other prospective parents, Katlyn was relieved to hear that theirs wasn't the only embryo that had been destroyed—and felt guilty for feeling that way.

"Did anyone see who did it?" Matthew asked.

"Yes, but not enough to identify him. He was dressed like staff, and the guard got to the lab in time to see him running out a back door. Usually it's locked. The guard said he was of average height and weight. There were no fingerprints. The destruction was meticulously planned."

"That's it?" Matthew asked indignantly. "That's all they know?"

"Only one other thing. The forensics investigator told me they found a small smear of blood on one of the tabletops near some broken glass—but not until after the cleanup started. It's possible that the person who broke the vials cut himself in the process, but it could have been someone who works there."

"Are they going to try and find out?"

"Of course." Alter's intercom buzzed loudly, startling Katlyn. He took the call, then put it on hold.

"I'm sorry," he sighed, "but it's one of the other couples. I'll have to take it in the other room."

Matthew looked at Katlyn, who was staring past Alter as if it didn't matter if he ever came back. Alter stopped at the door and turned to face them.

"When I return I'd like to talk about where we go from here. Until yesterday the process was going perfectly. Fertilization was achieved and the progress of the zygote was very encouraging. I'm ready to begin again as soon as you are. Please. Let's think about it."

"We will, doctor. You can count on that," Matthew said quickly, but when he saw Katlyn's face he wasn't so sure. They hadn't even come close to discussing it.

Alter nodded and left the room to take the call.

After he left Katlyn stared dejectedly at the pictures of children on the wall. Alter's challenge was unexpected, but it sounded remote now. It was hard to even think about another attempt. They'd come so close and the journey had been so difficult.

It started after almost a year of failure to conceive. At first Matthew had blamed the stress of both their jobs, but eventually their infertility was traced to scarring on both of her fallopian tubes, the result of the removal of several large cysts when she was in her late teens. When they heard about Murray Alter, they contacted his office, and began their wait.

Ten months went by before his office called, and from there she was given hormones to stimulate her ovaries to release as many eggs as possible, not just the single one that is the result of a normal cycle. Her eggs were then removed prior to ovulation and incubated in a special growth medium. At the right time, Matthew's sperm was added. A fertilization had occurred on their second try, and the egg was then placed in an environment that replicated the womb as closely as possible.

After that, the process was still perilous. The resulting zygote was to be inserted through the cervical canal back into her uterus. All told, the chances in favor of a full-term pregnancy were about twenty percent. They'd been well on the way to beating the daunting odds.

"We *can't* start over again now," Katlyn finally said to Matthew, "not while everything else is going on."

"Don't make any decision on that now. In a few weeks maybe, when things settle down." He paused, then added, "What happened at the lab might have nothing to do with the other things. You might feel better about—"

"Of course it had something to do with it," Katlyn interrupted angrily. "What are you thinking? That someone else just *happened* to do this at this same time?"

"All right, Kate. But what do we do, stop the most important thing in our lives just because we're scared?"

She was tired, very tired. "It's not our choice anymore, don't you see that? Starman is in control, not us. He dictates everything we do, even whether I'm going to keep working or not. What do you think our days have been all about since the break-in? And our nights? What do we talk about all the time?" Her eyes were brimming. "When was the last time we made love?"

They heard footsteps and Katlyn turned away before Matthew could reply.

"Sorry I took so long," Alter said when he entered the room again. He saw wet streaks staining Katlyn's cheeks. "I've obviously interrupted."

"I don't think we can make any plans right now," Katlyn said summarily. "It's just not the right time. We have to see what happens."

Alter stroked his chin. "Maybe you're right. Perhaps dealing with it right now would be too stressful." He turned to Matthew for confirmation but didn't see it.

"While I was outside I got another call from the hospital," he said, changing the topic. "One of the medical secretaries wanted to tell me before she called the police."

Katlyn rose to full alert. She wondered what could possibly be worse than what he'd already told them.

"This morning the secretary noticed that the office where we keep the medical records had been broken into. The office is pretty far away from the crime scene, and even though the door had been pried open it wasn't visibly damaged." He clasped and unclasped his hands nervously. "I don't know how else to say this . . . but the records are gone."

Matthew braced. "He took all the records?"

"No, not all of them. Just yours. I'm sorry."

Both men looked at Katlyn. She looked wretched, as if she had been expecting it.

"Well, I guess that tells us a lot, doesn't it," she said, shooting a harsh glance at Matthew. She stood and moved to the door. "Talk to you in a while, Murray. But I don't think it will be that soon." She left without closing the door.

Matthew stood, but waited when he saw Alter still deep in thought.

"You haven't told us everything, have you?"

Alter shook his head wearily. "I couldn't bring myself to tell Katlyn. The lab team has just finished their work with the broken vials. Each of them was labeled with a tape of the parents' names. The technicians found the names of all of my patients—all but one."

Matthew slumped to his seat and put his head in his hands. "I don't fucking believe this—"

"What they're thinking . . . is that your vial wasn't smashed. The person who broke in? Well, he probably took it with him."

TWENTY-TWO

"I t's time for you to get off the Starman story for a while," Conroy said, as if it were the beginning of a routine conversation.

He had waited until after the weekend to call her to his office and make her declaration of independence for her. Katlyn was taken completely by surprise.

"What happened to the 'hang tough' routine you gave me last time?"

"That was before. Now, things are different."

"You're afraid it's going to get even worse, is that it?"

Whatever Conroy believed didn't show on his face.

"I can see what's happening to you. You're on edge all the time, looking over your shoulder."

He'd noticed more than Katlyn had realized. It was comforting and disconcerting at the same time.

"And, speaking professionally, I know your audience can see, too. I've discussed this with Lockhart and he agrees. The strain is showing up in your broadcasts."

The critique came from out of the blue. Up

until then she thought she'd been doing a good job of hiding her inner turmoil from the camera. She felt defensive—and suddenly realized how protective she was about the possibility of losing her job.

"I'm having trouble concentrating. Memorizing. If I could read the TelePrompTers more easily, maybe I wouldn't—" She stopped abruptly. "Forget I said that. The last thing I want to do is use that as an excuse. Actually, it has nothing to do with it. I'll just have to be more careful from now on."

"Kate, anyone would have trouble focusing with what you're going through. And I don't think you can just decree it away, either. Anyway, I'm thinking it might be a good idea for you to lie low, but only for a while. Take a leave of absence for a few weeks. Get your face off the screen for a while so whoever's out there won't have a stimulus."

"Is this Sermac's idea?"

"Are you kidding? He'd work you until you dropped. And if you tell him we had this conversation, I'll deny it."

The irony was not lost on Katlyn. Now that Marty had come around to her point of view, she felt a tremendous letdown. But what he was saying was reasonable. Things had gotten woefully worse, personally and with her broadcasts.

In her own mind there was still no doubt that it was Starman who had visited the station. And since then she'd been scared from the time she stepped out of the elevator in the morning until she left at the end of the day. And all the way home.

"Are you ordering me off the program, no matter what my decision is?"

The directness of the question brought him up short.

"I'll listen to anything you have to say, of course. As I always do."

"Okay. I'll hold you to that. I've given it a lot of thought and I've decided to stick it out for a while. Not because I'm all that brave, though. I *am* very scared. It's just that I believe I can do more good for myself and everyone else by staying with it—at least for now."

"Is that how Matthew feels?"

Marty knew where to shoot his arrows.

"As a matter of fact, no. Matthew feels the way you do, only more strongly. We fight about it all the time."

Marty let her pronouncement settle for a while before his expression softened. Then he looked up at her and said, "And even so, all things considered, you want to continue?"

She looked at him for a long time. "This could be the dumbest thing I ever did. But I'm tired of running from something to nothing in my life."

Marty nodded, still holding his cards close to his chest.

"There's something else, too. I didn't know I had it in me, Marty, but lately, I've been getting mad. I mean, really mad."

Marty picked up a stack of papers on his desk, maneuvered them into a neater deck, then handed them to her abruptly. "In that case, we'd better get to work, hadn't we?"

He checked the look that his speedy turn-around put on her face, and then busied himself tidying his desk.

"You were testing me, weren't you? You knew what I was going to do all along."

Marty rubbed the side of his forehead with a great hairy hand. His eyes were deadly serious. "I had to be sure, Kate," he said softly. "And I had to know you were sure. The stakes are getting higher."

TWENTY-THREE

The six days since the theft of their embryo at
the lab had passed without further incident,
but the earlier events continued to take their
toll, at home and at work. Matthew's mood had
deteriorated to the point where all conversa-
tions were strained. At the station, she had lost
even more concentration, and each broadcast
contained more small mistakes.

Marty tried his best to be supportive now,
claiming that her slips humanized her all the
more, but she doubted that he believed it.

On Thursday morning, her work was disturbed by the feeling that something unusual was
going on. For one thing, her customary update
on Starman was not on her desk when she
arrived. That was puzzling since the Channel 2
Daybreak news program was already running a
story on another murdered young actress. In this
case, however, an enraged boyfriend had admitted to the killing, and police had been quick to
reassure the citizenry that it was not Starman.

Also, Marty had not come to her office all

morning and had studiously avoided her in the newsroom. For the last hour he had been in conference with Jude Sermac. Normally their unscheduled meetings did not last that long and took place in the executive conference area. This time, after their conference they left together, and Sermac had his arm on Marty's shoulder.

Fava was also acting peculiar. She was absent from her desk until after ten, and when she returned she stayed glued to her computer screen. She gave Katlyn a lame excuse about having to run some errands, then left hastily. She was obviously covering up something and was a terrible liar.

Doug's sudden conviviality was the final tip-off. Since she replaced him as anchor he had been predictably distant. But this morning he turned on the charm.

The workup on Starman finally arrived at ten-thirty. By then her concentration was almost completely shot, and she had to read some of the paragraphs two or three times before they sank in.

A short time later, still restless, she went out into the newsroom to look for Fava. Her computer was on, and the folder icon she was working on was still on the screen. It was labeled STRMN. Katlyn clicked on it and a dozen files filled the screen. She randomly clicked on one named STRMN 7.

The information on the first page was

research on violent stalking crimes and the characteristics of several of the stalkers. All of the cases identified involved female victims. Fava was working in an area that exactly paralleled Starman's victims. At least that made sense.

Katlyn closed that file and scanned the others in the folder. One she had not noticed before made her stiffen. It was named STRMN-KR.

Katlyn read the information and left the file open. She bent down and typed *Talk to me, K.* at the bottom of the page.

TWENTY-FOUR

Katlyn waited in Marty's office for him to return after his long meeting with Sermac. His room was somewhat smaller than hers, she noted, a point which Marty had brought up himself for its instructional value. He told her the news business was like professional sports: the stars get the perks because no one pays to watch the managers play. Marty was big on sports analogies. His wallpaper design motif was little Lakers logos.

"I want you to listen before you say anything," he said, when he finally came back. "And don't be negative."

"I'm already negative," Katlyn snapped, coming to her feet. "I'm the only one around here who doesn't know what's going on."

"Good, I knew I could count on your cooperation."

"No, you can't, Marty. Not this time."

"I've just spent over an hour with Sermac. A very unpleasant hour, actually. Not exactly male bonding."

"It didn't look that way."

"Never show the bad guys what the family is thinking. I learned that in *The Godfather.*"

He steered her with a firm hand to the sofa before she could say anything and stood in front of her with his arms folded.

"Sermac's been stewing with an idea ever since that thief broke into your house. And the crank call to the Larry Lynch program has spurred him on to even greater depths. In short, he smells the opportunity of a lifetime."

"What opportunity? For whom?"

"Ever since we started you on the Starman story the ratings have gone through the roof. Everyone knows that. Now Jude's talking about doing a special, something he refers to as 'The Hunter and the Hunted.' Are you with me so far?" Marty stole a peek at her out of the corner of his eye.

"I don't think I believe this."

"He wants the news reporter to become the news. What it feels like to be a stalked woman."

Katlyn was flushed with anger. "Sermac has the ultimate exclusive on the Starman story and I'm it, right? The mercenary slimeball."

"Mercenary slimeball, *sir*. But it's a perfectly logical idea, if you run a television news station and have the ethics of a boa constrictor."

"So what does he want?" She looked back at him. "Exactly what?"

"A news special on Starman with you as the topic. An up-close-and-personal type deal. What it feels like to go from reporter on a stalking story to becoming a target."

"You want to know what it's like? It sucks.

And isn't it ironic that Sermac is the only one who believes the person after me is Starman."

"I wouldn't go as far as to say he *believes* it. It's just that no other station has a news anchor being stalked by someone who *might* be him. It pays for him to believe it."

Katlyn shook her head in disbelief. "Of course you said *no.*"

"Absolutely. At least a dozen times."

"Thank you."

"For starters, I said the idea could ruin your credibility as a reporter. And Sermac agreed. But he also said what you'd lose in credibility you would more than make up for in audience empathy. And that your credibility had already taken a hit with that unfortunate *editorial* after the Lonnigan story. He had me there."

"There's never been any contest between my credibility and his profits."

"I also pointed out that it would compromise your ability to deal with future sources, like Stryker. He said that happened already, too, at the press conference, when you embarrassed Stryker by making Starman's previous track record public."

"He's rationalizing, and you know it."

"Anyway, when I couldn't reach him on a professional level, I told him it would be immoral to exploit your privacy for a special, and that you don't do something like this to a member of the family."

"What did he say?"

"That there was nothing immoral about running a business in a way that kept all the family members employed, especially the ones making the big numbers."

His message was clear. Sermac had ordered Marty to get her to cooperate if he wanted to keep his job. And he'd had to cave.

"The last thing I tried was your personal safety. I told him we were dealing with a lunatic and couldn't predict his reaction."

"Like he cared."

"Actually, I think he did. Jude's bad, but not that bad. Or maybe he just didn't want it on his conscience. At least he had thought about it long enough to call the Threat Management Unit and speak to their criminal psychologist."

"Ruth Dubois?"

"Yeah. How'd you know?"

"I've scheduled an interview with her. She has very impressive credentials. Consults with law enforcement offices all over the country."

"According to Jude, she told him there was no way to be certain about the effects of a program like that. But she also said that more publicity on your story could actually scare away the creep who's been terrorizing you. I don't know if that's true or not."

"Did she happen to mention what the chances are it could do the opposite?"

"No."

"That's very reassuring." Katlyn looked at Marty directly and said, "Does she think it's Starman who's been coming after me?"

"Didn't say." Marty massaged his paunchy stomach and grimaced. "Kate, I don't know what to tell you. In my opinion, Sermac should be thrilled that you're still at the station at all. I'm not ordering you to do anything, just telling you what went down and what he wants."

"Okay. I got the message."

There was no point in debating it further. She'd known that as soon as Sermac's name was invoked. Marty was caught in a trap that included food, clothing, and pre–college age children.

"The format is an interview—if you decide to do it. You and Doug, Barbara Walters–style. Doug asks the question and you respond live, no script. No chance to edit."

"And what am I supposed to say to him?"

"Whatever you want. Anything you're comfortable with."

Kate shook her head. For the sake of realism she would be put on the spot big time.

Marty shifted his large frame and said, "Look, in reality, you only have two choices. Get involved personally, or let Doug do the story without you."

Katlyn was infuriated. Evidently the program was already a done deal, and no one had asked her permission.

"They'd do it without me, wouldn't they?"

Katlyn stood and stormed across the office toward the door and back again. She could see herself sitting across from Doug in front of the cameras, baring her soul to millions of voyeuristic viewers while Sermac gleefully rubbed his hands. She had a powerful urge to throw something.

She saw that Marty watched her expectantly. As repugnant as the idea was, his analysis was right, as usual. If the story was going to happen anyway, it was better to help shape it. As far as stories on woman killers went there had probably never been another reporter who understood the fears of her audience better than she did.

"If I say yes, I want to know what the questions are going to be," she demanded.

"I'll do better than that. You write them, I'll rubber stamp them. By the way, I already asked Fava to do some background. Check with her."

Another missing piece of information about the morning had just been filled in.

"As far as the interview itself, don't feel any pressure to talk about anything you don't want to. Mainly it's about reaching out to all the women who've ever been stalked or attacked by men. How it feels in general, not the specifics. That will take the edge off." He reached for her hand. "Call Matthew. Talk it over."

"Oh, that'll help a real lot. Thanks for the advice."

Marty went to his desk. "I'm not happy about this either, Kate, but all things considered, I think doing it is the right choice."

Katlyn looked him in the eye. "And suppose—just suppose Matthew is right. It just so happens that so far I'm not all that hooked on this wonderful world of being a TV personality—like most people around here are. Quite the opposite, as a matter of fact. And suppose I've begun to think that small town college life wasn't so bad after all?"

"If that's where you come out," Marty said after some serious thought. "You and Matthew, of course."

He had her there. She hadn't begun to resolve the question of how Matthew would be able to work in a small town. She edged to the door and stopped as she opened it. "How much time do I have until the interview?"

"This evening. Right after the six o'clock broadcast."

Katlyn felt her muscles tense. She was about to explode.

"Unbelievable!"

Outside the office, Katlyn was aware of a sea of eyes on her. The chaotic newsroom had become eerily quiet. One face separated from the crowd, a very sober Doug Driscoll, who wanted to talk.

"I had nothing to do with the idea, Katlyn," he shouted as she strode briskly ahead of him and he tried to catch up. "If there's anything I can do to make it easier, let's talk."

"No, not now, Doug. No talk. Hell, we've got all afternoon."

Katlyn marched away, furious with Sermac— and someone else who had let her down by not plugging her in. Claire Fava, the human information expressway.

TWENTY-FIVE

Claire Fava reflected on all the evidence that revealed a spectacularly uneventful life—her own.

At thirty-three she was still killing herself for a broadcasting career that had thus far turned out to be a nonevent. She had $3,056 standing between herself and welfare, an apartment furnished with family hand-me-downs, and a broken-down ten-year-old Volvo that she couldn't afford to fix.

And back in April, when many couples were arranging their marriages, she had broken up with a man with whom she'd planned to spend the rest of her life. It was Katlyn who had finally helped her see that John Alonzo "Shithead" Reyes would never commit to a lifetime with her, and Katlyn who took her in after he punched her and then disappeared.

Now she found herself conspiring, albeit unwillingly, against the one true female friend she'd made in years.

"You're supposed to be on my side," Katlyn stormed when she flew into her office and slammed the door. "You knew about the interview and didn't tell me."

Fava held out both hands, creating the impression of a barrier. The way Katlyn looked she could knock her silly if she was inclined to. "Marty said he thought he could talk Sermac out of it. He made me promise not to say anything. Said if I talked I'd be writing for Big Bird from now on."

Katlyn didn't laugh. "Dammit, Fava, if I can't trust you—" She pressed her hands to the sides of her head. "I don't need this, not now. But I guess I should have seen it coming."

She made a beeline for the couch and collapsed, her feet up on a cushion.

"I got your message on the computer," Fava said warily. "You might want to think about going into surveillance."

"If you try to cheer me up I'm gonna smack you."

"Roger. No more cheer-ups." She pointed to an inch-thick pile of papers on Katlyn's desk. "But since you're doing this gig, there's some background you might find helpful. Doug's been asking me for it all morning, but I wanted you to see it first. Stalking stats, comparisons with Starman. Stuff like that."

"How do you know I *am* doing it?"

"A hunch, honey. That's all."

Katlyn threw her a derisive look and rifled through the pages. "Must have taken days. Anything interesting?"

"Two and a half days. And yes." Fava was glad

to see that the other Kate was making a come-back. Once she got into the project she would make the interview with Doug something to remember. "For starters, the stats on stalking in general are incredibly lopsided on female victims. Might be something you'd want to reference."

"Why? I assumed that."

"Not numbers this high. At any given time, two hundred thousand people are being stalked somewhere in the country, ninety-seven percent women."

She had Katlyn's attention.

"And that's without any agreement on what constitutes a stalking crime in the first place."

"Why isn't there?"

"A legacy of our founding *fathers*, if you catch my drift. Before the mid-eighties it wasn't even against the law in most places to beat your wife. That's only a dozen or so freakin' years ago!"

"Pretty hard to believe."

"Hey, you can't get arrested for damaging your own property."

"What about the laws on stalking?"

"Get real. Let's say a creep sits in his car out-side your bedroom window and doesn't do any-thing but stare in. To you it's a clear threat, a stalking, especially if there's bad blood between the two of you. But there's no law against it. It isn't even stalking in most states, not even if he follows you everywhere you go. And in the ten states where it is considered stalking, they don't even make a first offense a felony."

"What about here?"

"In California there has to be a threat of great bodily injury. The law calls it a credible threat."

Katlyn thought about the TMU. "If that's the case, how did Los Angeles supposedly end up with the best stalking unit in the country—according to Stryker?"

"Ironic, isn't it? California was one of the last states to adopt antistalking laws, but Los Angeles is the first place with a separate unit just for stalking. If you think about it the reason is obvious."

"Celebrities."

"Bingo! Lot of rich, influential celebrities—like you. If you're being stalked and want someone to give a damn, be a star in Hollywood. And if you're a police administrator in a city like this, you'd better be antistalking—and damn vocal about it."

"I never considered myself a celebrity."

"It doesn't matter what you think, darlin', television turned you into one. It has also given all the nut cases out there an intimate experience with you, right in their own living room—not something Myrna Loy had to worry about."

"After tonight it will get a lot more intimate."

"I know. The interview will narrow the distance between you and the scumsucker even more."

Katlyn fell silent. At a time when she needed to relax about the program, her nervousness was growing exponentially. "I have this awful feeling things are going to get worse. That's what Matthew's been saying, and now I'm afraid he was right all along, that something awful has been planned for me." She reached for the hand of her only real friend. "I'm scared, Fava."

Fava hated to add another piece of bad news she'd found in her research, but she had to.

"While we're on Matthew, I think you should look at what it says at the end of the next to last page. I don't want to bum you out completely, but it's better you should know."

Katlyn thumbed to the page and read a paragraph that Fava had underscored.

A concomitant concern in stalking, according to the director of the Sex Crimes Unit in the Manhattan Prosecutor's Office, is while stalkers are generally intent on their intended victim, they will frequently become violent toward whoever stands in their way. In that regard, an additional danger may exist for a third party.

TWENTY-SIX

"She's very pretty, isn't she, Bo?"

"Yes, Arthur. And very clever, too."

Arthur leaned closer to the TV screen and studied the young woman's face. He was particularly drawn to her eyes.

"Do you think so? She looks like she's just afraid to me."

He hadn't meant to disagree so directly and waited for a reproach. When he thought about Bo being angry with him the pain started again. It felt as if a small animal was inside his brain trying to eat its way out.

"I think you like her, Arthur. Tell me if you do. I always want you to be honest with me."

"Of course not, Bo," Arthur said quickly. He knew enough not to be that stupid. "I was surprised, is all. She's not like the others, is she?"

Something about Katlyn Rome struck a comfortable chord in him. She seemed like someone you could talk to, someone who would listen, maybe even like him.

"If that's what you think you're making a big mistake, Arthur. Trust me on that."

He had to respect the warning. Bo had never been wrong before. Not about Anne Marie and

Jennifer, and Victoria and Pam. The three in Florida. The two in Maine.

"She's very dangerous. More than any of the others."

Arthur continued to watch the program, afraid to say anything more. As the interview went on, he began to feel sorry for what had happened to her, even though she was blaming Starman. He was confused.

"It's me she's talking about, isn't it?"

"Of course it's you, Arthur. She's been talking about you for days. She hates you, don't you know that?"

"Why, Bo? I didn't do those things. You know I didn't. You better than anyone."

For a fleeting moment he wondered if it was Bo who had visited her and not told him. It was possible. He considered confronting Bo with it directly but quickly decided not to.

"Look at her, Arthur. Look hard. She's as wicked as they come."

Arthur nodded but studied the face on the screen in confusion. He wondered how Bo could see so much more than he did. Katlyn Rome's face was beautiful, and not in a cheap way. She reminded him of someone he cared for very much once, someone he had let down in a way he did not want to remember.

He tried not to think about it. He could only think about the animal that was eating its way toward the back of his head.

"I'll visit her, Bo, if that's what you want," he said at length.

"Yes, Arthur, and very soon. But there's someone else you have to see first."

"Another one? Worse than Katlyn Rome?"

"Yes, Arthur," Bo said.

There was a chill in the voice that turned his blood into a river of ice.

"This one is very, very wicked, the worst of them all. This one is the Antichrist, Arthur."

TWENTY-SEVEN

By the mid-nineties the Hollywood Bowl had become a 116-acre tract with seating for eighteen thousand people. Once a hilly and uninhabited section of land, the small mountain that originally surrounded the amphitheater had been carted away, truckload by truckload, to accommodate growing audiences. Now, to block the noise from the freeways that had encroached on the complex, there was a plan to rebuild the mound.

In 1916, the idea of a woman headlining at the just-completed Hollywood Bowl would have been equally absurd. It would take eighty-two more years for the female rock performer Christa to become the entertainment spectacle of the summer season.

Christa's act started where Madonna's left off. To a flagrant sexual appeal, Christa added a religious theme and her own brand of feminism, a mixture that united both liberals and conservatives in an attempt to have her performances banned—and in the end of course resulted only in a faster sellout.

To control the crowd, security was the tightest in the Bowl's history. In addition to the dedicated security force, 150 regular police were to be in attendance, and a series of new checkpoints at all entrances were created.

The elaborate security system had only one flaw. On some weekday afternoons, the public attended free rehearsals. From the place they sat it was just a short distance—past rent-a-cops who were little more than props—to the backstage dressing rooms that would be used by the performers later that night.

But no one was concerned. Normally only a few dozen people showed up for rehearsals, a group easy enough to keep an eye on. And nothing improper had ever happened in the afternoon.

The single performance of "Christa Rising" was scheduled from ten o'clock to midnight on the evening of Friday, July 3, the kickoff to a long, hot holiday weekend.

The free rehearsal began at four in the afternoon.

The early attendees enjoyed it immensely.

All three thousand of them.

TWENTY-EIGHT

The world's preeminent female rock artist stood in total darkness, unable to move. On the other side of the fifty-five-foot curtains, the rising cry of the audience was music to Christa's ears. In moments the greatest illusion in the history of the rock stage would commence.

No one would be disappointed, Christa had promised her fans in an unprecedented publicity barrage. The grand finale at midnight would be a stunt that required a team of Hollywood special-effects technicians. A spectacle of *biblical* proportions, pun intended.

For the feat, a towering aluminum cross had been installed into the stage and painted to replicate timber. The horizontal member was fastened with six carbon steel bolts. Together they formed a crucifix nearly fifty-five feet high, enough to invite comparisons to the 125-foot-high statue of Christ the Redeemer in Rio De Janeiro.

Standing on two steel footholds, Christa was bound to the huge cross with high-tensile copper ropes at the ankles and steel wrist bracelets painted flesh color. A similar band encircled her neck and was attached to the riser. Three gleaming brass spikes, one angled upward below each wrist, and one just under the point where the ankles crossed, had been coated with a thick layer of red gel to make it look as if they had nailed her in place.

The mechanical apparatus was the crowning achievement. An inch-thick titanium guide wire was attached to the top of the cross, part of a system of pulleys and weights like those used for elevators.

When the curtain opened, three dozen Roman candles would ignite simultaneously. Moments later, two three-hundred-pound weights would be released, and, as they descended, the cross would slowly be lifted from the stage, and Christa would rise to the top of the dome.

As an added thrill for the crowd, the tattered shawl that covered the upper part of her body would fall away about halfway into the ascent. In the dazzling light, her hard, siliconed, glycerin-coated breasts would glisten like bronze.

Standing alone on the darkened stage, the prospect of what she was about to do stirred a memory in Christa. She was fourteen-year-old Elizabeth Duncan, in the backyard of the rural home her family had finally been forced to sell. As it turned out, it was the last time they'd all be together. Her mother had called out for them to form a circle, Alexander, Bethany and Jenny, Cory and Jesse, Sophia and Harold and her. She came out of the house clutching a bouquet of balloons, each a different color. She handed a balloon to each of them, then looked back at their home.

"We are like these balloons," her mother said. "Now each of us has to fly away."

She opened her hand, and her balloon rose into the late autumn sky. One by one, they each let go of their balloons and watched them climb over the place where they had been a family together. Through the years, the winds had taken all the balloons in different directions, and Momma's and two others had been lost. Somehow, Elizabeth Duncan's had gotten caught in a current that lifted it higher than the rest and in a few seconds would ascend to heaven itself.

The musky scent reached her less than a minute before midnight, a sharp, foul smell that reminded her of a partially decomposed mouse she once buried as a child. Someone was drawing near her in the darkness. The break with procedure triggered a wave of anger.

"Who's there?" she called out, her voice drowned out in the music.

In a moment she could make out a tall, thin figure staring up at her. His eyes were deeply set and eager. Swiftly, he moved a wooden box close to the cross and stood on it, holding something she couldn't make out.

"Who are you," Christa said. "What do you think you're doing?"

She felt the point of a long, thin spike against her wrist, then a lightning bolt of pain pierced her skin and struck bone. Her mouth opened wide, but the sound was muffled by the band. Her other wrist was speared, and her whole body felt as if it were on fire. A third fire bolt found the spot where her ankles crossed.

She had only a vague awareness of her loin cloth being torn away. Something hard and cold being forced deep inside her. Dimly, she could feel something sting the tip of her breast.

I know who you are.

On schedule, the Roman candles ignited simultaneously and the wire latticework bore her up. Near the end, she felt like a little yellow balloon.

TWENTY-NINE

Elliot Stryker sprang out of the back seat of his unmarked car and quick-stepped to the entrance of the building at the corner of La Cienega and Washington. For the second time in two years, his holiday plans had been ruined at the last minute. The year before it was a hostage situation. This time, Starman had killed the queen of rock and roll.

The ground floor was leased by Ultima Video Enterprises, well known to area residents and police as an outlet for the pornographic films produced by its parent corporation in a dingy studio a few blocks south.

Stryker, and his bodyguard, Sgt. Paul Garmirian, took the twenty-eight steps two at a time. When they got to the landing, Garmirian waited outside.

The office on the top floor had nothing to do with X-rated films. The cramped quarters were a temporary satellite of the Threat Management Unit, the last place in the city the press was likely to look for the office. The secret location was also the reason why the video store and its production facility hadn't been busted.

Three metal folding chairs were clustered in

the center of the room around a vinyl bridge table that served as a desk. A number of large envelopes and assorted fast-food litter covered its surface. A three-cushioned couch, one of the cushions deeply stained, sagged against the far wall near the only window. The room looked as if it could be a set for the videos sold on the ground floor.

When Stryker entered, LAPD Capt. Michael Conaway stood reverently, but Lt. Dan Jarrett stayed seated with his arms wrapped around the back of a metal folding chair, rocking back and forth, causing the chair to make an annoying creaking sound. Two other officers nodded respectfully and stayed at their makeshift desk shuffling papers.

"All right, what have you got?" Stryker snapped.

The captain showed him a large plastic bag. It contained a blood-stained metal hammer that looked new.

"The murder weapon—part of it, at least," he said.

Jarrett lifted another bag that contained three lengths of brass rods. They had been ground to a point at one end. He hefted it, then dropped it with a loud clang. "Gives a whole new meaning to 'heavy metal,'" he said. Conaway grinned at Jarrett's pun, but Stryker scowled. He read insolence in the casual way Jarrett handled the bag.

"This is the way it looked," Conaway said, handing his boss a photo more respectfully.

Stryker's sullen expression deepened. It had been a long time since he'd been to church, but the position of Christa's body looked remarkably similar to that of Christ on the cross. Starman was a good deal sicker than anyone had given him credit for.

"It was planned to look this way as part of the show—which is why no one stopped when they saw it," said Conaway.

"She bled to death—right before their eyes," Jarrett added, drumming his fingers on the metal back of his chair. "Just as everyone was cheering their brains out."

Stryker's expression didn't change. Either he'd seen a lot worse, or didn't give a damn anymore, Jarrett thought.

"The way the Bible tells it, Jesus took a long time to die," Conaway said. "A slow, lingering death. But not Christa. The spikes penetrated her arteries. The medical examiner said she lost an amazing amount of blood and was probably unconscious before the cross got to the top of the place. The floor of the stage was like something out of a chain saw movie. Made some of our guys sick."

"Which means the killer must have been covered with blood, too," Stryker snapped. "How did he get out without being noticed?"

"A workman found some blood-soaked coveralls which Starman must have ditched. We sent them to the lab."

"That's the first time he's left anything at the scene. I want it looked at under a microscope and looked at again. If there's any chance that some of the blood is his, I want to know."

"Naturally," Conaway said. "But there's no indication of a struggle, so I doubt we'll find anything more than the woman's."

"Do it anyway."

The captain removed a familiar object from another envelope. Stryker looked dumbstruck when he saw it.

"Is that a night stick?"

It was blood-stained along its entire length except for where it had evidently been held.

"They found it inside her vagina," the hard-bitten captain said with difficulty.

"Sick bastard," Stryker said. He went to the couch and saw the filthy cushion. "How the fuck do you sit on this piece of shit," he shouted, and walked away.

"We're trying to figure out why he used a billy stick," Conaway said.

Jarrett rocked back in his chair again and said, "He wasn't just sticking it to her, so to speak. He was sticking it to us, by using one of our own weapons. Right, chief?" he said to his boss.

"Let me see the fucking note," Stryker ordered, ignoring him. "You said it was in her mouth?"

The captain nodded and reached for a small

plastic bag. The piece of paper inside was the reason the TMU had become involved. The murder investigation itself was being handled by the regular force.

Stryker held the bag to the light and squinted as he read the crumpled page. It was from the *L.A. Times* TV listings. The 6:00 P.M. heading for the channel 10 News had been circled with a red marker. Next to it was written, *Cops will fiddle, Rome will burn.*

"Have the reporters seen this?"

"No, we got lucky. They were there in droves for the show, but the coroner was the first one to find the note, and he held it back."

Stryker threw the plastic bag on the table. A shooting pain down the back of his right leg told him that his sciatica hadn't turned out to be the temporary condition his doctor had predicted. "Well, this is fucking great. With every cop and street slime we're paying to look for him, he kills a celebrity right in the goddamn Hollywood Bowl and leaves a death threat on top of it. Jesus, God," he bellowed, "this guy must have an ego the size of an elephant's dick!"

To a degree, Jarrett could sympathize with Stryker. Christa was wasted in front of all of his men and a threat was left to taunt police. Local television had reported the story overnight and fed it to the networks. After that the newspapers hit the streets with the death photo, and the word was, the commissioner had *suggested* Stryker apprehend Starman in forty-eight hours.

All things considered, it couldn't have happened to a nicer guy.

"Did forensics turn up anything new on the Rome incidents?" Stryker asked Jarrett.

"Well, maybe. They're making a big deal out of it, but I'm not jumping up and down."

The surprise news caught Stryker off guard, and he perked up.

"One of the criminologists who went over the scene at the TV station found a human hair in the envelope with the Valentine—the one addressed to Rome."

"What does that net?"

"Ordinarily, not a big deal. But this one came out from the root and had some skin cells still attached. Ordinarily, all a hair can tell you is sex and race. Also if there are any drugs in the suspect's system. But now they're gonna analyze it with something called a Mitochondrial DNA Test, which should give us a DNA read."

"With which we'll do what?"

"Well, if we ever catch somebody, we can take another sample. If it matches, then we have a tie-in."

"Big fuckin' deal."

"Yeah, that's what I thought. This forensic bullshit isn't all it's cracked up to be. But don't tell Guano I said that."

Stryker turned to his captain. "Anything from your end?"

"Uh-uh. Like every other time. No finger-prints or saliva. No one ever hears any noise. It's like he's invisible—except for that odor he gives off. The lab guys have never seen, or smelled, anything like it."

"What about semen? Did they ever get a DNA from that? All those women were raped, weren't they?" Jarrett asked.

"And sodomized," Conaway added. "Nothing there, either. They think Starman douches his victims after he rapes them. Thoroughly. Or else he uses a rubber. There's never a trace of semen. You'd think he'd have gotten sloppy somewhere."

"And he didn't rape Christa?"

"No. Not enough time. Or maybe because even if he did it fast he wouldn't have had a chance to clean up."

The room fell quiet until Conaway broke the tension. "It's not going to look good if Rome goes public with this."

"Not *look* too good?" Stryker mimicked. "It's gonna get the city fucking crazy, not to mention the commissioner."

"What about Rome?" Jarrett broke in. "Don't you think we should talk about her? She's the one who got the death threat."

Stryker recoiled. "And get this whole city bat-shit before we have a plan to deal with it?" Stryker scanned the faces and saw that his knee-jerk reaction had not been well received. "Okay," he said more pointedly to Jarrett. "You're the bad-ass who thinks *out of the box.* What do *you* think we should do?"

Jarrett looked at his boss closely. It was obvious Stryker didn't have a clue what to do about Rome. In his own macho, sarcastic way, he was actually asking for his help for the first time.

"I don't know, Elliot," he said. "I really don't know." He took the bag with the note in it and placed it neatly on top of the grisly pictures of Christa. "But I think trying to save Rome's life might be a hell of a good place to start."

THIRTY

Katlyn had first become suspicious when Stryker requested that the small group meet in Jude Sermac's office. Evidently, what he intended to propose involved station policy, a policy which so far had been total exploitation. Now, when he entered the plush room, he walked directly to where Katlyn was sitting. He was holding out a plastic bag.

"Sorry to have to show you this. It would be too dangerous not to."

The bag contained the note that had been left at the murder scene. Katlyn read it and felt dizzy.

When he saw her face, Marty inched closer, but she waved him off.

Stryker stepped back and addressed the group. "Unfortunately, Ms. Rome's earlier fears have been borne out. It's obvious now that we can't just sit around and wait for this madman to make his next move."

His explicit admission that it was Starman shocked Katlyn. From the beginning he had been the strongest holdout. Her eyes traveled from Stryker to Dan Jarrett, then Jude Sermac, who was observing the meeting with uncharacteristic silence. He must have known about the note before the get-together.

Ruth Dubois, the criminal psychologist consulting on the case, was also part of the gathering, an earnest-looking woman who held herself ramrod straight. Her air of confidence reminded Katlyn of tenured college professors she had known who did not fear the establishment and spoke their minds.

"I want to meet Starman's challenge with our own," Stryker continued. "Dr. Dubois believes there's a good chance we can flush him out and drive him to act irrationally. We've devised a plan that should do just that."

He paused to observe the reaction. Except for Sermac, he saw expressions of incredulity. And he was just getting to the meaty part.

"What we propose is for Ms. Rome to address Starman in a special television broadcast. We think we can provoke him to do something reckless, and when he does, we'll be waiting for him."

Marty sputtered in disbelief and stood. "You want to use Katlyn as bait for Starman? Are you out of your mind?"

Katlyn was stunned.

"If you will just hear us out," Dubois said loudly. "I think you'll see—"

"You people must be pretty goddamn desperate," Marty interrupted. His eyes darted to Katlyn's, sharing her indignation.

Jude Sermac leaned on his elbows, his milky-white hands clasped under his chin. "It's outrageous, Martin, I agree. That's exactly what I thought, too—at first—when Chief Stryker told me about the idea."

Katlyn ignored him. For all she knew the plan had come from him in the first place, for business reasons. "Is anyone interested in *my* reaction?" she finally said, and the room fell silent.

"Of course," Stryker said, backing off. "You have to be convinced that this will work, or we won't go on with it."

"Well, how can I be? How could anyone? None of us has a clue to what Starman is all about. So how can we presume to know what's in his mind?"

"We have models, Ms. Rome," Dubois said quickly. "I know that sounds rather theoretical, but they are usually remarkably good at predicting behavior for individuals like this."

"*Usually?*" Marty countered.

Katlyn echoed his feelings and looked at Dan Jarrett. For some reason it was suddenly important to know what he thought. Jarrett was the only person who hadn't taken a position. His expression was stoic.

"We've laid this out completely with Ms. Rome's safety in mind," Stryker said. "Once she does the broadcast, we'll have as many men covering her as we put on the president when he was here."

"And would that be *more* or *less* than you had at the Hollywood Bowl?" Conroy asked pointedly.

Stryker bristled. "This is completely different. This time we'll be the ones who are waiting."

Katlyn felt a wave of despair. No matter what they speculated, the plan was incredibly risky. It sound to her too as if the police were grasping at straws.

"If you know about the extra coverage, then Starman knows," she said. "He isn't stupid. He's obviously been able to work around the police so far. That is the problem, isn't it?"

"There is absolutely no chance he'll be able to get to you. Not one chance in hell," Stryker said, turning to Marty to quiet him.

"With all due respect," Marty said, "we have a number of dead presidents that prove that anybody can get to anybody."

His statement had a chilling effect on the room.

"I'm not blind to that fact. That's precisely why we'll be removing Ms. Rome from any possibility of attack." He turned to her, lowering his voice. "We're going to take you to another location right after your broadcast. We've identified a safe house where you'll be able to live comfortably, you and your husband, of course, until Starman either makes his move or we catch him for other reasons—which sooner or later we will."

The new twist caught Katlyn off guard.

"What makes you think Starman won't find out where I really am?" Katlyn said. "He always knows everything about his victims."

"Starman *will* know where you are, at least he'll think he does. He'll have every reason to believe you're still living at home because, in effect, you *will* be." He saw their confused glances and returned them with a coy look. "Two police officers will be doubling for you and your husband, staying in your house—living your lives, so to speak. It will look as if you never left. We'll bring you and your doubles together at the right time to make the exchange, during both of your regular schedules, so nothing looks out of the ordinary."

"My husband doesn't have a regular schedule," Katlyn said sharply.

"Then whenever and wherever you would normally get to the same place," Stryker allowed.

"And what if Starman gets to your people? What if he kills them?"

"Believe me, the people we have doubling for you can take care of themselves. Plus, there will be a lot more like them waiting for him to come every step of the way. Once he makes his move he won't know what hit him."

"The reality is, there's a bigger risk in doing nothing," Dubois finally spoke up. "In a case like this we have to be proactive, and take control away from Starman."

"That's a lovely theory, Dr. Dubois," Marty broke in, "but you're asking Katlyn to bet her life on it. Given Starman's track record, I'd bet on him doing something none of your models can predict."

"How do we know we won't just be driving him underground, until another time?" Katlyn asked. She felt lightheaded. For a brief instant the faces in the room went in and out of focus.

"That is a possibility, I admit. However, Starman fits the profile of other violent stalkers whom we've studied extensively, and sooner or later they all reach a point where their game changes. After their early success at escaping the law they begin to feel invincible, and their egos take over. We think he's already reached that point—after the Christa murder. It was the first time he left a message."

"But suppose you're wrong and it takes longer. How do we know when? What if it takes a month? Six months?" Katlyn turned to Stryker. "How long will you be able to keep your men around me if nothing happens right away?"

"As long as it takes."

Katlyn shook her head despairingly. He was probably lying, but it didn't matter what he said anyway—what anyone said. Nothing could give her the assurance she needed.

"It's possible that the televised interview you did may already have caused Starman to act rashly at the Hollywood Bowl," Dubois chanced. "I think we can consider that a trial run."

The room dimmed further. "Well that's just great. I do an interview on television and he kills somebody. And that's your idea of a successful experiment?"

"Of course, I didn't mean—"

"And what makes you think he won't see right through the new broadcast? You're underestimating him. He's smart."

"I won't lie to you, Ms. Rome," Dubois said. "We're not dealing in absolute certainties here. But our experience suggests that in your case his warning is intended to provoke a reaction. We want to give him one that stimulates him to act without his normal caution. We don't think it will take long."

When Katlyn didn't respond, Dubois softened.

"I'm sorry to put this so bluntly, but I believe Starman has already made up his mind to murder you. For some reason, in your case, he's decided to torment you first, to prolong your anxiety. All we're doing is trying to change the conditions of his final attack in our favor."

Katlyn noticed her hands were shaking. She had felt from the beginning that Starman was coming to kill her, for uncovering the evidence that connected him to many celebrity murders, for reporting on him after that. Dubois was right. The only issue was where she would be the safest when he came.

Katlyn's mouth went dry and she was suddenly perspiring. She noticed that everyone in the room was staring at her. A few voices called to her to see if she was all right. She tried to answer but couldn't. Everything went dark.

THIRTY-ONE

Katlyn Rome watched the title of the WMTC news special, *Hostage to Fear*, scroll up on the station monitor. Out of the corner of her eye she glanced at the show's producer, Ron Lockhart, whose oversized headphones looked ridiculous on his bald head. His index finger was poised high in the air for the cue. It was thirty seconds to an intimate talk with a celebrity killer.

With difficulty, she tried to organize in her mind exactly what she was going to say. More than for any other broadcast, it was crucial that she keep her thoughts in order, a task made even harder by what had happened at home since she agreed to talk to Starman.

On the previous night, Matthew had flown into a blind rage over her broadcast. She'd never seen him that out of control. Afterward, he slammed out of the house and returned drunk at four in the morning. They hadn't talked since.

To make matters worse, Matthew had been asked to attend an important party late in the afternoon with the staff and producers of Trio

Pictures, to perform his music for them live. He couldn't say no. After that, according to the plan she had outlined to him, he was to be picked up by the police and taken to the safe house. For reassurance, he was supposed to call her when that was done. Despite their fight, she knew he would.

Doug Driscoll was alone on the Team Ten set. Ratings experts estimated the audience at three million viewers. To help reach Starman wherever he might be, Sermac had agreed to a simulcast by the major radio stations that played to the Los Angeles metro audience. He was in his glory.

Driscoll started, his voice unusually grave. "In a report made public today, Los Angeles Police said that a note was found on the body of murdered rock star Christa. The note named the killer's next intended victim, who is thought to be this station's reporter Katlyn Rome.

"Recently, Katlyn Rome was interviewed in a special program here after a series of incidents that suggested she was the target of a celebrity stalking. Police now believe that these incidents were the work of Christa's murderer, the celebrity killer known as Starman.

"Tonight, in an unprecedented broadcast, Katlyn Rome will air a special message to the killer who has been holding her—and the women of Los Angeles—hostage to fear. Now, a message to Starman."

Driscoll's image faded and was replaced by a full-length shot of Katlyn seated in a specially constructed set that suggested a living room. This Katlyn Rome was the antithesis of the one who appeared on Team Ten news. She wore a sheer silk blouse, the first two buttons open, which clearly indicated the contours of her upper body. A clinging ankle-length skirt, slit for about half its length, was open enough to reveal long, well-formed legs which were crossed provocatively. Her hair was unpinned and spilled down to her shoulders, and her makeup included eye shadow and lipstick that accentuated the fullness of her mouth. The blatant sensuous concept was Fava's, to entice Starman. The degree of execution was Katlyn's. She hadn't told Matthew.

Seeing her new face on the monitor jarred Katlyn and made her pulse race. All eyes were trained on her as she took a deep breath.

"Ever since you've begun to terrorize innocent people in our city I've tried to learn about the kind of person you are, and what could have made you that way. I've done this as part of my job as a reporter and as a woman whom you have stalked."

Katlyn paused. She hoped that the slight tremolo in her voice hadn't already revealed the panic she felt down to her bones.

"From what I now know, you are outwardly an extremely intelligent man, healthy and physically very strong, gifts that in a normal man most people would admire. But for reasons of your own you have been compelled to use these talents in the most perverse way imaginable."

She settled back in her chair long enough for the camera to draw closer.

"You believe yourself to be unique, and that for some reason you have been chosen to inflict punishment on the people you select. Perhaps you are directed by God or some voice that only you can hear. But you are not unique or special in any way. You are like a few other wretched individuals which nature produces a few times a century who have had the same thoughts as you and a remarkably similar personal history.

"Like others of your kind, you have not been successful in relationships with men or with women or in the jobs you may have held. And, whenever you met failure, you always blamed others.

"You believe that men should do one thing, women another. You have few interests and an unnatural fascination with weapons and the thrill of the hunt.

"By any normal definition you are sexually impotent and deeply ashamed of your dysfunction. The only way you can perform the normal functions of a man is to brutalize women with whom you cannot establish intimacy.

"Your violent acts of aggression began in your youth, possibly directed against animals at first, then children and women. As you grew older your need for violence became progressively more uncontrollable. At one time you may have actually believed the things you were doing were wrong, but by now you have convinced yourself that your victims deserve your violence, and you have turned into a diseased and sadistic killer without any trace of human remorse.

"Now your savagery gives you only a temporary rest from the feelings of rage and worthlessness which force you to kill and kill again. And now, as when it began, your victims are those who cannot defend themselves. In this way, you are, and have always been, a coward.

"Perhaps there was a time in your life when someone might have helped you, but that time is past. All that matters now is that you are no longer able to distinguish right from wrong, and that you have placed yourself beyond any possibility of help or compassion."

The camera backed off and held Katlyn perfectly in frame when she stood up and approached the lens.

"When the police learned I'd be addressing you on television, they permitted me to offer you help in exchange for your surrender. They told me I could say you would not be harmed if you gave yourself up voluntarily.

"I thought about that for a long time, and finally refused. That's because I don't believe you deserve leniency of any kind. Because I don't consider you human in any way.

"Your deranged attacks against defenseless women prove to me that you are only a rabid animal, and therefore, the only solution is for you to be destroyed."

Katlyn challenged the camera frontally, her words and body playing to Starman on two levels at once.

"A few nights ago, when you threatened my life directly, you forced me to make another difficult decision. That's why, effective immediately, I'm leaving my work at this station to spend all my time helping with your inevitable capture and extermination. I promise, I will not rest until that happens."

Katlyn fixed her eyes on the camera lens, her expression taunting.

Just before the screen faded to black, the camera moved in for an extreme close-up.

"There is nothing you can do to make me afraid of you."

THIRTY-TWO

The migraine started when the reporter began talking to him, and it got worse as she continued. It felt as if the small animal in his brain had found another juicy piece of meat, a center cut, and was sinking his razor-sharp teeth into it. Arthur thought about smashing his head against the wall until either the animal died or he did, whichever came first.

"It's never hurt this much before."

"It's her, Arthur. She's doing it. I hope you see that now."

Bo's voice sounded as if it came from someplace close. The closest place possible.

"Yes, you're right . . . it must be her."

"You shouldn't have warned her. You gave her too much time."

Arthur bowed his head. This was the first time he'd done something without Bo's approval, and it had been a mistake. Leaving a note with Christa's body had been his idea. He felt deeply ashamed.

"Listen to what she's saying, Arthur."

He tried, but it was impossible to concentrate. Even through the pain, however, he could see how beautiful the reporter was. And deadly.

"*Listen, Arthur. She doesn't sound very smart, does she?*"

Arthur forced himself to pay attention to Rome's words but didn't really understand what she was saying. Only that she was ridiculing him.

"Why Bo? Why do you think so?"

"*She's saying you can't separate fantasy from reality. Do you hear that?*"

"Yes, I hear her."

"*But you can, Arthur. We both know you can.*"

"Can we, Bo? I'm not sure what you mean."

"*Fantasy is thinking you can't get to her, Arthur. Reality is that you can.*"

THIRTY-THREE

A man with hairy wrists and a balding crewcut sipped a lukewarm cup of coffee on the far side of the newsroom. After the broadcast the undercover officer would become the point man of Katlyn Rome's escort to the street. So far his attempt to blend in with the news staff bordered on the burlesque.

At the loading dock, one level below the street, an overweight Hispanic driver with a wiry mustache scanned the freight bays and sweated into a starched white collar a size too small. Every four minutes, two cars approached from opposite directions on the street and crossed exactly in front of the loading bay. One was a four-door BMW containing a yuppie couple and two empty children's safety seats, the other a late-model Buick that held two men in their late twenties. It had taken only a short time for the precise police choreography to be established earlier in the afternoon.

According to plan, once her broadcast was over Katlyn would return to her office and wait until she received a message from Matthew. Then she would exit by the elevators, arrive at the freight dock, and be driven twelve miles to a secret residence in Laurel Canyon, a place she'd never seen. The intended safe house had been the property of a drug kingpin, seized by the county for auction. It was chosen, Jarrett told her, because it was in an isolated community and stood in the center of a large, cleared lot. Thus it was relatively easy to protect. More of Stryker's legions were already in position there, waiting for her.

The transfer was scheduled to start as soon as the broadcast to Starman ended. But at twenty-five minutes to nine, Katlyn Rome was still in her office. And Matthew still hadn't called.

"It isn't like him. We had a terrible fight about the broadcast, but I can't believe that would stop him from calling. I don't understand why this is happening."

Fava could see she was close to the breaking point. It had been a rough night without Matthew adding to it. "It'll make sense when you find out what happened," she said, trying to sound reassuring. "It's probably just something innocent."

"No," Katlyn shot back. "Something is wrong." She took her eyes off the phone and gazed vacantly at her office. It seemed like an empty and accusing place now, the symbol of the trouble she and Matthew had found. After all this time, spaces for art work still hadn't been filled. Wallpaper and upholstery samples lay in a pile on the floor. The walls were a blank screen on which she projected Matthew's enraged face.

"Matthew was right. None of this is worth it. I don't know why I didn't listen to him."

Fava didn't say anything. It was Katlyn's fear talking, she thought.

Katlyn remembered that the police were supposed to wait outside the hall where Matthew was performing. After his show ended he would be transferred to an unmarked car and taken to the safe house in Laurel Canyon where he would call her from a secure phone. He'd be disguised as a police officer when he left the Trio function, with a real officer in the car already looking remarkably like Matthew Demarco. After they dropped Matthew off, that officer would continue back to their real house and begin his new life as Matthew.

It was simple and foolproof. *So why hadn't he called?*

"He was so irrational last night that I was afraid we wouldn't be able to put it right again."

"He was worried about you. That can make a man overreact."

"He accused me of being incredibly gullible and threatening our marriage. He couldn't believe I could love him and still have agreed to the broadcast." Katlyn looked past Fava and saw two plainclothes policemen outside near the office. They looked edgy.

Ten minutes later, when Matthew still hadn't called, Katlyn disobeyed one of Stryker's strictest orders and picked up the phone. She didn't have the number of the hall where the function was being held, so she dialed information. The Trio Productions' number rang several times before a recording advised her that the offices were closed and to call back in the morning.

"I'm going to tell Stryker to send his men into the party and look for him," she announced, slamming down the receiver. "I don't care whether it compromises security or not."

"I don't blame you," Fava said. She turned to the newsroom and saw Dan Jarrett walking briskly toward the office. "Why don't you ask him what he thinks first," she said, nodding in his direction. "I think he'll give you an honest answer."

Katlyn watched Jarrett approach. Something was wrong. Whatever it was had caused a thin line of sweat to form at his hairline. He wasn't the type to sweat easily.

THIRTY-FOUR

Wilma Sue Schroeder was a robust, no-nonsense policewoman who had come armed for the trip. She sat on the far side of the back seat next to Katlyn and said little at first. When she finally spoke she was surprisingly soft-spoken and empathetic. But by then, Katlyn's anxiety over Matthew was all-consuming.

The news Jarrett had come to the office with had added a harrowing new twist. Even before Katlyn had requested it, he spoke to his men at Trio, and, according to them, Matthew never arrived at the party. Two young parking valets had no recollection of his car, and the producers themselves were miffed over his seemingly ungracious absence. It had taken the police team most of the time she waited in her office to verify his absence. Then they called the station.

After getting the frightening news, Katlyn left the office in a trance. One thing was for certain. No matter what state of mind Matthew might have been in over her broadcast, he would never have missed his performance at Trio and risked his hard-won success.

There were a few possible explanations for

his absence that still gave her hope. Given the frenetic nature of his business, he might have been rerouted at the last minute by someone at Trio before he got to the affair—a manic producer who wanted him to go back to the studio to change the music. Even so, he would still have arrived later at Trio, and the police would have seen him. It would have set the schedule back, but not obviated it.

The most likely of the innocent scenarios was an accident on the road. But it would have had to be a serious crash for him to stay out of touch this long. He might be lying unconscious somewhere—or worse.

There was also the more remote chance that Matthew had been involved in an unrelated crime, a victim of one of the car jackings that had become epidemic in L.A. She shuddered when she realized what a ghastly thing this was to be hoping for.

A sudden thought about the tape they found in the car at their mountain house terrified her. At the time, they assumed the message was a threat to *her* life. Now the notion that Starman might have intended the 'hunting' reference for Matthew was a very real and frightening possibility.

In the end, the idea that Starman had intercepted Matthew was the most plausible. Somehow he had learned about the plan and outsmarted them all, as she feared he might from the beginning. If so, he would have found out that she was to be heavily guarded after her broadcast. So, unable to get to her, he did the next best thing and took her husband.

A wave of guilt inundated her. If Matthew had been kidnapped, it was her fault, completely her fault. There was no other reason.

She closed her eyes and settled into her desolation. The twenty minute drive from WMTC eventually took them north on Laurel Canyon Road. Along the way she prayed silently that somehow, despite how unreasonable it was to believe it, Matthew would be at the house when she got there. She saw vividly the shadow at the foot of the stairs the night of the robbery. She wished she'd gone downstairs with the gun blazing.

The car reached the top of the hill that traversed the canyon, then turned onto Mulholland Drive. Soon they were on a long, winding driveway of loose stones that made the tires spin as the car wound its way to a rocky escarpment hidden for most of the way by thick bushes. It was already dark, but a single light burning in the distance at the safe house entrance made her heart leap with renewed hope.

At the top of the incline the driveway ended in a large open oval. An older model Landcruiser that she recognized as Dan Jarrett's was waiting at one side of it, along with four other police vehicles. Several uniformed men were visible around the perimeter of the house, attentive.

Dan Jarrett walked slowly out of the house as her car coasted to a stop. The blank expression on his face said it all. He looked as if he had lost a close personal friend.

PART 2

HOME IS THE HUNTER

THIRTY-FIVE

LAUREL CANYON
Friday, July 17

At the beginning of the second week at the safe house, Katlyn pulled back the drapes of a living room window and stared out onto a surreal, alien world. In the short space of time since the hellish chain of events had begun, she'd lost her husband, her job and, now, even her home. More than ever, she yearned to go back in time, to return to the small college town that she once thought was so suffocating and that now seemed like the ultimate safe haven.

When Dan Jarrett appeared at the door that afternoon it was clear that he was her best and possibly only hope of finding Matthew. The simple fact of his presence indicated that he had been chosen by Stryker as the person responsible for her. What she did not know was whether he considered it an important job, or merely thought of himself as a glorified nurse-maid.

They settled in the living room next to one of many oversized steel encased windows. A hazy gray sky visible outside and the dreary amber glaze on the walls added a brooding ambience to their meeting.

"I was hoping they'd allow the prisoner a visitor," she said with false bravado.

Jarrett's rugged smile softened just a bit. He allowed his eyes to linger on her a few seconds too long and caught himself.

Even in her present state, Katlyn Rome was a remarkably beautiful woman, he thought. But the stress had taken its toll. There was a very noticeable difference in her physically from the first time they met.

He unbuttoned his timeworn brown leather jacket, but still looked ill at ease.

"What about Matthew?" she asked. "Have you found out anything? Anything at all?"

Jarrett leaned back on the sofa and put his hands flat on the cushions. "We found your husband's car a few hours ago," he announced straightforwardly. "In the parking lot of the Hollywood Bowl."

"Oh my God."

"We don't know anything more than that," Jarrett said quickly. "For all we know it could have been there since he's been missing. It was the last place anyone would have thought of looking for it."

"Was there any sign of a fight?"

"Not as far as we can tell. But it's looking fairly certain now that he was intercepted on the way to the Trio party. Given when he was supposed to get there, that probably puts it between six-thirty and seven."

The implication of the time registered right away. "So whatever happened, it wasn't because of my broadcast to Starman?"

"No. It was before that."

The revelation brought only fleeting relief before another harrowing possibility suggested itself. "Do you think that Starman drove him there? He took Matthew in his own car?"

"Possible, but not likely. If I were Starman, I doubt I would have risked it."

"So he did something with him first, is that what you're saying?"

"It's possible he left Matthew somewhere, then drove the car to the Bowl," Jarrett said, choosing his words carefully.

"But he could have killed him."

Jarrett hesitated. "I think you have to prepare yourself for that. He might have."

Katlyn recoiled. She closed her eyes.

Jarrett waited in silence.

"What if he did take Matthew with him in the car," she asked finally, "to someplace else before driving to the Bowl? What if he decided to keep him alive?"

"If he set out to only kidnap your husband it would be a first for him, at least recently. But maybe."

"Why the Hollywood Bowl?" she asked painfully. The answer dawned on her almost as fast as she said it. "Because that's where he left the death threat. This is his way of sending another message to me."

"Or another challenge to the police," Jarrett said. "Returning to the murder scene was the most audacious thing he could do—the most blatant way of saying he isn't afraid of being caught."

"What did he do after he left the car? How would he get away?"

"Switch to another one he had planted there earlier. Or just get on a bus. Buses go everywhere in the city from there."

There was so much to understand. The questions came one after another, all part of the torture Starman had undoubtedly planned.

"Was there anything of Matthew's in the car?"

Jarrett's silence seemed to confirm her fears. "I don't want to scare you. There was some blood, mostly in the area of the driver's seat. But not his," he added immediately.

She closed her eyes and waited.

"When the criminologist showed up he took a sample, and I drove back with him to a lab to do the test right away. I was hoping the blood type wouldn't match Matthew's, maybe even that it belonged to his abductor. Turned out it wasn't even human blood. It came from a male deer."

Katlyn stiffened. "Where would someone get it?"

"A deer was found slaughtered at the Griffith Park Zoo the night before last. Up until now it just looked like some sicko. But it's too much of a coincidence."

"He planned this, didn't he? He tried to make it look like he butchered him. It's not enough for him that he kidnaps my husband!" she shouted.

Jarrett looked down too late. His expression already telegraphed his agreement.

Katlyn cradled her head in her hands. "How can someone hate me so much? What did I ever do that made him hate me?"

Jarrett didn't have an answer. She wasn't expecting one.

"What are you going to do to find my husband now that there's a good chance he's still alive?"

"For what it's worth, the whole city is on it. And the state police. Every officer has Matthew's picture. But I don't think it's too wise for you to get your hopes up. Anything could have happened by now."

"What about the FBI?"

"They're already involved, on the earlier murders. Doing their own investigation and keeping a low profile on purpose. But we can't use them for Matthew, at least not yet. So far your husband is just a missing person. There's no hard evidence that he was even kidnapped, let alone—" He stopped short, without finishing the obvious thought. "Not even a ransom note."

Katlyn's eyes turned fiery. "Damn it! Does

there have to be a ransom note to prove he was kidnapped? Or a body? Can't you act on the likelihood that he was?"

"It doesn't work that way. Besides, the FBI wouldn't be a good move now. The last thing we need is someone new coming in and blowing the plan we've set up."

"But the plan is no damn good, is it? It took my husband away from me before it even got started."

Jarrett stared at his shoes and looked helpless. Katlyn was suddenly sorry she had been so sharp. The plan had not been Jarrett's idea. If anyone was to blame, it was Stryker—and herself for listening. Stryker and she made the decisions, and Jarrett simply fell in line.

"I'm sorry you don't like me," Jarrett said all at once after a strained silence. "But I'd like to think you can still trust me to tell you the truth."

The remark caught her off guard, and she quieted. She hadn't intended any personal attack. And she didn't dislike him at all. In fact, she realized, she had actually admired some of his qualities from the beginning, without even thinking about it. She liked his courage and iconoclasm and was intrigued by his unassuming strength.

"I only really know about you from your reputation."

Jarrett gave her a cautious glance. "Don't believe everything you read. Or write."

In an indefinable way, his answer and his manner felt comfortable, and it broke down a small barrier between them. Katlyn relaxed. Underneath his toughness there was something about Jarrett she connected with. In a way, he was an exaggerated version of herself, she thought. Not wanting to play by other people's rules. Now they had both gotten caught, each in their own way, and had both paid a price.

"If your husband is still alive, we'll find him. I promise you that."

She looked up at him and he seemed to react physically. "What do you really think? Was the broadcast a bad idea? Was all the publicity on it beforehand the reason Matthew is missing?"

Jarrett looked at her intently, weighing his answer. "As a matter of fact, I thought it was an incredibly bad idea," he said finally.

Before she could respond, the phone rang in another room. Schroeder picked up on the third ring, enough time for the trace to start. In a few moments the policewoman stood at the top of the stairs and called Jarrett's name. He excused himself and took it at the far side of the room.

He stood with his back to her and spoke inaudibly at first, then uttered a few terse questions into the receiver. Usually he had so much nervous energy he couldn't stop fidgeting.

When he put the phone down and came back to her his demeanor had changed dramatically. "They think they just caught the person who broke into the hospital lab. I have to go downtown."

Katlyn gasped and reached for his arm. "Who is it?"

Jarrett appeared deeply perplexed. "If it's Starman, it's got to be one of the strangest things I've ever heard. As crazy as it sounds, it's a woman."

THIRTY-SIX

Katlyn paced the floor waiting for Jarrett to return. Undoubtedly, his delay was caused by the law enforcement and judicial bureaucracies which had to be rigorously precise in the treatment of their suspect. Still, the idea that at that very moment someone was in custody who might be Starman, might know what had happened to Matthew, and that she couldn't get to talk to her, was more than she could bear.

When Jarrett finally did return, close to six o'clock, he greeted her anxious look with a solemn shake of the head.

Once inside, he handed her a small photo. "Do you recognize her?"

Katlyn reached for it quickly, her hand shaking.

"It's a duplicate of the one taken when she was booked—an unauthorized duplicate," he added while she studied it.

The woman in the photo was in her late thirties, early forties. Her face was weary, with once-pretty features that had become soft and puffy, and she appeared to be a good twenty or so pounds overweight. The skin at the corner of her mouth had drooped, giving her an almost clownish exaggeration of sadness. But her eyes were clear, nothing about them that signaled she was crazy enough to be a killer. There often wasn't any such signal, she knew.

"I don't know. She's vaguely familiar. I may have seen her before. I'm not sure."

"Her name is Helen Kahn. Does that mean anything?"

Katlyn struggled to make a connection. "No. I don't recall it. Did she say anything about Matthew? Did you ask her?"

"No, I'm sorry. We can't question her until the doctors let us. She didn't volunteer anything."

Katlyn had tried to prepare herself for that outcome, but the effect of Jarrett's news was still shattering.

"When she was arrested, the officers had to call a paramedic to the scene to sedate her. She was in pretty bad shape emotionally."

"How long until you can question her?"

"It's not a question of time. When she calms down she'll have a lawyer, and it will depend on which way he decides to go with it."

Katlyn turned away, despairingly.

"But there's a very good chance she'll be pressured to confess, once we tell her we found your pictures in her apartment."

Katlyn snapped to attention. After the disappointment about Matthew she hadn't expected anything positive.

"The pictures from my albums?"

"I saw them myself. That, together with broken glass taken from the lab, is pretty conclusive."

Katlyn felt like she had been slapped hard in the face. Matthew had told her about the in-vitro vial that had been taken from the hospital lab. Now she knew what had happened to it.

"We also found a mask at the bottom of a clothes hamper. The face and head of a man without any hair," Jarrett said, aiming a portentous look at her.

"Like the descriptions of him. And the shadow I saw on the floor that night."

"You remember that small piece of fingernail I told you we found in your library?"

"Yes."

"It's a good guess now that it's hers, not yours as we thought. Plus I think the forensic people will be able to confirm that her blood is the same as the sample found at the lab."

"How could you know that already?"

"They've finished running DNA scans and tried to match it to someone on the hospital staff, and none of them correlated. When I got to Kahn's apartment I looked around and found a used razor in her shower, one of those disposable ones. Figured it might come in handy for a blood match, which I knew we might have trouble getting once she had her lawyer. I gave it to a friend in the forensics lab, and we'll know soon."

For the first time Katlyn had a taste of what it was like to be on the receiving end of Jarrett's unorthodoxy. Taking Kahn's razor had cut days off the identification process.

"How did you catch her in the first place?"

"We didn't, her landlady did. Kahn rents an apartment in her house and she saw your interview on TV, the first one when you talked with Driscoll about being stalked, and about the in-vitro. This morning, about two A.M., she woke up to the sound of glass breaking and her tenant shouting obscenities in the room above hers. She was already suspicious because of the woman's odd hours, and because she skipped her last rent payment. So after Kahn went out this morning she went to her room and found pieces of glass in a trash bag under the sink—including one that still had the label *Rome-Demarco* on it. She made the connection right away and called the police. We staked the place out and nabbed her when she came home."

Katlyn again felt an inexpressible sense of loss about her embryo, a feeling that had been waiting for concrete news of its death.

"I still don't understand how Starman could be a woman."

"Assuming she is, I wouldn't have believed it, either, but there have been others like her. She's not big but very strong. And from the way she acted when she was arrested, capable of violence."

"What about the things that were done to the victims? The sexual part of it. You'd think only a man— "

"I've seen a lot of strange things. You can't rule it out."

Katlyn felt cold and gathered her arms in her hands. She tried to digest all the information that was coming at her, information which still did not shed any light on what happened to her husband.

"Where is she from? What else do you know about her?"

"Only what we could tell from an expired driver's license, her only ID. She's from Bakersfield. We ran a trace on her fingerprints, but she's not in any of the computer files."

"What about the landlady?"

"Dead end. All she knew was that the woman took the apartment a month and a half ago and kept to herself."

Katlyn did the math and felt her skin crawl. Six weeks earlier was when the reign of terror had begun. It was a coincidence that was too hard to ignore.

"You've got to let me see her. If I can talk to her I'll know if she took Matthew. I'll see it on her face."

"There's no way I can do that. She's locked up so tight they're not even letting Stryker's men in."

Katlyn felt the weight of impotence settle

over her. There was nothing she could do but wait, like everyone else. What happened next was preordained by the system.

"But what if she could tell us something?"

"I'll try to stay close to her, and the interrogations. If she knows something, someone will get word to me."

"How are you going to do that?"

Jarrett looked up at her, a quiet confidence behind his eyes. "I'll find a way."

Katlyn nodded and fell silent. Something about the way he said it, and his confidence, made her trust him.

Or maybe it was just that she had no choice.

THIRTY-SEVEN

"We don't have to talk about anything," Fava said when she paid her first visit late Saturday afternoon. "I just came to be with my friend." It was ten days since Katlyn had moved in, and it wasn't exactly the truth.

"Stryker wasn't too happy about you coming," Katlyn said. "I had to threaten to leave, just like I did for them to bring Monty. That seems to be the only way I can get what I need."

Fava nodded knowingly. She could see that Katlyn was unkempt, by her normal standards, even a bit frayed around the edges. She wore a plain white T-shirt that was only partially tucked into brown denim jeans. The jeans themselves appeared to have been worn for days. She had answered the door in her bare feet and had been perspiring; all in all a little too down-to-earth, even for Katie.

Later, as they sat in a lavishly appointed sitting room, a mewing announced Monty's entrance from behind a large chair. He immediately jumped onto Fava's lap.

"Well, look who's here," she said. "I'll bet your mistress is glad to have you around."

"More than you know," Katlyn answered,

looking at her pet fondly. "Matthew and he are real pals."

Fava stroked him under the chin, and he leaned against her hand.

"Anything been happening with the Kahn woman since we spoke?"

"Not really. I'm still mad that they wouldn't let me talk to her," Katlyn said with a caustic edge. "There was a chance that one-on-one I might have gotten her to tell me where Matthew is—if she took him. They let me look at her through the glass, but that didn't tell me any more than her picture did."

"What's she like?"

"From what they tell me, a strangely sad and introverted person. Not insane I don't think, just incredibly bitter about something." Katlyn smiled ruefully. "Like I'm getting to be. There's definitely something familiar about her, though. I've been racking my brain."

"She's still saying she doesn't know anything about Matthew?"

"Yeah, but they've matched her blood with the sample taken at the lab."

The shock on Fava's face showed she'd been out of the loop.

"The police think she'd go for a deal on stalking charges, but obviously, nothing to do with the celebrity killings. Or Matthew."

"What's their guess—that she really is Starman?"

"Deep down, the police don't know what to believe. They can't get past the fact she's a woman." Katlyn massaged a knot in the back of her neck. Her whole body ached, the result of many nights of restless sleep. "If I could only figure out why she came after me. Somewhere there's a clue that might lead to Matthew."

Fava sat back without knowing what to say. At the moment she was bothered by one of the other reasons she came, a reason other than friendship. Dan Jarrett had called her to say Katlyn was acting strange. The guards had reported it to him. She had stopped going out for exercise and was staying up half the night. The visit gave her a chance to see for herself if Katlyn was in trouble.

Fava rested her elbow on a pillow covered with a swatch of Oriental rug fabric. "Nice place," she said. "A person could get used to this."

"What? Solitary confinement?" Katlyn answered right away.

"You think this is bad, try eating every meal with a freakin' parakeet." Fava looked toward the inner rooms. "Wanna give me the grand tour?"

"Truthfully—no," Katlyn said. "This place gives me the creeps. Why don't you walk around while I get us some more wine."

"Good. And when I get back let's get stinkin'."

"Deal."

Fava's exploration started in a large central

hallway flanked on both sides by enough rooms to accommodate her extended family and their friends. The architect had obviously been infatuated with large open spaces, soaring ceilings, and twice as many windows as were needed for light. Everywhere, privacy had been traded for vistas.

The bed in the upstairs master bedroom was enormous, probably the worst thing in the world for someone to sleep in alone, Fava reflected. On the way to the bath she passed twin closets in a dressing room. The door to one was open, and she could see a few of Katlyn's outfits inside. Next to them she recognized an old sweater that she remembered Matthew wearing, and a soft alarm went off in her mind.

A connecting door led to a spacious bathroom with twin vanities.

"Am I drinking alone?" Katlyn called from the sitting room.

"Coming."

As she was leaving the bathroom, a man's electric razor caught her eye. She picked it up and examined it. It was spotless and could have been brand new. On a hunch, she opened a second medicine cabinet and was shocked when she saw that it was lined with a set of personal items, including medicines, brushes, lotions, the kind of sundries a man would use.

Two of the prescription drugs had Matthew's name on them: Seconal, a strong painkiller, and a half-used bottle of Halcion, a tranquilizer.

Evidently, he was less placid than he appeared. There was also a package of Nicorette.

The cabinet contained everything Matthew would need; everything had been taken from his own bathroom and put there for him, before anyone knew he would never arrive.

THIRTY-EIGHT

"The end of your speech blew everybody away," Fava exclaimed. "When did you decide to leave the station?"

She sat cross-legged on the couch and finished the last bite of her Johnny Rocket's cheeseburger, which had been delivered lukewarm through the security net by police.

"Sorry I couldn't tell you about it beforehand. Marty convinced me that once I did the broadcast I'd be a sitting duck if I kept coming to work. Too regular a schedule. It was my call to announce that I was leaving as part of the speech—for impact."

"Trust me, you got impact," Fava said.

"How are things going there, anyway? Anyone notice I've been gone?"

"Only a couple of million viewers." She could see that Katlyn was trying hard to look interested, but her mind was elsewhere. "Team Ten is in total disarray."

"I didn't mean to wreck things for the rest of you. I'm surprised I made that much of a difference."

"Sermac is hot to trot to leverage your story. That's his buzz word these days, *leverage*. He wants updates on you during every regularly scheduled news segment, a *Rome Watch*–type thing. He asked me to invent an emotional lead-in for each sequence, but I told him to get somebody else."

"Jesus, Fava, don't go doing anything stupid." She covered Fava's hand with her own. "You need your job. And I can't run interference for you. Besides, nothing Sermac does matters much anymore."

Fava nodded, then walked to a window and peered outside. She could see how large the property was, and why it took over a dozen men to protect it. Thus far, she'd seen only a few of them, however. They must have made themselves deliberately invisible.

"I can't wait any longer for Kahn to tell us something," Katlyn said in a while and with unexpected energy. "And I can't count on Stryker. I know now that I have to help find Matthew myself. "

Fava noticed the muscles in her arms were taut, her eyes intent.

"Whatever you want to do. I'll help you."

"I'm depending on that. I can't do it alone—from here."

Fava swallowed hard. "And just for the record, if anyone thinks they're dealing with two helpless women here they've got a lot to learn."

"We're not the worst detectives in the world, are we?" Katlyn said.

"Not the *very* worst. And, holding that thought"—Fava reached down and dug into her bag on the floor—"I brought you something I thought you could use right about now."

She took out the picture of Katlyn beating the boys in a race when she was a kid. She had taken it from her office as an afterthought.

Katlyn took it and put it on her lap. For some reason it made her sad now. "I've been thinking a lot about everything. I keep having this feeling that we've missed something obvious. Maybe we could go back to the research and take another look."

Fava grinned confidently. "I've already started. I have a few new angles I'm working on."

Katlyn nodded her appreciation.

A sudden knock at the front door made Fava jump. It was followed by four more thumps, the code the guards used.

"What's that?" Fava asked.

"Bed check," Katlyn said with a sigh.

"Who goes to bed at eight-thirty?"

"Inmates."

THIRTY-NINE

In mid-July, a cold, high-pressure air mass formed in southern Manitoba, and by the time it moved south and crossed into the United States, a weather balloon had reported pressure in its center at 31.54 millibars, a record for that time of year.

Covering an area of approximately two million acres, the system's winds were nevertheless wound tight. Typically, it would take a turn to the east, and if it held together, it would eventually become part of a Bermuda high that would lock the East Coast into days of oppressive heat and humidity.

But so far, the powerful system had gone relatively unnoticed.

Instead, the attention of the U.S. Weather Bureau was focused on a tropical storm in the warm waters of the Gulf of Mexico that had surprised everyone and become a powerful hurricane.

With winds clocked at 115 miles per hour, Hurricane Eunice stalled over the Gulf. For two days the computers predicted a move to the northwest, but for two days Eunice just spun.

On Wednesday, July 15, around 5:00 A.M., the

storm moved inland. Fifteen hours later it had spent only a portion of its fury on Texas, and, nourished by moist winds from the Gulf, it continued north and slammed into the equally strong high-pressure front advancing south from Canada.

For another day and a half, the storms churned against each other in place. Where their peripheries were contiguous, winds rose to a steady 90 miles per hour and roared into the Sierra Nevada mountain range, where they were forced up the steep eastern-facing slopes.

Rising quickly, the deeper layers of air cooled, and the moisture in them condensed. Prodigious amounts of rain pelted the normally dry mountain passes. Emptied of all water, the air was forced violently downslope on the other side of the tall peaks, and, without moisture, warmed quickly and blew more strongly.

Until one of the two pressure systems moved there was an inexhaustible supply of air to feed the tempest, and with no further barriers between it and the coastal plain, it would be only a few more hours until the wind reached Los Angeles and became known as *Santa Ana*.

FORTY

The Laurel Canyon Safe House

It hadn't rained since a month before Anne Marie Warren. The wind was dry and had been rising steadily, sucking the moisture out of Arthur Combs's skin. It didn't matter. This was the part he liked best. When he was close and his prey was still unaware.

From where he stood there was no chance the security guards would discover him, even with their special nighttime binoculars. He had learned from the best, and by the time the masters of insurgency and their snappy little covert military unit found him unfit to serve, he had learned everything about the fine art of not being. The secret was being one with the forest; covering a human scent with a stronger natural one; not infecting a killing ground with even a microbe of one's individuality.

And practice, practice, practice.

Most important was the mop-up. In his case, an intensely sanitary scrub. It was laborious, woman's work, but the reward was commensurate with the task: Every time he did it properly, he got to hunt again.

When he turned his face into the gale, the scent of the woods stimulated his senses. The swirling currents picked up debris from the ground and made the dead forest come alive again. Beneath his feet, fallen branches had turned to kindling.

For the third time in an hour, Arthur unzipped the pocket where he kept the medicine. Just enough to dull the pain, he assured himself, not enough to make him need more before he was finished. On this night especially, he did not want his judgment impaired.

He glanced at his watch and saw that the medicine had blurred the numbers. No matter. He knew within seconds what the time was. Still, the face on the watch reminded him that he had to walk the thin line between pain and caution. The drug could cause him to make a mistake, miss a detail.

And detail was everything.

Launching himself into the treetops again, he used the faint light of a crescent moon to guide his steps on the branches. Before he'd gotten far, the wind came in a more intense gust, more sustained, and countless bits of airborne matter made it nearly impossible to see without goggles. When his vision cleared again he saw the house at the top of the rise, and felt an invigorating rush of adrenaline.

Her face had been in his dreams since he

and Bo had watched the news program together. The things Katlyn Rome had said with the whole world watching had haunted him. Her performance proved that Bo had been right all along: Katlyn Rome was the cause of the pain.

Soon, she would be the antidote.

A short time later, when he had come down from the trees and moved as close to the house as he could, he crouched and rested against the prickly bark of a fallen blue spruce. The pain in his head was down to a dull roar, and he could feel the warmth of his blood surging in his veins. Pain and pleasure. Always together near the end.

Arthur held out his hands and studied them in the pallid light. They were steady, as they had been all the other times. The conditions were perfect. Nature was his sanctuary, and he felt safe. He was one with the forest.

Remarkably, the man who had led him to this secret place was the very best guide he could have hoped for. The chief of detective's car started out from the same place every day, and no one seemed to care about the nondescript vehicle, borrowed for the occasion, that followed at a long interval. Eventually Stryker turned off the main roads, then turned again. From there, on foot, it was only a matter of spotting the guards to find the house that contained the trophy.

He had to admit that his enemy was not completely unintelligent. The ambush they had set up for him at Rome's real house almost succeeded.

Ironically, what first alerted him was an unexpected lack of security. At a time when there should have been an army to guard Katlyn Rome, the TMU team that had been stationed there was suddenly taken away. Or so it was supposed to seem. The police had done everything but hang out a welcome sign.

The telling evidence came when Matthew Demarco himself stumbled going up the steps to his front door. To most, it would have been an insignificant misstep, perhaps, but to him it was inconceivable that someone who climbed those steps every day could have misjudged their height so badly. The mistake had alerted him to the police treachery. Later, an even closer inspection revealed that the people in the house were not who they seemed.

Focusing on the safe house from the thicket of branches in which he now rested, Arthur had a partial view into a window on the top floor. Perhaps she was there now, he thought, even though she was not visible at the moment, a beautiful canary in a cage—soon to sing a last plaintive song just for him.

The thought stirred his loins and brought him back to full alert, his senses razor sharp. Opening his duffel bag, he took out a costume borrowed just for the occasion, stripped, and put it on. The next time it came off it would be for a better reason than camouflage. A much better reason.

All together, the special gear weighed twenty-seven pounds and was oppressively hot, even in the coolness of the forest. The last piece that came out of the bag was the heaviest. He wouldn't put it on until absolutely needed.

Arthur had to wonder what Stryker was thinking. With all of his planning, there was a gaping flaw in the security—and it had nothing to do with how many men were guarding the house.

His hand worked into a deep top pocket of the uniform, and his fingers closed on the very special present he had brought for Katlyn Rome. He caressed it, just as he would shortly caress her.

It was such a little present for such an important visit, but one a person could depend on when the time came.

Zippo lighters were famous for working in the wind.

He looked past the tree line to the sentry post nearest to him. The two men who occupied it could easily be dead any time he wanted. They were not paying attention to what was just ahead of them in the forest.

Arthur cupped his hands to shield the lighter from the gale. Holding the top and bottom with two fingers, he pressed them together until the top one slipped off and the lid sprung open in a counter reaction. He spun the wheel a quarter turn and the wick flared brightly. He snapped it shut again instantly and with satisfaction.

"First time and every time," he recited, remembering the old commercial.

FORTY-ONE

The wind had risen after Dan Jarrett left the last of the sentry stations and kept walking toward the trees. He was checking for holes in the security net. Bits of airborne matter stung his eyes as he stepped off the perimeter of the property and crept a few more steps into the woods, alone in the dark. There was something about the night that was creepier than usual, he thought. Something instinctive he felt that he could not put his finger on.

The darkness had always bothered him, since the night when he was seven and burglars woke and terrorized his whole family for two heart-stopping hours before they fled. No one had been hurt, at least not physically, but since then he never felt comfortable sleeping without a small light on. Dan Jarrett, the hard case who kicked ass, took names, and slept with a night light.

For once he had to admit that Stryker had done his job. His security teams were L.A.'s best and positioned in a tight cordon around the entire property. Their radios kept them in constant communication with both local command and a police dispatcher at SWAT, where more help was available at a moment's notice. Beyond that, the entire grounds were under twenty-four-hour video surveillance.

The safe house had also been a good choice, he thought. It offered as much protection as was reasonable to expect from any place other than a jail. The grounds were open on all four sides, protected on the perimeter by dense woods on three. The fourth side was a boulder and root-strewn slope that dropped precipitously to a long dry stream choked with fallen limbs—a difficult approach, a more difficult retreat if one were being pursued.

But nothing was perfect. The Achilles' heel of this safe house was the forest itself, he knew. Its density and height made complete surveillance impossible. Given that, it was possible that an unauthorized visitor could get to the very edge of the property if he wanted to, if he could ever find the safe house. But if someone could, he would come from the trees.

At the edge of the forest, Jarrett stopped and listened. The only sound was the constant whine of the wind and the crackle of a voice on a police radio somewhere behind him, between the perimeter posts and the residence. He'd used the Night Owl lens only once before, the night he'd found his drug dealer hacking away at his delinquent customer in a vacant lot. The night he blew several large holes in the bastard, and one just as big in his own career.

He brought the special binoculars to his eyes and slowly adjusted the focus until the forest was miraculously visible in an eerie yellow halo. The wind arranged the trees into shapes that could have been anything.

Moving slowly, he raised his line of vision and peered into the uppermost parts of the treetops. From there, with patience, he pushed the lens slowly to the right, where the property ended, then started back the other way.

He was about to put the lens down, when, for an instant too brief to be certain, he thought he saw the slightest flash of light at the very top of the canopy. It looked like a small flame. But when he blinked it was gone.

FORTY-TWO

For the dozenth time, the words on Fava's monitor became indistinct clusters of type, and she had to blink hard to clear her vision. On a Saturday night she had been hoping to find information on Helen Kahn, but even after three hours, as with Jarrett's search of police records, there was nothing on her to be had.

Out of desperation, she went back into files she'd compiled when she originally tried to build a profile on stalkers for Katlyn. Within that large pool of information there might be something relating to the Kahn woman that would now jump out of the research. It was a long shot, but she was out of ideas.

When a recent psychological interview on the stalking personality came up on the screen, Fava remembered having read it. It had been part of a longer background article on acute personality disorders in psychiatric patients that eventually had turned them into violent stalkers. The specialty of the author, psychiatrist Dr. Ellen Lundon, was schizophrenia, and the article had been one of the more interesting. At the time, of course, Starman was presumed to be a man, so after perusing the story, she simply filed it away among the myriad of others that seemed like a dead end.

Fava clicked on the article and scrolled down until she found one part she remembered. Marty Conroy had once called her a human Polaroid camera. Sometimes it was a curse. This time it turned out to be a blessing.

Lundon's portion of the account dealt with stalkers from a point of view of the *persecuted personality,* as she had labeled it. What made Fava remember the article was that, among the patients that Lundon discussed, there was one woman she'd seen who believed herself to be a victim of the news media. To protect the privacy of her patient, Lundon did not name her.

But the story said she'd seen her recently.

Fava was brought up short at a specific reference to the vehemence of the patient's claim. She said that unfair news reports had ruined her life, and also mentioned that they had come from a television station in Los Angeles. The moment Fava read that she realized she was an idiot for not remembering it before, and she quickly went back to the first page of the interview. It was dated June of the current year, only a month ago.

She reached for the phone, her heart pounding.

If it was a recent patient, as Lundon had said,

and allowing a month for publication of the story, the woman had probably been a patient sometime in April or May.

The attacks on Katlyn had started only a few weeks later.

FORTY-THREE

The sky had had a brooding quality all day and by late afternoon had turned a sickly gray-brown. Katlyn peered out of a western-facing window and saw that a dust storm had reduced the visible world to the edge of the property. There were no guards in sight. She wondered if they had left their posts for better cover.

With Schroeder off for the night, she was left alone to deal with the questions that stalked her as relentlessly as Starman had. If Kahn, or Starman, had been only going after beautiful young movie stars recently, why had she targeted a newscaster? What had triggered her incredible vindictiveness toward Katlyn, and why had she decided to play cat and mouse instead of just killing her like the rest? Why had she transferred her revenge to Matthew?

She also wondered why Stryker hadn't allowed her to come out of hiding. With the evidence mounting that Kahn was the one who'd come after her, did he still not believe that she was the celebrity killer?

As she had many times before, Katlyn turned to the pile of documents accumulated since the break-in. She hoped that some obscure or overlooked fact that might lead to Matthew was some-where in those papers.

Rereading a transcript of an early report she did on Starman right after her press conference with Stryker, she realized again how quickly she had chosen to alienate the powerful cop. Her public condemnation of him was actually the way she introduced herself. No other reason was nec-essary to explain the antipathy she could sense in him ever since.

The verbatims on her impromptu editorial after the Lonnigan story were equally revealing. It was incredible how reckless she had been, part of the same pattern, she had to admit, that had governed her behavior since she took the job at the station.

Yet, in her mind, neither event even came close to the stupidity of the Starman interview and challenge. And, in the end, Matthew, not she, had become the victim. For that more than anything, she would never be able to forgive her-self.

Lost in thought, Katlyn did not hear the knocking on the front door until she heard a man shouting her name. It was Jarrett, calling to her urgently between fits of coughing.

She could hardly understand what he was saying. Something about a fire.

FORTY-FOUR

Dr. Ellen Lundon was a sturdy woman in her late forties with completely white hair pulled back into a tight bun. She stood ramrod straight in the entrance to her office, which occupied the main floor of a four-story commercial building in the heart of Westwood.

"I'm not really comfortable discussing my patients," she stated, even before they went inside. "But given the circumstances, I've decided that your friend's interest takes precedence."

"I appreciate that, Dr. Lundon. It's very important," Fava said.

"And no doubt I'll be doing this again shortly with the police."

"No doubt."

Lundon let out a long breath and was resigned to her fate. She led Fava to an inner office where her consultations with patients took place.

"First of all, I'm puzzled about the name you mentioned when you called," she said when Fava took a seat on a platform couch opposite her. "The woman in custody is Helen Kahn, but that wasn't the name of my patient. What makes you think we're talking about the same person?"

"I'm not sure we are. But how many women could there be who feel so persecuted by the media that they seek counseling for it?"

"I have no way of knowing that." Lundon thought about it some more and added, "I guess not too many."

"I figured someone like that could harbor so much resentment she might eventually come after the reporter she blamed for her problems—that is, if she was too late for therapy to help her," Fava added respectfully.

Lundon nodded but didn't say anything.

"Would you have known if she wasn't using her real name?" Fava asked.

"No, not necessarily. A number of patients withhold their real names, at least in the beginning. Do you have a picture?"

Fava quickly produced the shot Katlyn had given her, the one that Jarrett brought back after the arrest. As it turned out, that same picture ended up all over television and the newspapers the next day.

Lundon studied it, then looked at the date. "I was out of town when this was published. Poor woman. I had the feeling she'd already made up her mind to do something before she came to see me."

"You mean that's her?" Fava said excitedly.

"She was very disturbed." London stood and walked to a file cabinet to the right of her desk. She opened a drawer and in a few moments took out several pages of notes still attached to a ruled yellow pad. She slipped on a pair of bifocals.

"Her first visit was on the sixteenth of April. I saw her only one other time, on May eighth. She was much more agitated on the second visit, so I was concerned when she never called again. She said she was thirty-six, although she looked a good ten years older. Attractive, in a world-weary sort of way. But intelligent, definitely in the superior range."

"How was she dressed? Did she seem odd in any other way?"

"She appeared to be indigent, but not unclean. More like she was down on her luck. Her clothes were quite threadbare, though, as I remember."

"Did that come up in your talks?"

"Yes, very early. She blamed her impoverished state on the story the reporter had broadcast about her. The one I mentioned in the interview." Lundon looked down at her notes again. "Another curious thing was that she refused to sit during her visits. She paced the whole time, like a caged animal. Usually even the most agitated people get tired of standing at some point. Not her."

"I'm sorry, I don't know how to say this in medical terms. Do you think she was . . . unbalanced? Crazy?"

"I'm afraid that's not a very useful term," Lundon scowled. "In regard to her personality, the most extreme characteristics were anger and obsession. She made frequent references to a female TV reporter whom she never mentioned by name, but who was evidently the object of her rage. I tried to find out her name but she didn't want to tell me."

"What did she say the reporter did—exactly?"

"Spread lies about her in her broadcasts. She believed the stories on her had ruined her family and her life. And to be frank, after what she told me I have to admit I had some sympathy for her."

"I'm surprised you didn't make a connection to Katlyn Rome—after things started happening to her."

Lundon winced at the accusation. "Possibly, but to be honest, I didn't follow the story at all. I don't watch television much, especially local news."

"Did you find out how the reporter had hurt Kahn?"

"Yes, she went on a lot about that. She had worked in a day-care center in a small community, and as it turned out, a number of staff members were charged with child molestation."

With a shudder, Fava suddenly flashed on a story she remembered on the same topic. It was one of Katlyn's first stories well before she became news anchor. The amount of coverage Jude Sermac ordered on the story surprised everyone, and she had developed some of the background herself.

"The trial dragged on for months, very emotional. In the end the staff was acquitted, but by the time it was over, everyone who worked in the center had become pariahs—as often happens in small towns. Kahn had a daughter who was ostracized in school."

"Even though Kahn was proved innocent?"

"During the trial it came to light that Kahn once had an alcohol problem. All the publicity ruined her husband, who manufactured equipment for local businesses. His contracts were canceled and he blamed her. Later her husband sued for divorce and got custody of her daughter. So, in the short space of a few months, Kahn lost everything important in her life."

Just like Katlyn, Fava thought with a shiver. She thought about the police records that would have been developed on the case. They were probably expunged from police files once she was acquitted, which would explain why they weren't in Jarrett's police computer.

"I wonder if the name she gave you was her married name. And if she went back to using her maiden name, Kahn, after her husband left her."

"That's possible. I imagine it would be easy to find out. I've also been wondering why she focused on just one reporter. Don't most of the stations report the same news? You'd know more about that than I."

Fava did. "WMTC broke the story and made it the lead for much of the time the trial was going on." She read Lundon's look of disapproval. "Yes, I know," she said. "It wasn't a very popular decision. What happened to Kahn after that?"

"She left town and moved in with a sister in Santa Monica, in a run-down area near the beach. She told me that instead of diminishing over time, her feelings of rage toward the reporter became an obsession. She knew she was out of control and needed help, so she came to me."

"How did she get your name?"

"I have no idea."

"This is going to sound bizarre, but there's evidence in Kahn's apartment that suggests your patient could be Starman. There was a mask that matched people's descriptions of Starman. Also, she is directly tied to one of the most serious of the attacks on Katlyn, the theft and murder of her in-vitro embryo at a hospital lab. They found blood which has been matched to her DNA."

Lundon shook her head. "That's hard to believe, very hard. Nothing she said suggested a grudge against anyone but your friend." She continued checking her notes and shaking her head. She looked weary from the meeting, and years of dealing in human distress.

"There's not much else to tell you. Except I don't think Kahn was capable of murder."

"May I use your phone?" Fava said right away. "I'd like to tell my friend I'm leaving."

Lundon moved her phone to Fava's side of

the desk, and Fava quickly punched the number of the safe house, which she had memorized the first time it was given to her. It started to ring, but immediately became a continuous high-pitched tone.

She tried it again and heard the same sound. It was as though the line had been disconnected—or damaged. The trouble was probably because of the elaborate tracing setup, she told herself.

Still, she wondered why a drumbeat of panic was building in her chest when she rose from the chair to leave.

FORTY-FIVE

"**I** don't like the way it looks," Jarrett shouted.

He stared out at a fire that had definitely started in the brush somewhere between the house and road. Only a few minutes later, it had increased exponentially.

Katlyn went to the window and saw a large, smoky blaze moving rapidly up the hill toward them. While she watched, one of the largest trees became a fireball.

"Why haven't they sent a crew?"

"It doesn't matter anymore. It's moving too fast."

Jarrett had hoped the security guards would be able to buy the fire department enough time to do the job when they arrived, but he could see that the wind-driven flames had already forced them away.

"This place is supposed to be fireproof, isn't it?" Katlyn said.

"That's the theory. But we've got more to worry about than the fire." Jarrett looked up at the ceiling.

Katlyn understood. There was a fine haze where the rafters met the roof. And the musky smell of carbon had infiltrated the air.

"If the smoke doesn't get in too much we should be okay. The walls should keep out the heat."

Katlyn threw another worried glance out the window. "Shouldn't the fire stop at the tree line?"

"I don't know. I've heard about them jumping. I don't know how far."

Jarrett remembered the fire in Malibu a few years back, when the flames had hopped from one hilltop to another, as if someone at Disney had animated them.

He peered out the window again and was jolted by the progress of the blaze. The wind had carried it aloft, and basketball-size balls of fire were hopping from one tree to another. The whole eastern border was involved.

A distinct crackling sound came from his two-way radio and in a moment a voice sounded far away.

". . . dispatcher . . . units engaged . . . rest equip . . . fifteen mile . . . come . . . soon . . . possible."

"Dear God," Katlyn cried, as she ducked below window level. Thirty yards from the house, the tops of two trees lit up simultaneously and rattled the glass in the windows. The trees weren't burning, they were exploding.

"What happens if the windows go?" she cried.

"We'll be forced out."

"Out there? Dressed like this?" She was wearing shorts, canvas sneakers, and a light cotton shirt.

"Unless you want to suffocate."

She realized that they had been shouting. Like the smoke, the sound of the fire had invaded the house and made it difficult for them to hear each other.

Outside, Katlyn caught a glimpse of two security guards running through the thick haze holding their shirts to their faces. *If the house was so safe, why were Stryker's guards running away from it?*

"We're losing the guards," she yelled.

Jarrett tried to raise the security team on the two-way radio, but received only a short burst of static.

"Use the telephone," she shouted, not understanding why he hadn't already.

Jarrett picked up the receiver, then let it dangle by its wire for her to see. "I tried it before. The transformer probably blew with everything else out there."

As he spoke, a strong concussion shook the room, more of the forest going up. But the windows held all around. The backyard was beginning to look like the opening scenes from *Apocalypse Now.*

"It's getting worse," Katlyn cried the second she looked up. She pointed to the fine, churning haze that had collected at the top of the exposed beams that supported the ceiling.

"The wind must be forcing it in somewhere."

Jarrett had a good idea of what was happening. No matter how careful contractors were, every roof ended up with small openings from nail holes or tiny imperfections in the roof tiles.

The front yard of the house was completely obscured by a swirling black fog and intermittent showers of sparks. For a second, the dense curtain of smoke cleared enough for Katlyn to spot a last guard racing away. Then it closed again and he was gone like the rest of them.

Her eyes were tearing badly, and the smoke was burning her throat, so much so that she began to cough. They had to do something.

Jarrett looked up at the ceiling where the smoke had lowered about a third of the way down the two sloping beams. He put his hand to the window and could feel heat through the glass. He wondered how hot it would have to get before it melted. He tried to see through the noxious cloud in the front yard, looking for a place between the house and road where the fire had most likely started.

Perhaps it was only a cigarette tossed from a passing car, he thought. Or an ember from a barbecue.

Or maybe it was neither, he thought with sudden alarm.

FORTY-SIX

Fire Captain Tony Marchigiano acknowledged the news of the Laurel Canyon blaze with a sharp curse. Backup teams from his own cadre had already been split up and sent to Griffith Park and Coldwater Canyon. The officers in charge there would be reluctant to give them back so long as the strong winds continued.

The depth of coverage of all the fire companies in the area was, in fact, dire. With wind gusts above eighty miles per hour, and temperatures in the mid-nineties, there was a legitimate fear of another holocaust, like the one in Malibu in 1993. Because of that, the department had committed dozens of companies to locations more distant than the book called for, and much earlier. That had already reduced Marchigiano's own team, the one that protected the heart of Laurel Canyon, to a skeleton crew.

The first call on the Canyon fire was reported as a small but growing blaze a few hundred yards from the nearest house. Marchigiano immediately carved off a force of twelve men and two pieces of equipment and took off with them. On the way he'd been told that the house directly in the fire's path, and the people in it, had been given priority by the police. They wouldn't tell him why.

Seven minutes later, at the fire scene, what he saw made him instantly radio the station for his remaining force. The inferno had already engulfed the acreage above the road and was moving in a broad front toward a house at the top of the mountain.

Lack of men wasn't his only problem. The nearest water resource was on the road almost a hundred yards away, directly through the fire. The amount of water now en route on his pumper would have been useful if it were already there, but by the time it arrived it would be like taking a leak on Mount St. Helens after it erupted.

As he watched from the entrance to the driveway, one of the treetops on the eastern side of the house was blown to bits. Twenty-foot flames shot into the blackened sky. If the fire kept eating trees at the rate it was traveling, it would quickly encircle the house. After that, a distinct possibility was a firestorm, another name for a super-heated tornado.

Marchigiano had been in only one firestorm before—the first time the biblical concept of Hell had become real to him.

He jogged in his heavy equipment toward the thin line of men barely holding their own against the leading edge of flames. The wind was blowing directly into his face from the northeast, easily hurricane force and as hot as a furnace.

When he turned away from the gale, he noticed that a second fire had started well behind him and to his left and was building quickly. Driven by the same winds, the two infernos were moving inexorably toward each other. There was a remote possibility the lawn, cleared as a firebreak, might hold the fire back, but he doubted it. It would be only minutes before the fires combined and came at the house.

Caught between the two blazes, Marchigiano had a strange new thought. Even allowing for the flames' ability to travel through the air, it seemed as though the second fire had started too far from the first to have been spawned by it.

FORTY-SEVEN

"Cover yourself with the blankets, then we go," Jarrett yelled as loud as he could. Outside the fire sounded like the wailing of a thousand mourners.

Katlyn yanked open the doors of a linen closet, took out two blankets, then lugged them to the tub and turned on both faucets. While she waited for them to soak, she realized she hadn't seen Monty since the fire and frantically set out to look for him. She found him only a few seconds later, hiding terrified under a chair in the den. When she picked him up and returned to the blankets, he clawed her and tried to jump free.

Jarrett came to help her carry the watered-down load of blankets. At the front door he saw the cat and shook his head definitively.

"I'm not leaving here without him," Katlyn insisted.

"If he slows you down it could be the difference."

"Don't worry, he won't."

Jarrett took one of the blankets and put it over her shoulders, then covered himself with the other one. The front door faced south, he remembered, still the best avenue of escape. Coming from the opposite direction the wind would be partially blocked by the building once they were outside, but it was a capricious wind. The fire had created a cyclone, and the choking clouds could ambush them from any direction at any time.

"Take deep breaths," he ordered.

Outside there was a loud boom, like a hundred detonating caps going off at once, and Katlyn looked at him in terror. Monty dug his claws into her skin and clung to her for dear life.

"Are you sure?"

His instinct warned him to wait, but for once he decided to trust reason.

Before going out he turned back to Katlyn. "The little bastard will be safer with me," he said with resignation.

He grabbed the cat, and tucked him under his arm.

"Now," he barked and reached for the knob. It was even hotter than the window glass. The last place in the world he wanted to be was on the other side of that door.

FORTY-EIGHT

At the outer edge of the driveway, Marchigiano watched a ribbon of flame separate from the main body of fire and bridge the distance across the driveway. As if it had eyes, it touched down on a shed, igniting the roof. A wall of wind accompanying the curtain of flame knocked down two of his men who had been forced out into the clearing. Marchigiano crossed himself and gave thanks for the asbestos suits and Air-Pak breathing apparatus. Together they had probably saved his and his men's lives.

An apparition suddenly appeared from out of the smoke—John Richter, the lead man of the backup team and a veteran firefighter. He exuded an air of confidence despite having to deal with the glass of an air mask which was substantially fogged.

"Get the fuck out of here," Richter shouted to Marchigiano.

He studied the sky as if it were a human adversary. It had turned a sinister orange-brown, the classic warning sign of an impending firestorm.

"Tony! It's gonna blow, for Christ's sake!"

"There are people in there," Marchigiano

answered. He could barely see the house through the haze. "Lay down a stream on me so I can get to them. Do it now."

Richter shot a last quick look at the sky, then the house, and disappeared back into the smoke.

Marchigiano figured there was a fair chance he would never see the veteran again.

FORTY-NINE

Katlyn looked up at the rafters, and panic etched her face. The canopy of smoke was only a half-dozen feet over their heads, a churning killer fog.

Jarrett saw that the remaining trees on the south side of the house were a wall of flame. Their best escape route was now no better than any of the others.

At first the new sound seemed to be a modulated level of the howling wind. In another moment it became the familiar wail of sirens.

"They're here!" Katlyn shouted, suddenly jubilant. "They made it!"

"It doesn't matter, we can't wait."

"They must know we're in here."

"Too late." Jarrett pointed prophetically at the ceiling to a long, wispy finger of smoke that had dropped from the main mass and was testing the clearer air below at almost the height of their heads. Maybe the main body of smoke would stay above them, but any substantial change could happen in seconds. "Now!" he insisted.

He adjusted the cat higher under his arm and opened the door. Instantly, a torrent of black smoke billowed in and engulfed both of them.

Katlyn held her breath and made for the opening she could barely see.

The sudden pressure on her arm before she could step through was Jarrett grabbing her unexpectedly and holding her back. The reason became clear in a few seconds. There was a man running toward the house and shouting to them to stay put, waving his arms frantically. He was silhouetted in smoke by a powerful light behind him. A deluge of water from an unseen comrade was playing onto him, keeping the flames away.

When the fireman reached the front door, Katlyn saw that he was a captain. She also noticed that Jarrett looked relieved—amazingly relieved for someone who in a moment would have to go back the way the fireman had just come.

The reason for his relief was two pieces of equipment attached to the front of the captain's uniform. Two bright spanking-new air masks.

FIFTY

Katlyn had taken only a half-dozen steps when she could feel the hot stones of the path burning into the soles of her sneakers. All around her live embers, ash, and pieces of glowing wood littered the ground. Visibility was down to only a few yards.

The fire captain stayed in the lead, jogging and looking back, trying not to lose her. Jarrett was behind her somewhere. Katlyn held the heavy blanket tightly over her head with both hands, blindly following the yellow coat. The sound of her own breathing was barely audible in her mask over the fire.

She wondered how Monty was doing, if Jarrett could hold on to him.

The stone path that led from the front door to the driveway ended in a short drop. Katlyn stumbled over it, and loosened her grip on the blanket, which fell to the ground and began to smoke right away. Without its protection, the heat attacked her skin and she could feel it burning. Hundreds of hot ashes dug like burrowing insects into the unprotected areas on her arms and legs.

The blanket was smoldering when she picked it up. She yelled for the fire captain and Jarrett, but the noise of the fire swallowed her call.

There was no sign of either of them.

FIFTY-ONE

Dan Jarrett fought his way through the darkness in the direction the captain had indicated before he took off. He had tried to stay directly behind Katlyn, but the gap between them had widened in the blinding smoke, and by the time it cleared enough to see at all, she was gone. He could only hope that she was still close behind the fireman.

"Hang on, Monty, we're almost there," he said prayerfully. Monty had long since stopped putting up a fight, and instead had compressed himself as much as he could inside the blanket.

Jarrett darted ahead, pressing his forearm on the cat to hold him in place. After what seemed like hours he finally made it to a clearing and ripped off his air mask to suck in the unfiltered air. Smoke was steaming off his body. His blanket lay at his feet, a singed heap. He opened his arm and the cat fell to the ground. As soon as Monty touched the cool grass he scampered away in the opposite direction from the smoke.

Facing the house again, Jarrett searched for a sign of Katlyn and the fire captain. If he was out of it by then, they should be, too. Katlyn's frightened face became vivid in his mind. He imagined her lost in the smoke, searching for a way out. His panic struck with an intensity he hadn't expected, a personal level. He had to do something.

He could go back into the fire, as far as he could before his skin burned. The blanket was next to useless, but at least he had the mask. A few dozen yards. Maybe he'd get lucky.

Jarrett pulled on the mask and adjusted it for a seamless fit.

"Goddamn it!" he shouted and bolted straight ahead into the smoke.

FIFTY-TWO

Without the fire captain to guide her, Katlyn was completely lost. She tried to clear her mind and think logically. The wind had been consistently pushing her from behind. If she kept it at her back, theoretically, she would be taking the same track she and the fireman had taken before, away from the fire. Unless the wind had shifted. If that were the case, there was little chance she'd ever find her way out.

Moving forward again she was pounded on the back by a blast of air and sent sprawling to the ground. She broke the fall with her hand and screamed as her palm hit the scalding surface. Her face slammed into something hard that almost knocked her mask off. She could feel a trickle of blood move from her forehead down her cheek. She lay on the ground. She was going to die.

When she opened her eyes again, the fire captain was miraculously silhouetted above her. He floated down out of the smoke and crouched next to her, shielding her from some of the heat. With extraordinary strength, his arms went under her back and lifted her up. She kept looking at the large attentive eyes inside the glass, overwhelmed with gratitude.

Safe again.

FIFTY-THREE

Jarrett plunged ahead until he couldn't see anything. Neither Katlyn nor the fire captain had answered any of his calls. The air was like a blowtorch, scorching his skin until it was raw. Finding it nearly impossible to breathe, he was forced to turn back. He was sure the two of them were lost.

He tried to retrace his path back to safety. Every step required an effort of will. His legs felt as if they'd been worked over with tire irons and his lungs were burning. The mask no longer kept out all of the smoke.

An opening in the solid black curtain allowed a fleeting view of a familiar yellow shape. He wiped the glass of his air mask for a better look. The bright clothing moved diagonally away from him, toward the perimeter of the fire. The tall uniformed fireman was carrying a rolled-up blanket, something heavy inside—*Katlyn*, he assumed with a tremendous sigh of relief, even though he couldn't see her face.

"Hey!" he shouted as loudly as he could, and choked on smoke for his effort. "Here. Over here."

The fireman didn't acknowledge him and in a few seconds disappeared with his precious burden. Jarrett fixed his eyes on the spot in the smoke where they'd been and took off for it.

At least Katlyn was out of the inferno.

FIFTY-FOUR

There was majesty in the way he moved through the firestorm, she thought. Confident, powerful, like a modern-day gladiator. He held her firmly, as if they were forever bound together in time. Along the way they passed another fireman, who offered a respectful wave.

Eventually, the smoke thinned and distinct textures became visible—trees, a boulder, part of the lawn that had somehow stayed green. Either they were outside the fire zone or in an oasis that the fire had spared.

The fire captain walked a little farther, then knelt and placed her on a smooth section of earth that felt soft, like moss. Gently, he took off her mask, then reached for his own.

She imagined the face would be middle-aged, ruggedly working class, like the earthy older men she had known growing up. Instead, she saw the smooth face of a younger man. There was a boyish innocence in his eyes, which were intent on hers and full of wonder.

"You're even prettier than on television," the velvety voice said. "I had a feeling you would be."

When the mask was completely off, his head

was long and a bit too narrow. And completely hairless. Katlyn went rigid.

He turned sideways and one small, sunken eye came closer. A small bit of saliva was lodged in one corner of his mouth, and his tongue flicked it away, lizard-like. His smooth, warm hand stroked the side of her cheek.

"Get away from me!" she screamed. "Someone help me!"

His hand cupped her mouth tightly. In a moment his knee came down hard on her stomach, pinning her to the ground.

Without thinking, Katlyn drew her own knee to her chest and shot it forward. Her heel struck its intended target between his legs, and Starman bent over in pain.

Katlyn scrambled a few feet away before his hands were on her again, and he flipped her over on her back, as easily as if she were a doll.

She used her hands this time, slamming the palms into his face.

He shook off the blow quickly, and without apparent injury.

"That wasn't very nice of you, Katlyn," he said. "Bo always told me I was wrong about you."

Before she could react, his fist landed a crushing blow to the left side of her face, and she stopped struggling.

He knelt down beside her. His features sharper, his expression intent. Like he had work to do.

Deftly, his hands reached for the top of her shirt and ripped it open to the waist. She was not wearing a brassiere, and he was engrossed by her nakedness.

"What did you do with my husband?" Katlyn said weakly.

"Well, now. That's the sixty-four-thousand-dollar question, isn't it?"

Reverently, he cupped one breast and squeezed it like an adolescent having his first encounter with a woman's body. Holding perfectly still, she let his finger trace a line from her cheek to her neck, then draw a circle around her nipple. There was nothing she could do.

"Bo will like this," he said. He took out a straight razor from the pocket of the fire suit and opened it with a flick of his hand.

The sudden cry of pain made Katlyn jump. It came from her attacker. She looked up and saw that he had a deep cut on the right side of his forehead where a section of skin had been split open. A stream of blood had already worked its way down his neck.

"Jarrett," Katlyn cried when she saw him holding Starman.

His fingers were locked around the hand that held the razor, pressing it backward at an extreme and unnatural angle. She wondered if she were dreaming. In a quick reversal, Starman wrested control of the knife and turned it back at Jarrett's face with a slashing motion. He missed by only a fraction of an inch, but it forced Jarrett to lose his balance and let go of his wrist when he fell to the ground.

Starman got to one knee next to him before he could get up. He came closer, waving the razor menacingly.

"You can try to run but you'll never make it," he said softly.

Jarrett didn't move.

"Last chance."

Before his attacker could react, Jarrett's right hand shot to his wrist. He held it with an iron grip and twisted the bones sharply around until the razor faced the other way. Then he unexpectedly pushed back on the wrist using Starman's hand to carve a line from the end of his brow to his cheekbone. One eye rapidly filled with blood.

Still holding on, Jarrett turned the wrist halfway back, and pressed again until he felt it snap, and the razor popped free. The killer howled. Jarrett's rock-hard fist found the soft spot on the right side of his head, and Starman went down.

In a heartbeat, Jarrett got to his feet and had Starman's head in both his hands. He pulled him to a sitting position. "How does it feel, you lowlife son of a bitch," he said. He pulled him up as high as he could and drove his knee into the center of his face. Starman's mouth turned bright red.

"Don't kill him," Katlyn screamed before he

struck again. "He must know where Matthew is."

Jarrett still held the blood-soaked man in his hands. He looked first at Katlyn, then back to the killer. One eye was open, staring at him malevolently. He felt an unbelievable need to send him to his maker.

"Please, Jarrett," he heard Katlyn say again.

He held back on the final blow with his knee, but only a little. Just enough to put the bastard into a deep sleep.

And maybe get Katlyn her husband back.

FIFTY-FIVE

"Starman's real name is Arthur Combs," Elliot Stryker said, drawing a chair closer to Katlyn's hospital bed. He was the only visitor who had been permitted to see her right after she was admitted to the burn therapy center. "He matches the description: tall, thin, shaved head, late thirties. He looks younger in person, though."

"Is he saying anything about my husband?"

"Yeah . . . and it's one for the books. Claims he doesn't remember whether or not he kidnapped him, and I think he means it. He's just crazy enough to be telling the truth."

Katlyn studied Stryker's expression. Behind his normally inscrutable face she could see hints of confusion.

"He claims he talks to someone named Bo who tells him what to do, a best friend or confidant. He trusts him, listens to him. It's too early to tell if it's true, but he says Bo's been telling him which actresses to visit. He can't remember Bo telling him about anyone named Matthew."

"Multiple personalities?"

"Very possible."

"What does Dubois think?"

"She thinks Combs is very intelligent. Too early to call."

"He could be acting."

"Yeah, he could be playing mind games with us. He's still cocky as hell, even now that he's been caught."

Katlyn tried to make sense of it. "You've seen others like him. What do *you* think he did?"

Stryker didn't hesitate. "I think he's the one who took your husband."

"What about Kahn?"

"I never thought it was her. She's the type that's better at sneaking around. I don't think she could handle a direct confrontation that a kidnapping or murder would take."

The word hung in the air. Stryker realized it and looked sorry that he'd used it.

"Do you think Matthew is alive?" Katlyn asked in little more than a whisper.

"I don't want to give you false hope. It's not his pattern to keep his victims alive."

"It's not his pattern to go after a man, either. I'm not his pattern. I'm not a movie star."

"You're a celebrity. That may be the same thing to him." Stryker hesitated. "I think he may have gone after Matthew to get to you."

Katlyn felt an icy hand clutch her heart. Stryker was right. Somehow Starman had found out about the ambush and figured out another way to get to her.

"What about a lie detector test?"

"Given the circumstances we got the court's permission to give him one right away, a PSE."

Katlyn knew the abbreviation. It was short for Psychological Stress Evaluation.

"What did it show?"

"Not a hell of a lot. The technician who administered the test said it was unreliable, in his opinion."

"Why?"

"Combs's blood has a substantial amount of drugs in it, some weird concoction of painkillers and tranquilizers, which spoiled the reliability. Not counting that, the test absolved him of some of the murders and said he was lying about others. But it also failed him on simple things, like his name and the color of his eyes. I doubt it's something a prosecutor would feel comfortable using."

"What about him kidnapping Matthew? If he did it?"

Stryker nodded. "That was when he told us he couldn't remember. For what it's worth, he passed that question."

Katlyn had a terrifying new thought. "If Combs did kidnap him and decided to keep him alive, he would have been the one feeding him. Now that he's been caught, who's taking care of my husband?"

Stryker was morose. He'd thought of that and had no answer.

"What about Helen Kahn? Is it possible that you're wrong and she did it?" she asked.

"I wouldn't put too much faith in that."

"Why? She had no trouble murdering my embryo, did she? The next step could easily have been my husband."

"I can't prove it one way or the other. She's denying it, just like Arthur Combs. And, as I said, she doesn't strike me as the type to go beyond a certain point."

Katlyn felt a fresh wave of hopelessness wash over her. The cruelest irony was that the police now had two people in custody, either of whom might know what happened to Matthew, yet they were no closer to finding him now than when both were on the loose. It made the police look completely ineffectual.

"You can't wait for Kahn to confess," she suddenly blurted out. "Or for Combs to decide to tell you. You understand that, don't you? My husband may be dying. You have to find him now!"

"If he's still alive we'll find him. I promise you we will," Stryker said solemnly. "But at least you're safe now. Starman won't be bothering you or anyone else anymore."

Katlyn turned away from him and stared at the wall. As well intentioned as he was being, Stryker had misjudged her situation.

Her safety wasn't the point.

FIFTY-SIX

At ten the next morning, Fava and Marty arrived at the hospital together, each carrying a package. Marty's gift was a get well drawing from his twelve-year-old daughter. Fava brought Godiva cherry cordials and a cluster of unusual orange and salmon-colored blossoms. They were a variety of flowers Katlyn had never seen before and were already in a vase. Fava put them on the table next to the bed. "After people found out what happened, a ton of flowers were sent to the station," she said. "But these were delivered to your house personally. They're from Rachel Prescott, and I thought you'd like to have them." She handed Katlyn a small envelope. "This came with them."

Katlyn was surprised at the gesture from her kind but seldom seen neighbor, and it touched her. She opened the note and read it. *"These lovely Pavonia have always lifted my spirits. I hope they will help speed your recovery. I'm sure we will see each other before you know it. You are always in my mind. Rachel Prescott."*

Katlyn turned her attention to the candy. "I'm afraid you'll have to feed me for a while." She held up two bandaged hands.

In a short time the small talk became more and more strained. As much as they wanted to comfort her, no one wanted to discuss the obvious. Soon Fava could see that Katlyn was trying hard to be polite but that she was drained. The visit was mercifully cut short when a nurse came in with medication and Fava and Marty took their cue.

After they left, Katlyn drifted off and was still dozing when Dan Jarrett came quietly into the room. After a time she sensed his presence and opened her eyes.

He pointed to the bandages which were wrapped around her hands so many times that they doubled their size. "You look like you're ready to go a few rounds."

She managed a weak smile. "If you don't mind, I'll leave the fighting to you," she answered respectfully. "I've seen you in action."

"One of those little perks that make the job worthwhile."

Despite his smile, she could feel his awkwardness. She felt different with him now, too. What they had been through together at the fire had changed the nature of their relationship in some undefined way. Or maybe it had happened sometime before that.

"What about you?" she said. He had no apparent signs of injury other than badly bruised knuckles on one hand.

"It only hurts when I dance," he said. "And I never dance."

"Maybe you should try it some time." Katlyn reflected more seriously on what had happened. "I owe you my life. And I can't even shake your hand. Would a small kiss be good enough?"

The suggestion seemed to throw him into a moderate confusion, which he did his best to mask.

"I guess . . . if it'll make you feel better."

"It will."

He bent down and received the kiss shyly. Katlyn felt the warmth of his cheek as she pressed her lips against his skin. Something inside stirred and took her by surprise. For the first time she allowed herself to feel his presence as a man, and a much gentler, more complex one than she had ever suspected. Quickly, though, she thought of Matthew and felt a twinge of guilt.

"How's my cat?"

"Came out of it better than the rest of us. Took a while to find him, though. A friend of mine has adopted him until you get out of here."

"Thank you, Jarrett."

Like those who had preceded him, Jarrett had a gift under his arm, an unwrapped box. "Thought you might want a little souvenir of our adventure."

He opened the box and held up a little red fire engine. He turned it over and pushed a button on the underside. A small stream of water surprised him by shooting back at him, dampening his 1970s-style paisley shirt.

"How's that for showmanship?"

He sat down near the bed. Katlyn propped herself up on two pillows and fought the effects of the sleeping pill.

"I watched them interrogate Combs for over two hours. Some new odds and ends, but nothing really new came out of it."

"What's he like?"

"Well, his head is a different shape than it used to be. And his nose isn't too pretty. Got some broken ribs, too. A matching set, actually."

Katlyn didn't remember seeing Jarrett work on that part of Combs's body. He must have given him a few extra shots for good measure when she wasn't looking. All things considered, Starman was lucky to be alive. "You must have been pretty scared, given who he was."

"I didn't have time to think about it. Once I got going I was just trying not to get sliced up."

"Could you tell whether he's crazy or not?"

"He's hard to type, eccentric as hell. When we brought him into interrogation he measured every step he took. He was even careful about the exact position his chair was in before he sat on it and how he folded his hands on the table. Didn't like to be touched, either. One of the officers made that mistake, and it took three of them to calm him down—even with those ribs of his."

"I'm surprised he could walk at all."

"Once he was quiet enough to talk, you

wouldn't know there was anything that different about him. He was very at ease, even glib. Then, all of a sudden, he'd lose it again and have to be restrained."

"Stryker says he was on drugs."

Jarrett took the mention of Stryker's name with a sideways glance, then said, "Yeah. In withdrawal from painkillers. He told the doctors he takes them for headaches, evidently bad ones. He takes lots of pills."

"Did he show any sign of remorse?"

"Uh-uh. Only human beings do that. He did open up a little, but all he talked about was his agenda. Pretty weird stuff, like he was on some kind of a mission. Even his lawyers couldn't shut him up for a while."

"He's some kind of religious fanatic?"

"No. Nothing that simple. He seems to be empowered by a friend, someone he calls Bo." He saw she wasn't surprised. "Did Stryker tell you that, too?"

She nodded. "But not much more than that."

"No last name—just Bo." Jarrett went on. "He thinks this Bo can do no wrong. Tells Starman what to do, picks the victims."

"If Bo is a second personality maybe there's a way to get him to tell us where Matthew is, even if the real Combs won't."

Jarrett shifted in the chair uncomfortably. "Thought of that. But his main lawyer—a guy called Mike Butler—won't allow any moves that could jeopardize the case. He's a very smart and cautious man, evidently."

"Wouldn't you think they'd want to save Matt, if only to avoid another murder charge?"

"Kidnapping carries a death penalty, too. They have nothing to lose. And we can't force Butler to help us."

"Even if it means saving Matthew's life?"

"He's the defendant's lawyer, remember?"

"If the law protects someone like that over someone like Matthew, what good is it?" Katlyn said angrily.

Jarrett nodded. "There are a lot of us who feel that way."

Katlyn felt her body shutting down and fought it. "Sorry. It's the pills."

Jarrett got to his feet slowly, ready to leave. "I guess you know you'll have to see Combs, to identify him. You can take a few days until you feel up to it, but there's no way around it."

"They already told me." She looked up at him with intensity. "Will you be there? It would make it a lot easier."

The tone of her question as much as its content caught him off guard.

"Yeah, I'll be there," he said, putting his hand lightly on the side of her shoulder. "You sure you're okay?"

She made a small affirmative sound that wasn't very convincing.

"I'm here if you need me. Just call my name

and"—he looked at her, wondering if he'd gone too far—"you know, like James Taylor said."

She wanted to say something brave, but his sympathy triggered an emotion she'd been trying to keep bottled up, and she bit down hard on her lower lip to contain it.

"One more thing I've been dying to ask you," he said abruptly. "That."

He pointed to the flowers that Fava had put on the table. "Just what planet did they come from?"

"They're called Pavonia. They're from my neighbor, Rachel Prescott."

"Oh yeah. The flower lady. I met her when we checked out the area," Jarrett said somewhat vacantly. "I should have known," he added with a world-weary look.

FIFTY-SEVEN

Jarrett drove his vintage Land Cruiser to the aging brick-face building on Pico Boulevard. The two-and-a-half-ton companion of nearly a decade was closing in on the 300,000-mile mark. It was the best partner he had ever had and it had its own share of kills, including too many pulverized cars to remember, one super-stretch pimp limo, and one light plane that had been about to take off before its tail section was shattered by the invulnerable front bumper of the beast.

From curbside he looked up at the second-floor window through which Starman had observed his world. There was an extraordinary irony in the location, he reflected. It was less than three blocks from the undercover headquarters of TMU above the porn store. The worst celebrity killer that L.A. had ever known had been right under their noses all the time.

Upstairs, his friend Guano Dunellen sat in his customary Buddha position on the floor, surrounded by a neat arrangement of plastic bags and large yellow envelopes, all evidence compulsively neat. One large plastic container and several medium-size cardboard boxes sat nearby. Two men besides Guano were working in other parts of the apartment, which had a living room, a half bedroom, and a small, narrow kitchen.

Out of the blue, Dunellen's pile of evidence awakened a painful memory for Jarrett of the first time he had found himself immersed in the world of forensics, but on a deeply personal level. Less than two months after a wrenching separation from his wife, Beth Ellen, she was struck by a stray bullet fired blocks away as she drove home from work. He rushed to the hospital, but she died before he could tell her how much he wanted her back—how much he had regretted taking her for granted during their four-year marriage. He had let the job rule his life, and by the time he realized his mistake it was too late. That had been nearly two years ago.

After that he spent hundreds of hours, many of them with Dunellen, trying to trace the bullet back to its source. He never found the killer. And never got used to the randomness of events that could take anyone away at any time.

"Presumed fucking guilty," Guano announced, somehow knowing Jarrett had entered without turning to face him. At the moment he was stuffing small bits of unidentifiable matter into a glass tube.

"Nice to see you, too, Guano." He was careful not to touch anything on the way in.

"Congrats on your coronation. Try to hold on to it for a few days this time, huh?"

"Nah. It's never worth it."

Dunellen was referring to his imminent promotion to the rank of captain for his capture of Starman. The surprise announcement had been made by Stryker himself the day before in a photo op publicizing the arrest—which was mainly an op for Stryker, Jarrett knew.

"Does this mean you can go back to homicide?"

"There hasn't been any mention of that. We'll see what happens. What did you turn up?"

Dunellen's face brightened. "For starters, our boy was very big on mementos," he announced in a merrily macabre voice. "Quaint little reminders of the places he'd been, people he'd seen. Kept them all up there." He pointed to the ceiling.

"Hidden room?"

"Go to the head of your class."

"How do you get in?"

"Trapdoor in the bedroom closet. He's not the first animal to collect body parts, of course. But this sick son of a bitch has about the most exotic collection I've ever seen. Earlobes, nipples—something that looks like it could be an asshole for Christ's sake. A bunch of stuff ended up on a sort of charm bracelet."

"How old are the items?"

"From their condition I'd say most were from women he wasted a long time ago. Probably some poor souls we never even found out about. A few of them are still warm—so to speak."

"All women?"

"Are you kidding?" Dunellen gave him a condescending glance.

"I mean, are there any signs that any of the parts could have come from a man?" Jarrett thought about Matthew.

"No. At first blush, I'd have to say it's all female parts. Of course, an asshole is an asshole."

Dunellen's gloved hand opened the largest carton and fished out an envelope. He opened it for Jarrett's inspection. It was packed with clumps of long, medium-blond hair.

"Anne Marie what's-her-name?"

"Warren."

"Whatever. Fuck-face was very big on hair, among other things."

He picked a bunch of shorter strands out of a different bag and handed them to Jarrett, who put them in his palm.

"In case you think these look a little different, you're right. Vaginal. From the dark color we can assume they're not Warren's—unless she's got a good hairdresser. And don't go putting them in your wallet when I'm not looking." He grinned broadly at Jarrett. "They've got crabs."

"Jesus Christ!" Jarrett shook them off his hand like they were spiders.

"Just kidding."

"You sick bastard."

"Hey, you think you can be normal and work a job like this?"

"What else?" Jarrett demanded.

Guano reached for a smaller carton. "Our friend really did his homework each time. Take a look."

He found a large carton nearby and was into it with both hands, after which he brought out a half-dozen videocassettes. Blockbuster logos were visible on the ones that were still in their plastic cases.

"Some of these were made off television. His TV." Guano pointed to an older model Magnavox on a table stand. "The others were rented and never returned. Can you imagine the late fees this guy must owe? Dumb fuck."

"What's on them?"

"Hollywood babes, sex scenes, like that. Fairly tame actually, considering what you can buy just about anywhere. But ten to one all the women he ended up wasting are on these somewhere."

"What about the rock star?"

Guano's expression went suddenly leaden, conjuring something grim, even by his standards. "Now that's another matter entirely."

He produced a metal spike from inside a plastic bag. It was painted gold, and the sharp end was slightly blunted. Jarrett had seen others like it at the TMU office the morning after the murder.

"When he tried to bang it through her ankle he must have hit bone, but not hard enough to shatter it. Look at the tip."

"It's been stubbed."

"Besides that." Guano held it up for closer inspection. "See that brown spot on the end? Bronze doesn't rust. If that's not Christa's blood I'll give you a blow job in Macy's window."

"Thanks. I'm praying for blood."

"And guess what this is?" Guano said, preoccupied with something he held up in tweezers. It was a small nub of skin in the shape of a large dark raisin. It looked soft, recently detached.

"Christa's?"

Guano shrugged. "Didn't make it to the charm bracelet yet, I guess. What is it about these guys that lets them turn their entire room into exhibit fucking-A and think nobody will ever see it?"

"If you're not gonna get caught, you don't worry about it."

"Yeah, right. Guess that's why they pay you the big bucks."

Jarrett checked the labels on several of the envelopes, but didn't see what he was looking for. "You turn up anything on Katlyn Rome?"

"You know how it distresses me to be underestimated." In a moment he held up two other videotapes. "This one has all her recent broadcasts. For some reason he didn't tape the speech she made to him. The other has shots of her house made on a drive-by. He cased the place— even made some drawings of ways to get in."

"Any idea when they were made?"

"Hard to say. They're in pencil. Easier to tell the age when it's ink because of the way it dries."

"Anything else of Rome's?"

He fished a thin packet of papers out of an envelope and threw them to him. "All printed matter. Her bio from the station, head shots, plus clippings from the papers on her hard times with Starman."

Jarrett started to read.

"But wait, there's more," Guano interrupted, finding his new treasure quickly. "Lots of stuff on the husband. Places he went, addresses, phone numbers of his health club, music studio. Stuff like that. Maybe he was really after the husband, not Rome, the whole time. Maybe Starman cultivated a taste for boys."

Jarrett scanned the notes on Matthew. There were even detailed maps of Matthew's exercise routes, the exact times he ran past specific intersections. Combs had been closing in for the kill for a while—on one or both of the couple. It seemed to put to rest any question about Kahn doing the kidnapping.

Dunellen pointed to a carton on a nearby chair. "I think you might get a kick out of what's in there."

A number of grotesque possibilities paraded through Jarrett's mind.

Dunellen went to the carton and scooped out the baggie on top. It contained bright-red ladies' shoes with stiletto heels.

"Victoria Della Cruz, the porn goddess."

Guano closed his eyes and lapsed into a reverie. "As I recall, when she was wearing these she was on her back on the kitchen table and they were pointing up at the ceiling."

"You're a fucking deviate, you know that?"

Dunellen's expression suddenly got serious and his voice lowered. "Hey, Danny boy. If I took this shit seriously I'd be crying all the time."

Jarrett surveyed the rest of the room. From what had been found, they had Starman cold. Unfortunately, his lawyers would plead insanity. And this loony tune could show them signs of insanity in spades.

"Okay if I look around?"

"Sure. But if you find anything I missed I'll—"

"I know. In Macy's window."

Jarrett went directly to the only closet. It was empty, its contents somewhere in Dunellen's compulsively labeled boxes. The kitchen had been similarly stripped and dusted for prints. All of the utensils were piled in a heap on the counter next to a sink that hadn't seen a cleaning in years. An unseen roach's single long antennae wiggled through a hole in the drain, then disappeared. He had the urge to ask if the cooking gear had been used to prepare any *exotic* cuisine, but there was no reason to believe Starman was a cannibal, merely a vicious murderer.

Satisfied nothing had escaped the little

round man, Jarrett paced the length of a brick wall that had been painted white sometime before Moses. A window had been crudely punched into it after it was built, suggesting that the building had started as a factory or warehouse. The cheap canvas shade had turned the color of graphite, as did his fingers when he tugged on it. It shot up with a bang, and Dunellen hit the floor.

"Sorry about that," Jarrett said with some amusement.

The view was to the north, and not pretty. Below, and down the block, there was a Rite Aid discount drugstore with cheap folding chairs lined up for sale on the sidewalk in front. Flanking that was a news store that touted Italian ice in *diez flavores,* and a pawnshop with a broken window, its taped glass miraculously holding together after something major had hit it—like a body. Just left of center across the street was a building that once housed a fast-food restaurant.

Jarrett's eyes followed the building's facade upward. He was high enough to see two poles bolted into the litter-strewn roof supporting a sign thirty feet higher.

He gazed up at the large billboard and stared at it in amazement.

In the picture four professionally happy people were crowded together for a portrait. In the middle, wearing a highly tailored version of the program's dark blazer, was Katlyn Rome. Given its rough condition, the billboard had probably been up well past its normal rotation schedule. The headline was still readable, though, and a dozen feet high: *WMTC Team Ten News.*

From Jarrett's position in Combs's window, it was just across the street—and the last place in the world Katlyn Rome would have wanted to end up.

The randomness of it made him think of Beth Ellen, his poor dead wife.

FIFTY-EIGHT

For Katlyn, having to look at Starman was tantamount to living her worst nightmare all over again. Just the memory of his smooth, warm hands moving on her skin made her break out into a cold sweat.

More than a feeling of revulsion, however, she was afraid that once she saw him she would instinctively know if he had murdered Matthew or not. The approach of that moment scared her nearly senseless.

Jarrett was her escort for the trip to the lineup, and they drove most of the way in silence. Atypically, he was sullen and seemed distant. She could feel him churning over some unnamed battle that occupied his mind.

Less than a half hour after they left her house they entered a seldom used viewing room of the Los Angeles County Men's Prison. Soon they were seated in the small theater, Jarrett on one side, a detective from Stryker's personal staff on the other.

A door at one side of the stage opened and another officer entered from behind the glass barrier. He was followed by five men of roughly the same height dressed in civilian clothes. They were closer to her than she'd imagined they would be. She could feel the hair on the back of her neck bristle as they stared out at the unseen faces behind the glass.

"I can't stay here for this," Jarrett said while the suspects were still forming the line. "For obvious reasons. Don't worry, they can't see you."

"But I *want* him to see me," Katlyn said with a sudden rush of vindictiveness she had not intended to show.

Jarrett looked at her incredulously for a second, then turned and walked away without saying anything.

Her body was one tight muscle when she concentrated on the men on the platform. The first had small, agate-colored eyes set high on his face, not what she remembered. The second and fourth were taller than average, like the man who had tried to crush her skull. The third was more compact, thick in the limbs with a slightly protruding belly and a thin fuzz of light gray hair.

The last man was also tall and stood rigidly erect. She recognized him immediately. Arthur Combs stood just above the six-foot-one-inch mark on the wall behind him. He looked a little older than he had that day, closer to the thirty-nine years Stryker said he was. Under his clothing his body had a spidery quality, like the subject of an El Greco painting, and his face was sharp-angled and gaunt. His heavy eyelids closed halfway over deeply set small, dark brown eyes which seemed to grow more unsettled as they searched the void and didn't register a human presence.

"That's him," she said coldly to the detective next to her.

When she indicated her choice, the officer raised his hand and a loud voice from a source she could not see asked the man to step forward. He smiled inappropriately and complied, with a slightly insolent swagger. He seemed to be enjoying the effect he knew he was having on whoever was out there.

While all eyes were on the suspect, Katlyn sat back in her seat, took a breath, and closed her eyes. For a moment she allowed herself to slip into a vengeful reverie, her hand slipping into her jacket pocket, her fingers closing around a pistol, withdrawing it swiftly, holding it steadily in front of her, aiming it at the center of Starman's face. She could feel herself pulling the trigger this time, watching Combs's leering expression turn to shock as part of his face exploded, taking pleasure in shooting him again and again until his shirt was shredded on his chest and he pitched forward and collapsed on the stage.

Katlyn's eyes popped back open, and she pressed herself hard against the back of her chair in the viewing room of the Los Angeles County Men's Prison.

Combs's hateful face came slowly into focus again, unchanged from when she last saw it, very much alive.

The gun was still at home where it had lain untouched since the night their house was invaded and their lives dismantled, piece by piece.

FIFTY-NINE

When Katlyn opened the door, it was the first time Jarrett had seen her since his visit to the hospital. She looked better than he thought she would. The angry bruises on her face and arms had already begun to lighten, and the bandages on her hands were modest compared to what he first saw. Some of her energy had returned.

He stood outside for a time, stirred by a recurrent memory that she innocently rekindled about the way it was when the two of them were alone, when it was finally over on the day of the fire. For that brief moment in time when the whole world was burning, the professional distance between them had been erased, and they had shared an intimacy that only a life-threatening event could produce. Now that she was back in her own home, her own world, he realized that time would never come again.

She escorted him to the living room and waited with urgency on her face.

"Combs has decided to remember some more details," he finally said with difficulty. "He's claiming that *Bo* told him to kidnap Matthew and hide him somewhere. We tried to get him to tell us where, but he wouldn't."

Katlyn braced, but held herself in check. "Do you think it's true?"

"There was evidence in his apartment that he was tracking Matthew."

"What kind of evidence?"

"Notes on your husband's routine. A record of the hours he worked over several weeks, the routes he took when he ran. Very specific things."

"What about Kahn?"

"Turns out she was just someone else who had a grudge against you. She broke into your house and used a mask to make you think it was Starman. The piece of woman's fingernail in your library and the pictures from your album at her place prove that. And the blood match shows she was the one who took your embryo from the hospital. But that's as far as she went before we got to her. It's a pretty sure thing that Combs took your husband."

"Did he say why?"

"Bo told him to, that's all."

"Is there anything in his record that could point to a reason?"

Jarrett shrugged. "This guy's been in trouble since he was a kid. His sheet runs a few pages long. We're going over his history with a fine tooth comb, but so far he's always targeted women. If he's starting to cross over to men, this is the first time—at least the first time we know about it."

"Do you think he did it to get to me? Is that why he didn't kill him right away—at least, as far as we know?"

"Possibly. Or maybe he wanted some bargaining power, if he ever got caught. Now that it's happened, telling us your husband is still alive does give him some leverage, at least in his own mind."

"And in reality?"

Jarrett thought about it. "Yeah, I'd have to say it does. As much as a captured celebrity serial killer can get."

Katlyn let out a deep sigh of resignation. "How much control do you think this other personality has over Combs?"

"If you believe what he says, it has complete control. Bo tells him everything he's supposed to do, which means who to kill. And Combs is afraid of him for some reason. Maybe it's his darker side, who knows."

"How could it be any darker? The whole thing is insane."

Katlyn bowed her head and he saw that she was shaking. All at once he wanted to hold her. He remembered having that thought after the fire, again at the hospital. Before that.

"Is there any way you could get me a copy of Combs's record?" Katlyn asked after a while.

Jarrett said, "At this point in time that would be a very serious matter. Whoever took it would have a lot of explaining to do if he got caught."

He thought about it some more. "In other words, of course I will."

She looked at him with gratitude. "What if Combs does have Matthew hidden somewhere?" she said a moment later. "How are we going to find him before it's too late?"

She looked at him expectantly and long enough for him to think his heart was going to break. He had no answer. It was all he could do not to let what he was thinking show. Eventually she looked away and stared off into the distance in silence.

SIXTY

Arthur Combs sat in the nebulous light that emanated from outside his cell. His back was to the wall and his eyes were closed. But he wasn't sleeping.

The voracious animal inside his head had grown, and so had its appetite. He could feel little pieces of his brain being devoured, bit by bit, and his ability to reason being swallowed with each bite. Making it even more unbearable, the doctors had taken away his painkillers because he could not tell them about someone named Matthew.

He had been alone for too long, he knew. Solitude was the thing he feared most, the only thing. The prison authorities must have known what it would do to him. They had been right to protect him from himself in his prison cell.

He had studied his cell in the most minute detail over the hours. Every part of the walls of his cell was padded with a soft blue material, like the kind used for mats in gymnasiums, only thinner. There were no fixtures, no glass, nothing hard or pointed that could be used to help him in a final violent act that would rob the courts and the public of their spectacle.

Or so they thought.

Arthur had already identified three items in the room that could be used, if the time came.

First there was the porcelain toilet, which could be broken into sharp pieces with a well-delivered kick. One of the pieces could easily become a dagger, put to use before they came running at the sound.

There was the insulation just under the first layer of mortar on the walls. Once uncovered its components could be separated, the fiber twisted into strips, the strips into a rope, the rope tied into a hangman's knot.

And the bed.

Arthur rocked back and forth on his haunches, letting his head knock into the wall on each pass, scarcely feeling it.

The time would come, he told himself.

As bad as the pain was, it was nothing compared to the solitude.

"Where are you, Bo? Where are you?"

PART 3

A HUNTING WE WILL GO

SIXTY-ONE

Alone in her own home, Katlyn sat on the floor leaning against the couch. She had not moved from the spot since she had come in fifteen minutes earlier after shopping for groceries. It had been sixteen days since Matthew had disappeared.

She had been so lost in thought it took her all the time since she came in to finally hear the small, persistent beep coming from the office. The telephone answering machine had stored some messages while she was out.

The first call was from Fava. Empathetic as usual, she wanted to know if she could come by and talk about how they could help the investigation. A second call was a hang-up, probably a wrong number since her phone was unlisted.

The last message started with some unusual clicking noises and, for a fraction of a second, a word seemed to be shouted. It was cut off quickly by car sounds that made the message hard to understand. Still, she could hear that the voice was barely audible, mournful, of someone in pain. Each word took forever to complete, but the instant Katlyn heard the first few her body went limp.

"Caaannnt tallllllk forrrr lonnnnnng."

"Matthew!" The voice was his, she was sure. Somehow he was alive and had gotten to a phone.

"Mussst . . . releeeeease . . . Cooommmmbs . . . nevvverrrrr . . . seeee meee . . . agaaaain."

The unexpected warning cut short her exultation. It was obvious that someone else was with him—had forced him to make the call.

"Tellllll poooliiice . . . let Coooommmbs goooo."

There was a pause, then his voice seemed to be breaking. Maybe crying.

"Hurrrrry . . . nooot muuuccch tiiimmme."

The click of a receiver being put down.

Katlyn reached for the rewind switch but caught herself just before she pressed it. His call was the last since she had been out. The small window at the top of the phone caddy still showed the phone number of the person calling. The caller ID display was another safety measure they had installed since moving in.

She stared at it a second, then reached for a pencil and started writing.

The display had ten digits. The first three were 310. The call had been placed from somewhere in Los Angeles.

It could be traced.

SIXTY-TWO

BRENTWOOD
Monday, July 27

Just before noon, Katlyn opened her front door and saw Claire Fava's exhausted face.

"Stryker called and told me to watch out for you," she said, marching past Katlyn into the living room. "He thinks you've gone around the bend." She turned to face her friend. "Have you?" she said with a cautious smile.

Katlyn was taken off guard. "Because of the tape, you mean?"

"You think? Your ordering him to let Combs go really went over big. That and telling him to start looking for somebody else."

"What else could I do, for God's sake?"

"I know. Mainly, I think he sent me here to pump you for information, to see how dangerous you might be to him. He thinks the Starman case is over, he really does. Ever since he got Combs."

"How can it be over if we still haven't found Matthew?"

"I know," Fava said sympathetically. "I think maybe it's Stryker who's crazy not to realize that. Do you know that he once thought that you might have been involved in Matthew's disappearance?"

"What?" Katlyn shrieked.

"He found out the two of you hadn't been getting along at the time."

"How could he say that? We were fighting over me—wanting me to be safe!" She heard herself and paused. She knew it wasn't the whole truth.

"Stryker wanted to know what I thought about the voice on the tape, since I've had a lot more contact with Matthew than he has."

"He shouldn't have put you in that position. I know you can't be as sure as I am."

Fava didn't answer for a moment, then said, "I'm sorry. The tape was so bad. I think you would have to hear something beyond the voice itself to know for sure, as only you could," she added diplomatically.

Katlyn looked disappointed. "Jarrett told me that because of the tape Stryker *is* going to put more men on the case. But I know it's only a token effort to keep me quiet. I think he wants to use Starman's conviction to help his career."

"There's a big surprise. But I guess it's to be expected. If he hadn't caught him he would have been up shit's creek—excuse the French. Anyway, he really is convinced the tape is a fraud, Kate. And he really thinks you're around the bend, because of Matthew."

"What did you say to him?"

"I asked him what he'd be doing right now if his wife were missing."

"He's not married."

"I know. And when he told me that I said that was part of his problem. He had no idea what you were going through."

"Great. Now he hates both of us. All three of us, if you include Jarrett."

Katlyn went to a big stuffed chair, Matthew's favorite, and collapsed in it. She had the fleeting wish that she could just keep sinking down in the stuffing and disappear.

"He's afraid of you, honey. He knows you can raise holy hell any time you want."

"Believe me, I thought about it. But I didn't think it was smart. It could be a big mistake to show the person who has Matthew that I went to the police. It might panic him." She noticed Fava's look of suspicion. "*If* there is a new person, of course, not just another crank with a voice that sounds like Matt's . . . to me, at least."

Fava touched her arm sympathetically but did not respond. Her face turned sly. "Have you thought about going over Stryker's head to the commissioner?"

"Yeah. But I've got to believe that he has the same vested interest in Starman as Stryker does. And I doubt he'd be any more convinced by the tape." Katlyn stared into Fava's eyes. "You don't have to believe it, but I know it was Matthew—

even though it didn't exactly sound like him. I could tell."

"Like I said, you would know better than anyone."

"And I guess getting a little more help is better than nothing."

"What's Stryker doing for you, exactly?"

"He said he was getting some men from Threat Management to cover my house, which tells you what he really thinks—that it's another crank call. But I'm not in a position to say no to anything, am I?"

Fava didn't respond.

"It's hopeless to think Stryker's going to help. You'd think I would have learned that by now," Katlyn said. "Tell me what you think of Dan Jarrett," she added in a sudden change of direction.

"Aside from the fact that he saved my best friend's life? And his lemming instinct?"

Katlyn nodded.

"Well, I think his heart's in the right place. And his track record is exceptional. But with him there's always the chance he'll piss someone off before he gets the job done. Why are you asking?"

"I don't know. There's something about him I trust. In his own rough way, he's one of the purest and most ethical men I've ever met. And right about now I need someone who isn't afraid to go up against the system."

"Yeah, that's Dan Jarrett all right." Fava arched her back. It was aching worse than ever. "For better or worse, that's him."

"I do worry about the way Stryker feels about him—and how that hurts his effectiveness. If someone Stryker respected more went to bat for us we'd probably stand a better chance of getting help."

"Yeah, Jarrett's credibility with the boss man is a problem. Actually, I think Stryker looks at him and you in the same way—like you're both loose cannons. But I still think we're better off with Jarrett on our side than some suck-up academy cop looking to move up the ladder."

"Yes, that's where I come out, too," Katlyn said, then raised an eyebrow. "It's really up to me, isn't it? No matter what, I probably have to figure this out myself."

Fava shook her head emphatically. "Uh-uh. Up to *us*. As of now, you have me along for the ride. Full time, part time—as much as you want."

Katlyn looked alarmed. "You didn't do anything stupid, did you—at the station?"

"They can all go screw themselves, especially Sermac."

"What happened?"

"Somehow our illustrious leader found out about the call and decided to do a story on it—tonight, if you can believe it. When I went to him to complain, he threw me out of his office. I don't even know if I have a job. And I don't give a rat's ass."

Katlyn's worry intensified. "As much as Sermac would deserve to lose you, I'd hate to think of you getting fired for helping me."

"He is a sleaze, isn't he?"

"Dammit, Fava, doesn't he know what the hell he's doing? That he may be compromising our only lead to Matthew?" Katlyn rubbed her neck and pressed her lips tightly shut. She wanted to scream at the injustice of it all.

"He's still alive, Fava, I know he is," she said.

But she knew it was more a prayer than anything she believed deep down.

SIXTY-THREE

Elliot Stryker smoothed down a few errant hairs and thought about the thirty-five members of the media waiting in the conference area. They were a particularly bloodthirsty bunch now, he knew. They wanted headlines, and revelations to write them about. But they'd get just so much from him, only what he wanted them to have. He was better at that than anyone else in Los Angeles law enforcement had ever been.

He had already kept the press waiting twenty-five minutes when Ruth Dubois finally responded to his call and showed up at his office. By then he'd built up a full head of steam.

"First we catch the crackpot woman who was harassing Rome," he said, "then, the son of a bitch trying to kill her. We have all the evidence we need to link him to all the other attacks, including spying on her husband. And now she has the balls to tell me I have to start the whole investigation over again and look for someone else."

Dubois waited patiently for him to finish his tantrum. Eventually, after he was done ranting, he might even listen to what she had to say.

"This fantasy about her husband on the

answering machine is total bullshit. You know it as well as I do," he stormed. "The call traced to a phone booth in Venice, for Christ's sake. Any loony tune down there could have made the tape. I'll bet my ass that's what happened."

Stryker looked past Dubois to the corridor that led to his conference room where the reporters were waiting. A day earlier he had looked forward to another opportunity to publicize his capture of Starman. The press coverage would help fuel his run for higher office, first the commissioner's job, then, God willing, the mayoralty. Other public servants had boosted themselves on a less conspicuous success than he had already scored.

But that was before Katlyn Rome had burst into his office demanding a search for a second kidnapper and threatened to derail the campaign train. Even though it was lunacy, her fantastic request raised grave doubts about holding the press conference at all.

"She even had the nerve to ask me about releasing Combs! Do you believe it? Has she gone totally insane or am I missing something?"

"Are you at least checking out the tape? Trying to match it to something else Demarco recorded?"

"Of course I am, even though I've been told the tape's so bad it's a waste of time. But Rome knows she can use it as leverage to get more men looking for her husband," he said, clenching and unclenching his fists, and speaking as much to himself as to his guest. "If I don't play the game, her buddies in the media will have a field day with the story. Hell, she could hold her own god-damn press conference. Or come to mine."

He turned to face his expert on psychopaths. "Can you imagine me agreeing to start another search? It would be admitting Combs isn't the kidnapper."

"She wants her husband, Elliot. You didn't really think she'd just sit back and hope for the best."

Stryker stalked to the window and looked out. The sky was the same crummy mustard color it always was that time of year. He ground his teeth until he felt a tinge of pain from a cracked molar he hadn't had time to repair. "You and I have already agreed that her husband is probably dead, right?"

"Probably isn't enough for her. It wouldn't be for me, either." Dubois removed her glasses and looked less officious. "She's grasping at straws. She's had nothing to give her hope until now. Her life is completely changed, ended in every way she used to know it. And don't forget she's a reporter trained to think about remote possibilities, connections."

Stryker wheeled around to face her. "But she's not a trained detective, goddamn it! And there's a big difference. I value your opinion, Ruth, but the fact is, neither are you."

Dubois wasn't injured by his attack. She was barely listening, thinking about Katlyn Rome instead. She was truly touched by the young woman's situation, as she had been all along. Disciplined to react to violence with detachment, this time she had been unwittingly drawn into the human drama.

"Can you stop a minute and imagine what she's going through? She was already emotionally battered when her husband was kidnapped. Now she's an easy target for anyone out there who wants to play mind games with her."

"That doesn't change the facts."

"The irony is that if there was any evidence that Demarco was murdered, the poor woman could begin to heal. But so long as there's the slightest hope, nothing will stop her from doing what she can."

Stryker's face went sour. He sat at his desk and drummed his fingers on it. "What if she keeps thinking there really is someone else, even though I thought we all knew now that this Bo bullshit is another personality. You were the one who convinced me of that in the first place."

"And I still believe it. But we're not talking about what I believe."

"If she puts the word out to her friends at the station, it'll run on the news, and Combs's lawyer will go batshit with it."

"She's asking for help, and you're the only one who can give it to her," Dubois insisted, aware of the politics. Stryker was an expedient man. He'd do what he had to to get where he wanted to go. "You're going to have to deal with her. You have to give her something. Some more men. Some hope. Something."

The rap on the door came from Stryker's assistant, a trim black woman who opened the door and leaned into the room.

"The natives are getting restless," Leanne Dowdall said in a singsong voice. "And Jude Sermac is on the horn. Wants to know why you canceled the interview with his man Driscoll, the one we agreed to as a payback."

She saw Stryker's expression, took a hasty step backward, and waited.

"Tell the reporters something has come up. I'm sick or something. Tell them anything. We'll reschedule. Tell Sermac the same thing and set up a date with Driscoll later this week."

Dowdall saluted irreverently and was gone.

"Well?" Dubois said, aiming an accusatory look at him. Her previous challenge still hung in the air.

Stryker glared back at her. She could smell the circuits burning in his brain.

"And get Katlyn Rome on the phone, god-damn it," he shouted loud enough for Dowdall to hear through the closed door.

SIXTY-FOUR

A broad grin spread over the bartender's face when Dan Jarrett stormed in and ordered a white wine spritzer. He'd known the honest cop with the fiery heart for years, and although they'd never socialized, he considered him a friend. He'd gotten divorced at about the same time Jarrett's wife died, and they'd gotten past the level of bar talk in their commiseration.

He had also been the absolutely last rye and ginger drinker—until a moment ago.

Jarrett downed the fizzy Chablis in a single gulp and felt immensely unrewarded. To make up for it he ordered another right away. At least he was trying, he told himself. It was amazing what a person could give up when he was working on an ulcer. His stomach was as screwed up as his career.

"You can't outrun your past, Carlos," he said, the sour aftertaste spoiling in his mouth. His hands were clasped clumsily around the unaccustomed fragile glass. "Don't ever forget that."

"That's what they say, amigo," Carlos said, wiping the counter.

"Anywhere else they'd throw a parade in my honor for nailing that sick bastard. And you know what Stryker told me?"

"That you're a goddamn pain in the ass."

Jarrett looked up at him with surprise. "Yeah, how'd you know? That's exactly what he said."

"But he's making you a captain again, isn't he? That says something, too."

Jarrett let out a frustrated sigh. "Shit. It's not even worth a spot on the varsity."

He watched Carlos Perez, part-time bartender, would-be actor, fashion another sardonic grin and begin putting glasses away in an overhead rack—real glasses, like the kind that held whisky. Jarrett felt a muscle spasm in his neck and rubbed the area.

What was bothering him most at the moment was that morning's visit to Stryker's office. The chief had told him about Katlyn Rome's phone message, then didn't want him to say or do anything about it—this latest insult to the man who saved her life while all the other geniuses were pouring water on a fireproof building.

It was incomprehensible that Stryker had not asked for his counsel, out of sheer self-interest, if nothing else. The man didn't have to like him, but he had to know he could help him, especially since things were getting ragged again.

There was one bit of satisfaction, at least. Rome had threatened to use the tape to bust Stryker's chops. Just as Stryker was ready to take his walk in the sunshine, she'd crapped all over his parade.

"Why would a pretty and intelligent woman

ever want to be a TV newscaster, anyway?" Jarrett said, off and running on a tangential thought.

Carlos took a seat on a high three-legged stool, folded his arms, and listened, a faint grin visible.

"Sure the money's good. And maybe you can push your fifteen minutes of fame to a few years. But you gotta know that every second you're on, every creep in the world is having a wet dream about you." Jarrett glanced up and saw Carlos grinning at him. "What the hell are you looking at?"

"I don't know. Perhaps a cop with a woman on his mind. Perhaps a *man* with a woman on his mind."

Jarrett felt his cheeks get hot. "What the hell are you talking about?" he said, waving off the remark, but unconvincingly. He'd never had much of a poker face, he knew, especially when it came to hiding his feelings about women. He was the kind of guy who telegraphed his attraction, and he had lost out on more than one promising love affair because of it. "I didn't ask to be put on this case," he continued. "And it wouldn't faze me in the least to get off."

"Before you get in any deeper, eh?"

Jarrett dismissed his friend's comment with a scowl. "Her husband's been kidnapped, for Christ's sake. Have a little respect, will ya?"

Of course, what Carlos said was beginning to be true. Jarrett was painfully aware that at the present time his feelings about Katlyn Rome were not totally professional. Mostly, but not completely. But his friend putting it into words had forced him to another level of self-awareness.

"I'd have to be a world-class shitheel to be thinking about anything like that now."

"Yes, you would," Carlos concurred, without changing his expression. "World class."

Jarrett chased the thought from his mind. He remembered Stryker and his last order, which had been the capper—that he was to *observe but not participate* in Rome's new search for her husband. The chief was no dummy. He had to have known there was no way a guy like him was going to stay out of it. But the ball was back in his court. It would be suicide to violate Stryker's direct order. He had been clear about the penalty.

On the other hand, there was the not-so-insignificant matter of the lady's safety. Aside from his personal feelings toward her, which he would do his best to lose, he knew Katlyn Rome was no bullshitter. He agreed with Stryker that the Matthew message had probably been called in by some cheap thrill seeker, but if Rome kept up the drumbeat long enough, she was going to need protection from someone who would risk a few hits to keep her from getting hurt anymore. One lousy advocate somewhere in the whole damn police department.

Once again it had come down to the same old issue: honor versus obedience, at the bottom of the ninth.

"So what'll it be this time, Shirley?" Carlos asked him, batting his eyes coquettishly, which looked ridiculous on such a tall and handsome man. "A lime rickey or chocolate frappe?"

Jarrett raised his head from the empty wine glass and saw a hundred liquor bottles lined up in neat rows on the wall behind the bar. It had been more than eight hours since he'd felt the razor-sharp pain that was trying to turn his pancreas inside out.

For a split second, a thought from hell that he had been suppressing all day came to the surface and gave him a case of the willies. *What if Rome was right? What if there was someone else?*

"Seagram's and ginger," he commanded the startled barkeeper. "And fuck you, too."

SIXTY-FIVE

The executive offices of WMTC were the last place Katlyn expected to find herself after quitting her job. Nothing had changed except for the startled look on Jude Sermac's face when she stormed into his conference room.

The gatekeeper who had failed him was Margaret Dunphy, a nasty old bird who had started as a secretary and worked her way up to be the station manager's sergeant-at-arms. In appreciation, Sermac saw that she received a bouquet of fresh-cut flowers every morning and a modest raise every year.

When both doors to the inner sanctum suddenly swung open, Marty Conroy observed from his position at the opposite end of the table that Dunphy was slumped over her desk, and that her hair was sopping wet and strewn with flowers. It was going to be an interesting meeting, after all.

Guy Spenser, the station owner, and Jesse Orvitz, executive program director, were just as astonished to see Katlyn.

"You don't care about anything except your damned ratings, do you, Jude?" Katlyn exploded, and pointed an accusing finger at him.

Sermac reached leisurely for his coffee and

took a sip. He put the cup down, careful not to chip the fine china, and dabbed at his lips with a linen napkin.

"How nice of you to join us, Katlyn," he said. "Perhaps if you had informed us that you were coming we could have all started together."

"I'm starting now," she said, her voice raised a pitch.

"Please sit down, Ms. Rome," Spenser said quickly.

The station owner was ramrod straight and immaculately tailored. His bright blue eyes darted back and forth between the combatants.

"I've been following your story with great concern. I'm sincerely sorry for what you've had to endure." He turned to Jude. "I was also sorry to hear that Ms. Rome left the station."

"Well, I'm afraid that the station hasn't left me," she said directly at Spenser's station manager. "Has it, Jude?"

"I'm sorry, Kate," Sermac said, still unruffled. "I haven't got the slightest idea of what you're talking about. Why don't you just tell us *all* what's on your mind." He cast a glance at the man who owned eleven television stations and an untold number of newspapers, nodded, and folded his hands neatly in front of him. He looked as though he were ten years old and at the circus.

"Last night when you ran the story about my message from Matthew you put his life in jeopardy. Did you even consider you might have told the kidnapper I betrayed him by telling the world? Do you think this is all about business?"

"Why, Kate. How could you even think—"

"You authorized it personally."

Sermac looked around the room, inviting the others to share in his astonishment. "I assure you, I have no idea where that story came from." He turned to Conroy. "Do you, Marty?"

The sneak attack caught Conroy off guard. But he suspected that Sermac had had a heavy hand in the story all along. He hadn't seen the copy before it was broadcast, and it wasn't a stretch to think that Sermac had ordered it read on camera without consulting him.

"Actually, Jude," he said with a touch of malice, "I heard it for the first time when Doug reported it."

"There must be another explanation," Orvitz interjected.

Katlyn took the few remaining steps to the narrow conference table and stood directly across from Spenser. "Someone at the station must have found out about it—maybe through police contacts after I told Stryker."

"Is it possible that someone else here knew what happened?" Spenser asked.

"Only one other person here knew, and it's someone I trust," Katlyn said pointedly.

Sermac still wore the implacable expression of someone who believed himself to be in the presence of powerful friends.

"What about it, Jude?" his boss said calmly.

Sermac placed his beefy fists on the table and locked them together. Small beads of sweat dotted his forehead, and his normally sonorous voice was muted. "Anything we may or may not have done was in the best interests of the station," he said calmly.

"*We?*" Spenser asked. "Was there someone else involved in this decision?"

"I was using the word in the corporate sense, Guy. Naturally, I take full responsibility . . . for everything. But I assure you, there was never any intention to interfere with the effort to find Katlyn's husband."

His abrupt admission of guilt left the room quiet.

"As you know, Guy," he continued, "we operate in a highly competitive environment. I was merely trying to stay ahead of the pack. In other words, to do what you pay me for."

He looked at Spenser and waited optimistically for the decree.

The media baron lowered his eyes to the center of the table. In a few moments, Sermac read his silence as approval and added, "Incidentally, Guy, the early numbers on the broadcast are quite reassuring."

Spenser tapped a gold fountain pen on the table. Each time the metal tip hit it left a tiny drop of ink on the inlaid rosewood surface and Sermac winced.

"I'm not surprised, given the public's appetite for this sort of thing," Spenser said finally. "I congratulate you on your success."

Sermac was relieved. As usual, the bottom line was the bottom line.

"But not on your judgment," Spenser added right away. "My reputation aside, I happen to believe it's in our best financial interests to set a higher standard than our competitors. If I had wanted WMTC to be another *Hard Copy,* I would have hired a ringmaster to manage it, not a journalist."

He turned his intelligent eyes back at Katlyn. "This all comes as a very unpleasant surprise to me, Ms. Rome. Please accept my apology. I had no idea this sort of thing was going on in my name."

Katlyn glanced at Sermac, who looked as if he'd been hit in the face with a shovel. He glanced around the room and saw himself without an ally.

"All things considered," Sermac said, "the episode probably was . . . ill-advised. As of now the story is dead. We'll leave it to the other stations."

Sermac put out his hand to her in a mock show of reconciliation. But Katlyn had noted his final veiled threat to Spenser. Without warning she leaned across the table toward him, and slapped him hard across the mouth.

"Sorry," she said calmly when she leaned back again. "All things considered, that was probably ill-*advised*, too."

SIXTY-SIX

Fava rapped sharply at the front door shortly after three in the afternoon. Katlyn ushered her in and led her to the desk where she had been poring over Combs's record for the past few hours. The documents had to come as a surprise to Fava.

"How in the world did you get Combs's police record?"

"Jarrett got it for me. It's a copy."

"Isn't this supposed to be confidential or something? Like, didn't someone stop being president for taking stuff like this?"

"I think he actually gets a kick out of bending the rules. That's probably why he's gotten into trouble so many times."

"Anything interesting?" Fava said, peeking at the page on top.

"Mainly, it's amazing how someone like Combs could stay out of jail for so long."

She handed her the report, and Fava eased herself into a nearby chair. She was immediately taken by the similarities between Arthur Combs and the profile she had helped research for Katlyn's TV address. There were some notable exceptions, however.

"His history of drug abuse isn't that common," Fava observed. "There are many cases where drugs come into play later, like to deal with the letdown after a murder. But Combs used drugs from the beginning, even before he killed."

"His attacks were consistent from the start," Katlyn said. "All sexually based, all brutal. It started when he was fourteen and got caught abusing neighborhood animals. *Abusing* is a generous word. He enticed the poor creatures with food, then killed them and mutilated their genitals. Did it on four occasions. And his behavior slowly got more and more perverse over a long period of time."

Fava was sickened. She skimmed the next section. Four years later Combs pushed a female teacher down a flight of stairs and was expelled from school. The assault wasn't sexual, but sexually explicit letters sent to her prior to the attack proved to be in his handwriting. Three years after that he was arrested for fondling a minor and possession of marijuana, which got him a year's probation.

"There was a gap of five years, then he was charged with the statutory rape of a six-year-old girl. The case was plea bargained to a misdemeanor for some reason," Fava read out loud. "Probably to prevent any further emotional damage to the girl during a trial. This time Combs was stoned on amphetamines.

"He was remanded to the care of a relative, not his parents. Evidently, at that time, he was no longer with his original parents, or at least there was nothing in the report that identified who they were."

"Everything he did was against individuals he could physically dominate, without fear of a fight, which is typical," Katlyn said.

"I know. They're all really cowards at heart. And God knows what else he did that no one found out about, because the victims never reported it. Like happens so often with rape."

There was a gap of six more years this time before his record of offenses continued, another step in a violent progression. In 1994, he was accused of driving a seventeen-year-old female hitchhiker to a deserted warehouse, making her strip. Then he let her go and stalked her.

"The bastard hunted her—like she was game," Fava exclaimed.

"He raped and beat her and shaved her hair, all of it, head and body. And he took it with him! Could be the first time he took a trophy. He left her for dead, but she survived when a homeless man found her and called the authorities. She was able to remember part of the license plate of Combs's car."

"You're going to tell me he got off again, aren't you?"

"In a way. He plea-bargained it down," Katlyn remembered.

"This is such bullshit. On something as serious as kidnapping and rape?"

"Depends on how you look at it. He said he didn't know it when he picked her up, but the girl had a history of sexual misconduct. Combs claimed she told him about the warehouse, and the cat-and-mouse scenario was her suggestion. He beat her up to protect himself when she asked for money and came at him with a brick when he refused to pay."

"Pretty transparent."

"Of course. But between her background and the fact that a prosecutor would never be able to disprove the story, he got the charges down to aggravated assault. He was sentenced to fifteen months in prison, but never served it."

"Why not?"

"A drug test found that he was a heavy user at the time. His case was appealed on the grounds of impaired mental faculties. The judge split the difference, the same amount of time, but to a detention facility specializing in drug rehabilitation, the California Correctional Treatment Center at Glenmora, near Sacramento."

Fava scanned the remainder of the record. It was all as Kate had memorized. The warehouse attack had occurred in November 1993, the trial in February of 1994. Combs was sentenced in April and spent the next ten months at Glenmora.

The final entry reported an incident that occurred at Glenmora itself.

"He was the subject of an investigation into an assault on a female inmate," Katlyn said, "but there were no specifics. No mention of what was done to her or of any punitive action taken."

"Why do you think that's important? How do you know it was even him?"

"When I read about it I couldn't believe it." Katlyn pressed her palms together and leaned forward. "I may have found what I was looking for."

She flipped over a page and pointed to a section near the bottom.

Fava stared at what she read. "Well I'll be damned. There were two of them under suspicion," she said, with rapt attention, then looked up.

"Yeah, two of them. The report doesn't mention the other person's name, but whatever they were accused of at Glenmora, the authorities thought that they might have done it together."

SIXTY-SEVEN

//"Where are you, Bo? Why haven't you come?"
Arthur listened intently for a response from the familiar voice and tried to recall the serenity he felt when they were together. It had been quiet for a long time. Deathly still.

"*Are you angry with me? Is that why? Are you afraid I told them?*"

An idea that had been lurking just beneath the surface suddenly crept into conscious thought. In another moment it registered fully and with heart-stopping clarity.

Minutes later Arthur was still staring into the dark cell. For the first time since he had come there he knew the numbing truth. *Bo was never coming. Bo was gone for good.*

An old image played in his mind. He had seen it in a movie as a youth and never forgotten it. After a long chase, an African lion was holding an antelope by its neck between its great incisors. He had been fascinated to observe the complete absence of fear in the antelope. Instead, as his death drew near, the animal seemed to accept the eternal process of which it was about to become a part. It had taken Arthur until then to understand.

He held on to the image for a while, and eventually it brought him a sense of peace. Finally, he knew what he had to do and wasn't afraid.

Keeping the vision fixed firmly in his mind, he got up on the bed on his hands and knees. Gripping the raised part of the frame at one end, he bent down and worked his head into the space between it and the mattress. He took a last full breath.

"I can't do this anymore, Bo."

With a single powerful thrust of his legs, he pushed off the bed. His momentum forced his body up and over the frame with his head still wedged in the opening. His legs came down on the other side. Just before he heard the snapping of vertebrae that protected his neck he thought, *even lions have to die.*

SIXTY-EIGHT

The twenty-five-minute wait in the claustro-
phobic reception area was an exhausting
exercise in self-control. Now, when every second
could spell the difference between life and death
for Matthew, there was nothing she could do but
wait on a reluctant administrator.

The Glenmora facility was set twenty miles
from the nearest residential area on a lightly
forested tract of sixty-five fenced acres. From a distance the austere Neolithic bastion had looked
menacing, but inside it was well lit and painted in
a muted green that lent a softer ambiance. This
duality mirrored its twofold purpose, as a detention center for criminals and a beneficent dispen-
sary of taxpayer-supported therapy, something
between a halfway house and a lockup. For many
years, those who had walked through Glenmora's
doors were among the most fortunate of outlaws.

After making the two-hour trip to the center,
Katlyn was cleared at the security desk and
directed to a seat on a timeworn bench in a small

waiting station. From where she sat, a wall ran for about fifty feet to the facility offices, an unadorned surface broken only by a phone booth close to her. An amiable Chinese night porter had been the only other human presence since then. He made an abbreviated bow when she sat down and then went about his chores. She waited for almost ten minutes for another human presence.

An administrative assistant named Cynthia Stall, a squat, late-middle-aged woman with a suspicious nature etched into her face, didn't seem to recognize the casually dressed television reporter, and it was clear from the start that she wasn't going to part easily with any information she might have.

No, she wasn't at liberty to discuss Glenmora's past inmates.

Yes, of course, she had heard of Arthur Combs, although she did not remember anything about his stay there.

No, she didn't recall any trouble he may have gotten into.

Yes, as a matter of fact, she did have other things to do.

No, the center's administrator was not available, but Katlyn was welcome to see him another time.

Total time of interview: less than sixty seconds.

Out of desperation, Katlyn finally identified

herself as a newswoman. Stall looked at her, and with a sudden flicker of recognition, rose quickly and excused herself.

Before long another woman appeared and introduced herself as Nancy Hallberg, the procedural administrator. Slender, with very short dark hair, she was surprisingly young and contemporary-looking compared to what Katlyn had expected. She proffered a hand with a courteous smile and gestured to a hallway. In a minute they entered a large office with a painted cement wall whose focal point was a poster of Bon Jovi.

"I can guess why you came, Ms. Rome," Hallberg said. "I'd like to help you, but I think you should know that I was not even aware that Arthur Combs had been here until the recent publicity. I've only been at Glenmora little over a year."

Katlyn appreciated her directness. The woman was ill at ease, but definitely sympathetic. Possibly she was trained in the healing arts and ended up miscast as a bureaucrat, Katlyn thought.

"I'm interested in an incident that happened when Combs was here. His police file describes some trouble he got into, even though the investigation was inconclusive."

"I'll be completely honest with you," Hallberg said forcefully. "I'm not going to be able to help you very much. I know what you must be going through but—" She started to shuffle through a folder on her desk, then thought better of it. She was going through a stressful internal debate. "A memo from the administration on Combs was circulated after his capture, and we've been instructed not to discuss his case."

"I'm only asking for something that must be part of the public record—or was."

"I don't know anything about that. Right now, Glenmora is under intense scrutiny because of the . . . sensitive issues involved."

Sensitive was quite an understatement, Katlyn mused. Combs had received Glenmora's state-of-the-art treatment and had gone from being a sex offender to a mass murderer a while later. Track records like that were the stuff of which budget cuts and changes in administrations were made.

"The police report says there was another person involved with Combs. Can you tell me anything about him?"

"You'll have to go through channels for that." Hallberg said, sounding more and more like a reluctant bureaucrat before she stopped herself abruptly. "I'm sorry. I never thought I'd hear myself saying something like that, but I really have no choice."

"Then whom do I have to see to look at the full report?"

"The records administrator. Her office is a few doors down the hall."

A nod of her head indicated a location to her right.

"Do you have access to it?"

"No. It's locked."

Katlyn could feel their conversation was about to end and frantically searched for another way in.

"I know Combs had a partner in whatever he was accused of. It could be a matter of life and death for my husband that I find out who it was."

Hallberg sighed and said, "There are duplicates of our records at the district court in Sacramento. Some of them are still on microfilm waiting to be converted to computer files. I have no idea if they'll let you see them, but it's worth a try. I'd appreciate it if you didn't mention how you found out about them," she added.

"What if you called ahead for me? Told them to make an exception."

Hallberg shook her head. "My credentials wouldn't help you. These are legal matters."

She had given her one last chance to help, Katlyn thought, to help Matthew. Hallberg had gone part of the way, but not far enough, even though she may have wanted to.

"I don't think there's anything else I can do, I'm sorry. You'll have to try the courthouse."

"It's Friday afternoon and it could be closed for the weekend. I can't wait until Monday. Do you understand that?"

There was no response.

"The police record says that Combs and this other person attacked a female inmate. If you can't tell me who his partner was, can you at least let me know what they were accused of doing to her?"

"I'm sorry," Hallberg said, more curtly this time. She stood.

Out of desperation, Katlyn seized on a last idea—and a guess. "It was a sexual attack of some kind, wasn't it? Please, you don't have to say anything. If I'm right, just don't say anything."

A silent few seconds crawled by. Hallberg was caught off guard in a scheme that forced her cooperation. She looked flustered but her mouth did not open.

When Katlyn rose and left the room a brief time later, the silence was still deafening.

SIXTY-NINE

If his intent was personal aggrandizement, Stryker had chosen an ideal time for a meeting with the media, Jarrett thought. The pre-weekend ritual guaranteed that anything the reporters said about him would make the late broadcasts, and the public would have two full days to digest the story.

"Now that you've indicted Starman, word is you're looking beyond police work," a reporter from the *Los Angeles Times* said. "Any comment?"

The question was inevitable. The surprise was that it had taken twenty minutes.

Stryker held up his hands in a calculatedly dramatic gesture, a shield against the shocking allegation and the murmurs of approval it had stirred. In truth, he had counted on the question, having started the rumor himself as a trial balloon.

"I'd rather not get into that, fellas. I accepted the job of shaping up the department, and my work is a long way from finished."

Jarrett stood at the very rear of the media

gathering, disgusted. There was nothing more repulsive than the media sucking up to a public servant, unless it was a politician pandering to reporters. Any moment, Stryker would say, *If nominated I will not accept, if elected I will not serve.*

"Of course, if the citizens of Los Angeles asked me to serve in a greater capacity, it would be my duty to consider it."

When he finished, his hands were folded piously on top of the lectern, the pose of a proper servant of the people. There was a smattering of applause. Jarrett recognized some of Stryker's flunkies at large, who were responsible for most of it. One was the captain who had been at the secret TMU office after Christa's murder. Michael Conaway gave a knowing nod to his boss from offstage and made a circle of his thumb and forefinger. Stryker the shark, and one of the little sucker fish who swam along with him.

The conference was going well, and with good reason. Trial preliminaries had gotten off to a good start, with the judge allowing everything in Combs's apartment to be entered as evidence. There was no way Starman was going to walk. Even if he pleaded insanity and went to the funny farm, everyone would know who put him away. Not Dan Jarrett.

WMTC's Doug Driscoll strained to be recognized. It was common knowledge that he was close to Katlyn Rome and the others would discount the bias in his interrogation.

"Has Starman said anything yet about where Matthew Demarco is?" he asked predictably.

Stryker's solemnity showed the depth of his concern. He squared his shoulders and leaned into the lectern.

"I'm afraid he hasn't been very helpful. And let me just say that in all my years of police work, nothing has saddened me more than our inability to locate Mr. Demarco—even though we have tried very hard."

Stryker scanned the room and inadvertently caught Jarrett's eye. He scowled at the man he hadn't invited to the meeting.

Jarrett touched the corner of his forehead in a mock salute and toyed with the idea of asking Stryker a few last questions himself.

Question number one: Why wasn't Stryker trying for a court order to prevent Combs's defense team from holding back information that might save Demarco's life?

Question number two: Why was he distancing himself more and more from Katlyn Rome?

And his favorite: If Stryker had no aspirations for higher office, why had he already created a special slush fund to promote his future candidacy?

A sudden commotion offstage forced the foolish thought out of his mind. Jarrett turned and saw the captain conferring with an officer who had just arrived. He was quickly joined by a third man in civilian clothes and the three were very animated. In a moment the captain moved smartly to the podium and whispered something in Stryker's ear. Stryker's complacency was suddenly shaken. He took a moment to consider what to do, then turned back to the microphone.

"I've just received word that Arthur Combs has taken his own life. It happened within the past hour."

The room erupted. Quickly, he held up his hand for quiet.

"I don't have any other information at this time. Sorry, no more questions for now."

There were calls from the floor, but Stryker turned abruptly to leave the stage.

A final entreaty was launched before he could get away. It was not its volume that quieted the room again. It was the speaker's tone of contemptuousness.

"What about Matthew Demarco?" Doug Driscoll shouted from the gathering. "How are you going to find him now?"

Stryker slowed his pace for just a second, then kept going.

Doug Driscoll repeated the question, but it went unanswered.

SEVENTY

On a Friday afternoon at almost five-thirty, the recording clerk for the Riverside Hall of Records in the courthouse was still at her desk, possibly a bureaucratic first. Katlyn breathed a sigh of relief at finding the undistinguished clay-colored building before the weekend shut down her inquiry. It was the repository of all records, past and present, on the rehabilitation center at Glenmora.

According to the nameplate on her desk, the clerk was Joyce Bridie, a sharp-edged, nervous woman probably in her late thirties. Her ensemble for the day included a black polyester stretch skirt and a see-through blouse with a bad bra. Katlyn was certain the strong scent of Joy perfume was a knockoff.

Joyce didn't stop straightening her desk even when Katlyn introduced herself as a researcher and requested to see the Combs files. "Even if you had authorization to look at the records—which you don't—you'd have to come during regular business hours." She tilted her head toward the wall clock. "We close at three-thirty on Fridays in the summer."

"Then you're here very late," Katlyn answered,

not meaning it as patronizingly as it must have sounded.

"I love my job," Bridie parried sarcastically.

"Where do I go for the paperwork? And how long does it take?"

"If the county courthouse approves your request they'll give you the forms right away."

"An executive supervisor at Glenmora said she was sure you'd help me," Katlyn added, stretching the truth.

"You'll need authorization from the court." Bridie's desk was getting tidier by the second. "But they'll only give it to you if you're a relative, a friend of the court, or if it's a police matter. Are you any of the above?"

Katlyn shook her head. It was tormenting to know that the records were only a few feet away and she couldn't get to them.

"Then there's nothing I can do."

Katlyn had an idea and checked Bridie's left hand for a ring. "I see you're married."

"Which is why I have to get home."

"Suppose when you get home there's a message that your husband has been kidnapped?"

That stopped the clerk, who looked up at her incredulously.

"Then a week goes by, then two, then a month, and you're afraid that if he's not already dead he's dying, and that the only way to save him is if you can find out who has him. How would you feel about that?"

Bridie stared at Katlyn more closely and then, in a flash of recognition, said, "You're the one on the news program whose husband—"

"Was kidnapped by Starman," Katlyn finished for her. "Yes. And I think he's still alive, and I'm trying to find him. But if I have to wait for the courthouse to open on Monday it may be too late. Now, if you won't help me, at least tell me how can I get in touch with someone from the court right away."

"There's no way that I know of," Bridie answered, more respectfully. "The court's on summer schedule. I'm not even sure who you'd have to reach. Which judge, I mean."

Katlyn was losing patience. She cast a glance toward the next room and Bridie guessed her intention.

"Look, if it makes you feel any better, it wouldn't have mattered even if you had clearance to see the records. The ones you're looking for are on microfilm files, and the rolls got all messed up yesterday."

"How did that happen?"

"The same way it always happens. Someone broke the machine."

"Who?"

Bridie hesitated, then let down her guard. "I don't mind telling you, this was one conniving bitch."

"A woman?" Katlyn felt electricity surge through her body. She had assumed that if Combs had a partner it was a man.

When she got over the initial shock, she said, "Do you remember what she looked like?"

"Uh-huh." Bridie checked behind her, an office with a closed door. She lowered her voice. "Middle thirties, give or take, medium height, long dark hair. She had a good strong body, maybe a hundred thirty pounds. And one of those Cindy Crawford moles over her lip. Pretty, in a foreign way."

"What nationality?"

"Mediterranean, maybe. Italian or Greek."

"You sound like you really studied her. I'm surprised you remember so exactly."

"Trust me, I had reason to. My boss wasn't too happy when he found out what happened."

"What about her name? You must have a record of that."

A nicotine-stained finger went to a large ledger in front of her. "It was right in here, right where I entered it. She said she was looking for records on her sister. Had some court papers that looked good, at the time."

"Her name?" Katlyn asked again.

"I said the name *was* in here," Bridie said opening the book and thumbing through the pages. "It's the one thing I couldn't remember, and the page she signed is gone. She called me into the microfilm room when the machine broke and came out here to wait while I tried to fix it. When I came back she was gone—and so was the whole page she signed. Ripped out. Her court papers were missing, too, so I never even had a chance to check to see if they were legit."

Bridie found the place she'd been looking for, and showed the remnant of a torn-out page to her. "A week's worth of people. That's what ticked my supervisor off. I caught hell for it."

"It wasn't your fault."

"Yeah. That went a *real* long way."

Katlyn understood now why the clerk was still at her post so late on a Friday, and why she had taken so long to loosen up.

"She really did a number on our machine," Bridie said. "There's a whole roll of torn up film still jammed in there, too, from when she tore one piece out."

"Can you tell what's missing?"

"Hell, no. It's not like we have it on computer or anything, like everyone else. These are files that still have to be transferred. I still can't figure out why anyone would ruin a whole roll to get what she wanted. She could have just made a copy. That's what everybody else does."

"Not if she didn't want anyone else to find it."

Later, outside the building, Katlyn wrestled with a frightening thought. The incredible idea had been in her mind often since the visit with Hallberg, and was more compelling now—one final way to get the records. She couldn't do it by herself, she knew, nor could she possibly ask Fava. There was only one person left, but it would be asking a lot, even for him. This time they'd be talking about breaking and entering, not just breaking with procedure. By the time she turned on the car's ignition, she was in turmoil.

She started the engine, but before she could drive off Bridie rapped on the driver's side window. The breathless woman must have run after her. Katlyn pressed the window down.

"I forgot to tell you something," Bridie said, struggling for air. "You couldn't help but notice if you were in the same room with her. The woman that messed up the machine? I remember that she was wearing some kind of weird perfume, like something left out of the refrigerator too long, or maybe she hadn't showered in a few weeks. It was real gamy. Totally."

SEVENTY-ONE

The drive home took three hours, with heavy traffic. By the time Katlyn's Pathfinder turned the corner of her street it was after seven and she was bone tired. When she saw what was half a block ahead, right in front of her house, she screeched to a halt. It was the last thing she needed at the moment.

A makeshift police barricade of wooden horses stretched the distance of her property. Just behind the barricade were news vans from all the major TV stations, her own conspicuously absent. Her first thought was that it must be about Matthew. She was afraid to think what it was.

A dozen reporters spotted her at the same time and ran in her direction. She checked to make sure the doors were locked, and nudged the gas pedal down a little. The reporters had gotten a good head start on the police, and when they got to her vehicle they pressed against the car in a swarm. Their chorus of voices swelled, all asking the same questions: *How would this affect the search for her husband? What was she going to do now? How did she feel about Starman's suicide?*

A half-hour later, Katlyn peered out the window of her house and saw a new commotion behind the police barricades. Several officers had formed a wedge and were driving a path through the crowd. The face at the head of the wedge was Dan Jarrett's. Foolishly, several reporters got in his way and stuck microphones in his face. Jarrett grabbed two of the microphones and yanked them away from the reporters. Then he tied the wires together, and handed them back to one of the men. He took off again for the house. The remaining journalists were sobered by this long enough for Jarrett to get to the door unmolested.

Katlyn sat in a trance in her living room, wanting to sleep and wired at the same time. "When did it happen?"

"Early this afternoon. We heard about it during Stryker's press conference."

"I thought he was under a suicide watch. That it was supposed to be impossible."

"For anyone else it was probably was. But no one thought about his bed. He wedged his head under the frame and managed to snap his neck by flipping himself over. He died instantly."

Before Matthew was kidnapped, she had prayed for Starman to be caught and executed. Now it was the worst thing that could have happened. "Matthew is going to die with him, isn't he?"

Jarrett saw her tremble and instinctively

reached for her. For a few seconds he touched her shoulder, but withdrew his hand again.

"Did he leave a note? Did he say anything about Matthew?" She wasn't expecting an answer. She already knew the answer.

"He was never going to tell us. I didn't want to say that to you, but I was convinced of it." He saw the effect his words had on her. "I know this is going to sound farfetched, but in one way this could actually turn out to be positive."

Katlyn looked up at him, her eyes confused and filled with tears.

"The way I see it, this will put more pressure on Stryker. Now he has to find Matthew himself. He can't wait for Combs to talk anymore."

SEVENTY-TWO

On Saturday night, August 1, the California Correctional Treatment Center at Glenmora was a Picasso of fractured shadows caused by spotlights playing on the sharp-angled architecture. Except for a few lighted rooms on the top floor, and an occasional dark shape in the window, there was no evidence of any activity. Once inside, and for the hundredth time since he left for the complex, Jarrett told himself he must be losing his mind.

When Katlyn mentioned the idea of going there herself, he had reacted so strongly that he was sure she saw something more than his professional concern. He told her that she could be arrested for breaking into the place, and that she could get the records she wanted with a court order, even though it might take a few days. But a few days was too long, and that's when he lost the argument. Her urgency suddenly outweighed any personal risk.

In the end he volunteered to go because it was the only way to keep her away, and because the idea of her getting caught in her present state was too painful. And because he had nothing better to do on a Saturday night anyway.

In addition, the information that the police had received back from Glenmora to date in their investigation of Combs's past was sketchy and incomplete. Whether that was deliberate on the part of the institution's administration or just bad detective work was uncertain. His personal visit guaranteed a more complete dossier on Combs—if he was lucky enough to find it.

Before he left Katlyn told him what she remembered about Glenmora's security. After that, he knew that getting inside would require only a modest subterfuge.

The plan was simple. He identified himself as a detective and succeeded in getting an interview with the night administrator on a police matter too sensitive to discuss on the phone. When he got to the front desk the appointment was checked in a book, as it was with Katlyn, and he was admitted to the waiting area. If someone was there to personally greet him, he was prepared to have the interview and think of something else on the way out.

Once he was cleared to the waiting area, however, he was alone and found the public phone Katlyn had told him about. He canceled the appointment, with sincere apologies, and was then free to roam. The irritated administrator had no reason to suspect that one of Los Angeles's finest was currently on the premises, about to become a common criminal.

Seated in the empty waiting area, Jarrett's

sense of impending disaster escalated. For someone who had no trouble stretching every rule, he
felt unaccustomed trepidation over becoming
one of them. He envisioned Stryker's face if he
got caught and Stryker heard what his detective
had been doing—and for whom. Not pretty.

The area remained deserted as Jarrett finally
stood and walked deliberately in the direction of
the records office Katlyn described from her
interview with Hallberg. He found the door, the
top part of which was thick milk glass. The brass
knob was worn, a darker base metal showing
through in places. He looked around to make
sure he was still alone, then turned the knob. It
was locked.

The glass would be easy to break, he guessed,
but the noise would draw the security guards. His
brand new Visa card fit snugly into the door-
jamb, just like in the movies, but when he pushed
the plastic in farther the pressure mangled its
front edge.

Out of frustration, Jarrett tested his shoulder
against the door, but it held firm. Grasping the
knob firmly with both hands, he leaned back,
ready to push it in. As soon as he did, he heard a
distinct *click*. The door swung open and he was
home.

SEVENTY-THREE

The small pocket flashlight easily lit the modest-sized, very cluttered office. A large locked safe sat in the left corner, covered with a serious layer of dust. Jarrett hoped that what Katlyn was looking for was not inside it.

On the wall to his left floor-to-ceiling rusted metal shelves were filled with dozens of gray metal boxes neatly piled on top of each other. All had a year stenciled in black paint on the front and they were arranged in chronological order. When the pile became too high it was continued by the next stack. A few were out of sequence, but all were unlocked.

He selected the one marked 1994. Inside were roughly twenty folders. A quick perusal showed they were classified by date, not name. The police report said Combs had been admitted to Glenmora in April.

A sudden movement of furniture on the floor above sounded like a clap of thunder, and it made him jump. "Dammit!" he said, feeling his heart thump.

When he had examined about a third of the files, the name at the top of one in April caught his eye, and he opened it. A color head-

and-shoulders picture of Combs affixed to the bottom of the jacket greeted him. He shone the light on it, and Combs stared back at him eerily from the past.

The most striking thing was the extra weight he had carried. The present-day Combs had been in perfect physical condition, drugs notwithstanding. Also, his hair was close-cropped in the picture, and there was more dysfunction in his expression. Otherwise the face bore a strong resemblance, especially the eyes, which were deeply sunken and had an unfocused quality about them.

He wondered what had made Combs's personality deteriorate so radically after Glenmora. And whether his rapid progression to celebrity killer had actually been hastened by his stay and the well-intentioned doctors.

The first few pages were copies of the official documents that had landed Combs at the facility. After that there was a full medical profile including test results of blood workups, drug tests. On the first pass he saw nothing in the deck that referred to an investigation or any trouble Combs had gotten into.

Most of the half-dozen remaining pages were handwritten, and he was forced to sort through them slowly. They were all signed by the same person, Martin Schermer, a prison psychiatrist. The earliest date was two weeks after Combs arrived, the last almost ten months later, at the end of his stay.

The early pages detailed the history of Combs's drug use, the reason he had been sent to Glenmora and not a more secure prison. Starting with antidepressants, there was a list of controlled substances, including names Jarrett recognized as psychedelics and hypnotics. He had become dependent on cocaine and pain-killers by his late twenties.

Schermer had added a summary in short-hand at the bottom of the paragraph:

1. *Prog. Compl. withdrawal not pos. this time.*
2. *Delusionary.*
3. *Frequent migraine.*
4. *Risk of self-infltd. injury.*
5. *Rec. contin. maintenance, haldol.*
6. *Therapy uncertain.*

Some of the notes on the next page were highlighted in yellow marker, with a simple key at the bottom of the page, a yellow dot with *A.C.* next to it, suggesting that these were Combs's own words.

The first part was all yellow and covered the period until he was thirteen. He detailed a very beautiful mother whom he loved, and a father he had never known, who deserted the family after he was born. He lived in poor circumstances, isolated from other children. Most of his time was spent in the apartment alone when his mother was not home. He idled away his time watching TV—his introduction to a fantasy world populated by film stars, Jarrett speculated.

There was a long section exclusively devoted to his mother's failed career. She'd been an actress who made films to support them. Here, Schermer indicated that they may have been pornographic, something, evidently, that Combs might have alluded to. Later on, his mother couldn't find work and started using drugs.

Jarrett felt a chill when he read that Combs blamed other actresses for his mother's unhappiness. He said she should have been a star, and the others stole it from her. He also mentioned visits by his mother's friends and *noisy games* they played while he was locked in the bedroom.

The most chilling part came at age fifteen, again in yellow:

1. *Mother murdered/intruder, violent death.*
2. *C. woke to find her.*
3. *Throat cut, bloody.*
4. *Killer never caught/suspect female acquaint.*
5. *C. blamed actresses, as before.*

The sound of leather heels approaching outside the records room alerted Jarrett. He clicked the flashlight off and waited. If it was a guard and he was caught, he would never be able to talk his way out of it. For a moment he let himself imagine how Katlyn would feel if he lost his career helping her. The sentry paused by the door, then continued on and it was quiet again.

He checked his watch. It seemed like an hour, but he had been in the room for only twelve minutes.

The section on Combs's mother was followed by several progress reports which did not shed any new light. Disappointed, Jarrett found the place in the stack from which he took the folder and made a space to return it. Right before he slipped it in, he saw an envelope behind it with an official seal of some kind stamped on it. It might be part of the Combs file that had been placed outside the main file by accident.

The envelope contained one page, typed on the Glenmora letterhead, under which was the heading INTERNAL DISCIPLINARY REVIEW BOARD.

Jarrett read the single paragraph without blinking.

> After a review of the circumstances involving the assault and sexual abuse of inmate #34712, the evidence examined by the committee regarding the involvement of Arthur M. Combs and

inmate #34866 proved inconclusive.
No disciplinary action is indicated at
this time.

The report was stamped with an official
seal. The space in the design had a handwritten date on it.

Three weeks before Combs's release from
Glenmora.

SEVENTY-FOUR

Matthew lay perfectly still, riveted by the footsteps in the next room. Usually there were six before the door opened, which made the adjoining space around eighteen feet long, he estimated, half again as large as the one he was in. He guessed it was early in the morning, not yet sunrise. Time had become relevant only as the interval between her visits.

With great effort he sat up and pushed himself back to the wall for support. The room was in sharper focus, he noticed, as if a screen had been removed from in front of his eyes. Over the past day, the drugs had relinquished their hold on him, perhaps an oversight on her part. More likely, she did not think he needed them any longer. Even without them he had little strength.

The door opened and a plane of light dissected the room. The imprint of the unaccustomed light remained on the back of his eyelids when he blinked. She studied him for a few seconds, then came to the bed.

The object in her hand was the knife he had seen before. The cold sharp edge brushed his neck as she probed his skin for a soft spot, then pressed the point in until he was forced to lie flat on the bed again. Whatever she had planned, the game was being conducted silently.

When he was in the desired position, she took hold of a section of chain attached to his right wrist, and pulled his arm up so roughly he thought it had come out of its socket, but he didn't give her the satisfaction of calling out.

Fastening one of the links to the hook that was set into the wall behind him, she repeated the process for his other wrist, and he was unable to move at all. In a short time a match flared and the pungent scent of sulphur filled the room. After his long period of sensory deprivation, the intensity of the odor was a hundred times more vivid than anything he remembered.

He watched her light two small candles and place them on either side of the bed. The light etched the ceiling with grotesque shadows made by her hands, huge spidery shapes that scampered back and forth when the air was stirred by her movements. He wondered what kind of ceremony she was planning. And whether the knife was going to be part of it. He strained his wrists uselessly against the handcuffs.

Soon, she stood over him and reached for

the first button on her blouse, then the second. She wore no undergarments. Seductively, she pulled the fabric away from her body and let it fall from her shoulders. She stared at him expectantly, eager for his reaction.

Her upper body was well-proportioned, shoulders square and symmetrical with unexpectedly delicate musculature. Her skin was radiant where the light played on her breasts which were trim with long, fully erect nipples. Except for a modest roundness in its center, her belly was smooth, with elongated hollows on both sides. She was more fit than he had imagined her to be.

Once she removed all of her clothing she got onto the bed and straddled him on her knees. She touched herself without taking her eyes off his, her hand inserted into a thick, rough triangle of pubic hair.

When she reached for him Matthew willed himself not to respond, but he became aroused anyway and the feeling humiliated him. The ceremony she had in mind had become clear, at least the first part of it. The idea of being raped by a woman who held him captive struck him as absurd, but it was happening. He also thought about the female black widow spider, who killed the male right after sex if he could not get away fast enough.

Only the tips of her fingers touched him at first, tentatively, as if the male member were an object of curiosity to her. She grasped its head and rubbed the surface lightly with her thumb and forefinger. In response, his pelvis rose off the bed, and when she saw him grow further she manipulated him between the fleshy portions of her palms until her hands looked small by comparison. He fought against the increasingly pleasurable pressure, thrashing his head from side to side. But once set in motion, his body ached for release.

A threatening thought entered his mind. He had been stupid not to realize it before: This was the reason she had kept him alive.

A new sensation of warmth sent a heightened wave of pleasure through him. Her lips clasped him more softly than her hands had, her tongue hot, the air from her nostrils warm on his belly. Taking him away from her face, she held him with one hand and guided him inside her. He entered easily and completely.

Against all instinct, he tried not to help her move, but her thrusts were insistent, and before long his resolve was lost in a building need for completion. She moved over him, steadily, in increasing rhythm. In a last attempt to resist, he conjured Katlyn's face, and turned away toward the wall.

He forced his eyes to focus on a bright area at the edge of the window, a section where the wood had separated from the plaster. Beyond that, he suddenly had a tiny view of the universe outside; the tops of trees, a section of colored roof with a weather vane on it.

When the climactic moment finally came, he knew exactly where he was.

SEVENTY-FIVE

"**I** think we may have found Combs's partner," Jarrett announced as soon as he was inside the house. "And just like the person who stole the microfilm at Riverside, it's a woman."

The confirmation of what she suspected all along sent a rush of adrenaline coursing through Katlyn's body. It was the first time that anyone else actually allowed that Combs did have a partner.

"The attack on the female was a sexual assault, as you guessed. That's what the investigation was all about. I got enough from Combs's record to do some cross-checking and come up with the name of the woman who they suspected was with him when it happened."

She stared at Jarrett with a penetrating gaze. "Do you think they stayed partners? After they left Glenmora?"

Jarrett didn't hesitate. "Hell, yeah," he said.

Feelings of relief and dread swept Katlyn at the same time.

He reached into his jeans pocket and withdrew a small piece of paper. It looked like a passport photo. "After I got his partner's inmate number from Combs's file, I found this in hers."

Katlyn took the photo from him quickly and stared at it. The woman looked to be in her early thirties. Bridie had said middle thirties. She was Mediterranean-looking with a smug, tight-lipped expression. The clincher was the Cindy Crawford birthmark, just over her lip on the right side.

Katlyn looked up in astonishment. "The records clerk I told you about described a woman who looked a lot like this. Even the birthmark. It couldn't be a coincidence."

Jarrett shook his head. "No, I don't think so, either. Not anymore."

Katlyn looked at him suspiciously. After the way he had held off judgment for so long, she was startled by his sudden agreement. "What makes you so sure now?"

"Because her name would have to be just a coincidence, too. The photo was in a file for someone called *Bogardis. Rosa Bogardis.*"

Katlyn's mouth opened wide in sudden comprehension of what he meant. She thought about the sound and said it over and over again in her mind.

"Combs wasn't that crazy after all," Jarrett went on. "The Bo he was talking to was a real person. Rosa Bogardis. If he's still alive, she's the one who has your husband."

SEVENTY-SIX

BRENTWOOD
Wednesday, August 5, 8:45 P.M.

The call came in just as Katlyn stepped out of the shower. The woman identified herself as Ellen Dowling and said she had been on the team of therapists who conferred with Dr. Schermer on Combs when he was at Glenmora. Her voice was husky, like a smoker's, and she was given to frequent fits of coughing.

"I got a message yesterday from Nancy Hallberg. She said she met with you and asked me to get in touch with you, unofficially, of course. She didn't want anyone to know she had called me and hoped you would respect that."

"Of course."

"When she told me who you were I understood. Asking me to help you wasn't the most prudent thing someone in her position could do."

Katlyn was surprised, too, that Hallberg had made the request on her behalf. She must have had misgivings about not helping after all. "Did she tell you what I wanted to know?"

"Enough to know I had to call. At this point it isn't likely you'll get much information from

Glenmora, and if you do, it will most likely be an official version, if you understand my meaning. Naturally, since my retirement, I don't have the normal restraints."

"I'm very grateful," Katlyn said.

Dowling paused to cough deeply a few times, then cleared her throat. "I've followed your ordeal since the beginning. I watch television news all the time, and I always thought you were a genuine young woman. Also, I felt stupid. I heard all the reports about Combs and Bo—and never made the connection."

"The connection to Rosa Bogardis?" Katlyn asked, not wasting time.

The phone went silent. "You know about her?"

"An old file turned up. Some very good research. Is that what you were going to tell me?"

"Yes, mainly. What else would you like to know?"

"Just how close were Arthur Combs and Rosa Bogardis?"

"When the two of them were at Glenmora you couldn't talk about one without the other. They were inseparable whenever the men and women were allowed to associate."

"I didn't know they were allowed to associate."

"They aren't anymore. But at that time they could, once in a while, to help with their socialization. Don't forget, they were mainly in a drug rehabilitation program. Besides that, they found other ways to get together. They were in separate dormitories, but the security isn't what it is at penitentiaries. As I remember, they were caught together several times after hours."

"Why do you think they found each other?"

"They were two of a kind," Dowling said, then stopped herself. "No, that's not what I meant. It was more to do with the way they complemented each other. Both were incomplete personalities, and each filled in an important missing element for the other."

"In what way?"

"Arthur Combs was a very dependent personality. He was brought up without a father, and his mother dominated his life, and shut him off from the world. When she was killed he may have begun a lifelong search for a mother to replace her."

"Why did it take so long for him to find a woman like Bogardis?"

"I'd guess the pattern was set in adolescence. We knew that on the few occasions when he tried to make contact with women, he was clumsy and acted oddly. Possibly he was impotent, or so conflicted about his mother that he was unable to perform. Also, he wasn't the most handsome kid on the block. Women invariably distanced themselves from him, which no doubt fueled his anger toward them."

"A lot of people get rejected socially. They don't start killing people."

"Yes, that's true, of course. It's hard to know what sends some people over the edge. In Combs's case, a number of things could have."

"Like what?"

"His mother died a terrible death in their apartment a dozen feet from where he was sleeping. He woke up and found her with her throat cut—a terrible, bloody murder. Do you know this already?"

"Yes, but not much more than that."

"Combs blamed himself and was lost without her. Pitiful, really, as so many of these cases are. God knows he didn't receive any counseling. And we can see what he did with his unresolved anger."

For the briefest moment Katlyn actually felt a small amount of sympathy for Combs, the boy. She could scarcely imagine what his grisly discovery added to his already disturbed view of life.

"How did Bogardis fit into this?"

"She was the daughter of a housekeeper who lived on the grounds of her employer—in Hollywood Hills, of all places. Like Combs, she didn't have a father. He left his family for another woman. Because of where she lived she went to the rich kids' schools, where she was always an outsider, ridiculed for the way she looked and spoke.

"By the end of high school she had built up an immense resentment toward her peers, mainly the girls. She wanted desperately to be accepted by them, but at the same time hated them for their advantages, which she knew were only an accident of birth."

"She was smart?"

"Definitely in the superior range. Combs was no match for her intellectually. Anyway, after a while, in order to become popular she started on the drugs many of the kids were experimenting with, first as a user, and later, selling them to the other students. That gave her value to them, as well as the money she needed to compete. But she took her revenge, too."

"On the other girls?" Katlyn asked pointedly.

"Yes. She was good at pitting people against each other, setting them up to be caught. She would sell drugs to someone she had it in for, and then anonymously tip off school authorities about where they hid them. No one suspected her since she stood to lose customers by turning people in. Once she even set fire to the home of a girl who didn't invite her to a party."

"Did she get caught for that?"

"I don't know. She also paid someone to beat up the older daughter of the woman her mother worked for. Seemed very proud of it."

Katlyn wondered if her pattern of getting others to do her dirty work had been established then.

"Later, some of her classmates went on to become film actresses, a few famous. This incensed her more than anything else. She was tortured by the injustice. I think you can see how she and Combs might have hit it off."

Katlyn could. Two sick souls who found each other at a low point in their lives, both with a reason to hate a certain kind of woman, each with an enormous rage.

"What happened with them at Glenmora? They were investigated for a sexual attack on a woman?"

"It was an especially brutal attack. The girl had accused Bogardis of stealing some personal items and did it in front of Combs. A week or so later someone broke into her room in the middle of the night."

"What did they do to her? Exactly."

"The girl said she was heavily drugged at the supper meal, maybe with something like you hear about these days that's used for date rape. No one ever found out what it was or where it came from. When she woke the next day she'd been sodomized, but didn't remember it happening. Also, most of her hair had been shaved off. Whoever did it had all night to get back to their room—or rooms. The reason they investigated Combs and Bogardis was the fight she had had with the girl, and the fact that they did everything together."

"Do you think it was them?"

Dowling recovered from another bout of coughing. "There's never been a question in my mind. Rosa held a great deal of power over Arthur Combs. That was another way in which they were symbiotic. He needed to be directed. She needed a proxy for her acts of revenge."

"How could such a brutal monster let anyone control him?" Katlyn asked incredulously.

"Yes, I know it sounds bizarre. But you have to remember that he once lived only for the approval of a dominating woman. Bogardis's approval became essential to Combs's well-being."

"When did the attack take place?"

"Just a short time before the two of them left Glenmora. Maybe a parting act of retribution."

"Or practice for what was to come?"

"I'm not sure they planned anything like that at the time, but the rest may have evolved quickly."

It was so ironic, Katlyn thought. The two met at a rehabilitation center, and the result was one of the most shocking murder sprees ever. Now one of them was dead by his own hand and there was a good chance the other had Matthew. Or did once.

"What would Bogardis be like without Combs? What would she be like on her own?"

"This is also going to sound strange, I know, especially after what Combs has done. But in his own way I believe he had a conscience, of sorts. What I mean is, he was the type who would probably have to convince himself that his victims deserved his punishment before doing something to them."

"And Bogardis?"

"Completely the opposite. Bogardis was a sociopath. She had no conscience about anything. As bizarre as it may sound, despite what Combs did since leaving Glenmora, Bogardis is potentially the more violent of the two."

SEVENTY-SEVEN

Thursday, August 6, 3:00 P.M.

The pounding at the door sounded so urgent that even after Katlyn confirmed it was Allen Frazier, the TMU sergeant Stryker had given her, she opened the door with suspicion. Curiously, the TMU officer stood at a distance from the entrance, very agitated. There was a package in his hand which he held uncomfortably to one side.

"This was just delivered to your house," he said with an edge to his voice. "We kept knocking to see if you were expecting it, but you didn't answer."

"I was bathing. It took me a while."

"What about it?" he said, showing the package to her but not bringing it any closer. The parcel was a standard-size FedEx envelope that looked innocent enough. She could only guess who had sent it and what was inside. "It's possible. I wouldn't worry about it." She reached for it, but Frazier moved it even farther away from her hand.

"There are a lot of crazies out there. We don't want to take any chances."

The package was probably something from Marty, or, now that she thought about it, probably some more personal articles of hers from Rudy Gallico, the station wardrobe manager. Besides, if she worried about every move she made she'd end up in a straitjacket.

"I'll take it now, Frazier," she demanded softly. "I have a good idea who it's from."

Frazier drilled her with a disquieting look, then suddenly hefted the package for a clue to its contents. Abruptly, he walked a few steps away, turned his back to her, and tore open the strong adhesive. When he faced her again he was holding a black videocassette. He inspected it carefully.

"You're a nice guy, Frazier," she said when she saw him do it.

"You never know." He gave it to her reluctantly.

"Don't worry, I'll be fine."

There was no label on the tape. Strange, Katlyn thought. Marty or Fava were the most likely ones to have sent it. But they would have identified it, something news people did as a matter of course.

Alone in the house, she walked to the TV set in the library. She turned the tape over, found nothing more, and slipped it in the video player.

From the quality of the image that began playing she could see it was far from a professionally made movie. The scene had been staged indoors without enough light, and the frame jiggled, showing the camera had been hand-held. The picture was almost too grainy to make out. The central figure, however, was discernible as a man lying down. He was not moving. Katlyn had a dark premonition and slipped down to the floor in front of the monitor feeling her skin tingle.

After a short time the vertical hold went and the weak picture started to roll. The vertical control only slowed it down, but by synchronizing her eyes with the movement of the roll it was possible to follow the action for a few seconds at a time. The effort made her dizzy, and it took a while to get used to it.

Eventually, the frame stopped rolling and the image became steady. Probably by then the camera had been put down and set to keep running by itself. Even with the poor reproduction, she could see that a second person had entered the scene, joining the first on a raised surface which appeared to be either a couch or a bed.

When the new actor got up over the one lying down, the upper portion of a woman's body was visible. A short time later she began rocking up and down over the man. It was obvious that they were making love.

The lovemaking occupied the major portion of the tape. When it was over, the woman left the bed and approached the camera. The picture went dark for a while until there was a sudden flare of light.

The new image was in better focus than what had come before and much more illuminated. A white rectangular shape filled the center of the screen. The picture sharpened further, enough to see it was a large white index card and that there was writing on it.

One short sentence followed by a single letter.

FUCK WITH ME AND I FUCK WITH YOU. B.

SEVENTY-EIGHT

Long after the woman left the room, Matthew remained attentive to any sound that would tell him she was on the other side of the door listening. He was ravenous for the food that she had left deliberately within easy reach. The aroma of meat had worked on his mind more effectively than any of her threats, but if he touched the meal she would know that he was capable of feeding himself and tighten the chains again.

When he thought that enough time had passed, he opened his eyes and slowly began moving. Bending at the waist, he rolled onto one side, then tried to push himself off the bed. His legs responded feebly, but in time he came to a sitting position on the edge of the mattress and rested. The simple effort had winded him. It had been weeks since he had used any of his muscles.

The instant he got to his feet, a ribbon of pain traveled up the center of his leg, and the large muscle of his thigh went into spasm. Massaging it, he contemplated the reduced body that had replaced his own.

What he had seen through the hole under

the window gave him strength, however, and he edged forward toward it, cursing the clatter of the chains. When he went as far as he could, he used the chain itself to support his weight and extended his reach to where the small piece of plaster was missing.

The window was covered by an old piece of canvas nailed to the wood frame. With the right amount of pressure it could be ripped away, but there was a good chance parts of the frame would come with it, and it was therefore too risky. If enough of the plaster at the bottom of the window was removed carefully, however, it would yield a view of the outside world. Then it could be filled in again—not seamlessly, but close enough.

Matthew pressed his hand to the left side of the frame, just under it, and removed a piece of plaster about four inches long. Another large section came out unbroken, and another after that. After each new piece, he knelt and placed it on the floor intact in the order of removal.

When he was able to look out of the opening he drank in the air streaming in from outside. It was filled with myriad scents that staggered his senses. Soil, grass, bark, bougainvillea. He had never known how rich and subtle the scents really were. For one fleeting moment he considered smashing the main window and calling for help, but the noise would attract her attention if she was anywhere near, too great a risk.

He peered outside. The real world looked beautiful and serene. Later, if a small miracle was granted and the special visitor he'd been thinking about came into the area, he *would* break open the main window and reach out to it with both hands. He would then use the precious object that he had created from the only thing she had not taken from him.

Then his special visitor would become his messenger.

SEVENTY-NINE

Jarrett sat impatiently across the desk from his boss, tapping a reggae rhythm with his foot. His impending fight with Stryker was foretold by two ominous signs: a forty-minute wait that said, Of all the things I have to deal with, you are the least of them, and the way Stryker had looked at him when he was summoned into his office.

Wisely, he had not come to the meeting unarmed.

The chief—or was it *Hail to the Chief*—seemed preoccupied with loftier thoughts than a meeting forced by a subordinate. Eventually, however, he allowed Jarrett to update him on events. Then they watched the videotape Jarrett had brought together in silence.

"Why didn't she bring me this herself?" Stryker asked when it was over. "Not that this meaningless piece of crap changes anything."

"I think you just answered your own question. She doesn't expect you to raise your dress and show your panties every time she finds something. She doesn't even think you take her seriously anymore."

"That's because everything she's been coming up with is like this. A phone message that even the tech guys can't hear. And now a video-tape that probably came from some cheap porn store—or a bad home movie from some new ass-hole. How am I supposed to react?"

"What about the microfilm records stolen in Riverside?"

"I don't think it's that much of a stretch to believe they were taken by a reporter—maybe even Rome," he added pointedly, baiting Jarrett to react. "Or maybe even a TMU officer."

"If it's bothering you, check it out."

"Don't tell me what to do."

Jarrett made a quick decision.

"Combs was involved with someone at Glen-mora. A woman. The two of them may have attacked another inmate, and they might have stayed together after they were released. His part-ner's name is Rosa Bogardis. We think that's who Bo is."

Stryker stood up straight and absorbed the news with a look of dismay. In a moment he gath-ered himself again and leaned over the desk, closer to Jarrett. "*We?*" he said arrogantly. "What the hell are you talking about, *we?* You and Rome got this new information?"

Jarrett didn't answer.

"And just how did you and Rome get it?"

"She went there and got someone on her side, a retired shrink who used to work there and told her about what went on there. Then Rome told me." Everything he said was the truth. Only the name of a certain other participant had been left out to protect the guilty. He sat back and waited for a reaction.

"What did Combs and this woman do, exactly?"

"They drugged and sexually assaulted a woman. And they shaved her hair off and took it with them."

"You know that for a fact? Was there an investigation?"

Jarrett backed off a bit. "Yeah. They got off."

Stryker shook his head. If anything, he looked relieved, in a way that was clearly condescending. "Is there anything else that you're holding back? A vision maybe? A ghost that visited Rome and told her where her husband is? A talking dog that witnessed the kidnapping?"

"They did the assault. The staff knew it, they just couldn't prove it."

Stryker shook his head, relief turning to contempt. "Don't shit me, Jarrett. Officially, all you have is two people who were cleared of a crime— and the sound of part of a name that happens to match something in the mind of a raving lunatic. That's what I call a stretch. Gimme a fucking break, will ya?"

"You have to check it out, Elliot. There's going to be a major shit storm about this."

Stryker's expression was impassive. It was amazing, Jarrett thought. Nothing got to the man. He put his hands flat on the desk and said,

"If you want my opinion I think you should put Rome back in a safe house. Start checking out this Rosa Bogardis. Rome is basically uncovered where she is."

"No way. You can just forget that," Stryker said, suddenly exploding and slamming the desk with both fists. "When in hell are you gonna grow up, anyway? A hundred of my men are still looking for Demarco, or did you forget that? Even though we all know how much good that's gonna do. And I've got a full-time team on her house."

Jarrett had heard it all before. It all added up to not doing as much as he could if he really wanted to cut Rome a break.

"What do you think, that this is all I have going on here? Right now I got a dead celebrity killer in the city morgue who killed himself under suicide watch, an arsonist on Southside who's hit three buildings and one of them is still burning. And last night there were two drive-bys in South Central, and another tourist got shot right on fucking Sunset. And guess who's coming to visit next week? The goddamn president—and there goes a few thousand more of my men. And you're telling me I should shit a brick because Rome just got another hot flash about her husband? Bullshit."

Jarrett steadied himself in his chair. For a second it looked like Stryker was going to come across the desk at him, fists first. There was no way to attack the underlying logic of his argument. There were never enough men. It was always a matter of where to put the ones you had.

"Have you thought about what will happen if Rome is right and there is someone else out there? And she gets to Rome? Her friends in the media will crucify you. They'll say Rome warned you and you didn't care."

For the first time, Stryker seemed to be listening.

"Or what if she lucks out and actually does find this Bo? And it does connect to Combs and her husband. What if they find Demarco or his body? That's something the whole force hasn't been able to do," he added for effect. He stared at Stryker and waited.

Stryker was pensive. The color had drained out of his face. Maybe he was working it out, Jarrett hoped, every painful step, all the way to disaster at the polls.

"Okay, here's where it is," Stryker finally said in a studied calm. "Rome isn't getting any more men because I don't have any. In fact, she's getting one less. From now on, you're completely out of this. I can't have a solo act out there, doing whatever the fuck it is that you do." He narrowed his eyes suspiciously. "Besides, I think you've become too personally involved with this woman. And right now I don't want to even think about *how* involved."

Jarrett clenched his jaw and strenuously

fought the urge to tell the pompous chief of detectives what he thought of him and each link of his entire genealogical chain back to the slime that he came from. Only his last pronouncement stopped him from doing it. In actuality, Stryker had used the personal involvement shot as part of an excuse for getting him off the case, but without knowing it, he had hit on the truth. Now, if he said anything to deny it, he would only get himself in deeper.

Still, Jarrett had logic on his side. Sooner or later, no matter how pissed Stryker was, he had to see it.

"What if she is right about the woman," Jarrett said in a diminished voice. "What then?"

Stryker leaned across the desk threateningly. "Let me make this clear one more time. If I even hear about you being with Rome, or catch you in the same part of town, you're gone. And I don't mean to some other department or desk job this time. You're off the force—forever. And that's a fucking promise."

He was so close that Jarrett could smell the sardines he had had for lunch.

"And in case you're wondering about what you did three weeks ago, as far as I'm concerned, a lot of people nailed Starman. You just got your name in the paper."

Jarrett studied the malevolent face for a moment, then shook his head. He now knew for certain what he had suspected ever since he captured Combs—why Stryker had a bug up his ass at the very time he should have valued him even more. He had wanted all the credit for the collar.

"That's funny," he said. "I thought I mostly saw yours."

Stryker threw him a vicious glance and did a slow burn. "If you think that video is such hot shit, you take it to forensics and let me know what they say. I have more important things to do." He grabbed his jacket from the back of his chair and left the room without further comment.

When he was alone, Jarrett sat, tapping his desk, thinking. The man definitely had a self-destruct button, he decided, and he had just pushed it by kicking his best hope off the case—or trying to. Unfortunately, he himself did not respond well to threats, never had. Another of his many shortcomings was that he always took threats to be more like challenges. Stryker was not at the top of his game. Normally, he would have remembered that about Dan Jarrett.

Jarrett stared at the desk and focused on Katlyn's videotape, which still lay where Stryker discarded it after the viewing. He picked it up, using a handkerchief, just in case there was a fingerprint on it that hadn't already been ruined by the handling. He put it back into the plastic bag he'd brought it in.

Stryker might not have thought much of the tape, but there was someone else who might. Willy "Guano" Dunellen.

EIGHTY

"Sorry to bother you so late," Jarrett said when he paid an unaccustomed visit to Katlyn's house late Thursday afternoon.

Katlyn had just got out of the shower and met him at the door wrapped in a thick terrycloth robe. The faint but enticing almond scent on her skin made him reel.

He stepped in swiftly and walked right past her. "Got any coffee?" he said. *God help me,* he thought.

He sat in the kitchen feeling clumsy while she made coffee. "Stryker didn't think much of the videotape. I don't think it would have mattered if his mother were on it."

"Why am I not surprised."

"His mind is closed down on anything to do with reopening the case. And he's not all that thrilled with me, either. Maybe you should have hooked up with someone else."

"Uh-uh. No regrets." Katlyn looked at him closely. Something in his expression spelled more trouble for him than usual—which was a lot.

"Don't worry about it. It's nothing that hasn't happened before because of one politician or another who happened to control my life at the time. I didn't come here for that. It's unsafe for you to go out again. We know that, even if Stryker doesn't. I'd like you to consider staying home for a while."

His sudden escalation of concern took Katlyn aback. This time there was a personal component visible in his discomfort. While they were talking the distance between them had narrowed, and all at once he felt disturbingly close to her. The skin on her arms tingled, and something warm was happening at the nape of her neck.

For a few moments she found herself seduced by an old need—strong arms to take care of her. But that wasn't her anymore, she told herself. She would have to straighten herself out.

"I can't lock myself in here. I already did that—at the safe house. I might as well stop living."

"I don't think you have a choice anymore. The tape shows how bold Bogardis is getting. Something's going to happen. You're completely unprotected outside of this house."

She shook her head and was adamant.

"Dammit, Kate, it's too dangerous." He grabbed her shoulders and pressed them together.

Katlyn held him at arm's length. She told herself that Matthew had acted the same way, domineering, possessive. But with Jarrett it didn't feel the same way. They looked at each other, and for just an instant they started to move toward each other.

A sudden pounding at the door made them both pull away.

"What is it?" Jarrett called, letting go of her shoulders.

Frazier was barely audible behind the front door. "I just got a call from one of Stryker's men. He was asking for you and I thought you should know."

"What did you say?"

"That I hadn't seen you, like you told me."

"Be right out."

Jarrett stared at Katlyn with an intense look of concern. "If anyone asks, you haven't seen me either."

"What's going on?"

"I'm not supposed to be around you anymore, here or anywhere else. Stryker just kicked me off your case." He paused, then added, "He thought I was becoming too personally involved with you." *And he was right,* he wanted to add.

Katlyn drew back slightly. There was so much to deal with in what he said. She needed time to understand what it meant.

"Trust me, it goes back a long way between me and Stryker. That's what's really going on." Jarrett adjusted his light leather jacket, body language that said he had to leave.

"What happens now?" she said shakily, afraid of his answer.

"If you need to talk to me at any time, you can reach me here." He handed her a slip of paper with a phone number on it. She didn't recognize it as a police line. "If I'm not there, leave a message. I check in all the time."

"And that's it? You just walk away?"

"It's all I can do—for now. The only way I can get Stryker off my back."

"By running away?" she struggled to say. "It's just not . . . not like you."

"I promise I'll do what I can. You have to trust me on that."

He looked at her, as if there was more he wanted to say. He took her hand in his, squeezed it tightly, and slipped past her to leave.

When he was gone she could not take her eyes off the door. The sense of loss that his surprise announcement had brought on was deep and all-consuming. She felt hurt and alone. And as guilty as sin for what she was allowing herself to feel.

EIGHTY-ONE

By bracing his chest against the wall to free his hands, he had been able to remove pieces of plaster over a roughly two-foot-long area, first the ones that had been fitted back into place the last time, then the new ones. Finally, as he'd begun to do every afternoon, he peered through the opening below the window and started his vigil.

After an interminable wait, perhaps as long as an hour, nothing had happened. By then his legs were trembling so much they threatened to give way, so he had to leave his post to rest them. The vertigo had also returned, and the wall in front of him tilted slightly left, then right, when he looked up at it.

A short time later, when his legs felt stronger again, he returned to the window and put more of his weight against the wall. Scanning the grounds outside from one edge of the window to the other he saw no movement except for the swaying of trees in an occasional gust of wind. The thought that the woman might be nearby kept him in a constant state of anxiety. He could feel her eyes on him. If she was there, and found out what he was doing, he had no doubt that she would kill him without hesitation.

A sudden movement in a clump of distant bushes caught his eye and he narrowed his vision to that exact spot. The shrubs appeared to have stirred unnaturally, but he feared that it was probably only the wind, which had picked up since he first looked out. The air smelled musky, as if it was going to rain. The last thing he needed.

A few seconds later he watched in disbelief as an indistinct collection of colors separated from the thickest section of the same bushes, a rough mosaic of blacks, browns, and white. He shut his eyes tightly and opened them again. The object was still there and now more sharply defined. A fourth color, orange, confirmed the miracle. It was Monty. The animal slinked along the ground, his head fully extended, stalking something.

Matthew's heart raced. He had been over the idea a hundred times in his mind. He knew he had to move slowly. The crucial time would be when Monty was close enough to recognize him, but still far enough away to feel secure in the distance that separated them. If the cat became frightened at any unusual sound, he would bolt, and with him would go the only chance of getting out of the cottage alive.

Like a blind man, Matthew moved his fingers along the edge of the canvas cloth that had been nailed to the window frame, feeling for the best purchase. When he found a loose space, he worked his fingers between the nails, then pulled on it with one powerful yank. One corner of the canvas came away easily with part of the sash still attached. The original glass was behind it. After a few more pulls, all of the old window was clear.

Matthew put his face to the glass and peered out. Monty was still there, waiting, perfectly still. He had stopped when he heard the ripping noise, and his head was raised, staring directly in his direction. There was no way to tell if he could see past the glass to who was behind it. So far, he gave no sign of recognition.

With a silent prayer, Matthew made a fist and aimed it at the center of the window. The glass disintegrated. Monty crouched fearfully and became a statue, his eyes two bright yellow circles of reflected yellow light.

Matthew felt elation and terror at the same time, entranced by the cat's nearness, but afraid that the woman might have been in the area and heard the breaking glass. If so, nothing else mattered.

Carefully, he picked the largest shards of glass out of the frame until the opening was unobstructed. He leaned closer to the space and pursed his lips to make the kissing sound that always brought Monty running. But his mouth was dry, and the noise he made came out as only a small hiss. Pressing his tongue between his teeth, he was able to squeeze out just enough saliva to moisten his lips. He tried to make the sound again, a few short bursts, followed by the name, which he chanted softly.

Monty. Monty.

The animal raised his head and stared into the window. His hindquarters rose off the ground, and he took a step at half speed, keeping his body low. Matthew called to him again, and the cat responded with a soft, guttural sound. He trotted forward toward the sound, and stopped only a few yards from the window. Pieces of broken glass lay scattered in his path. He sniffed them. Something unseen suddenly caused him to crouch and look around. Small beads of water began to collect on his fur. It had begun to rain.

Matthew moved out into the opening where the glass had been until he was certain that Monty could see him. When their eyes met, Monty meowed. At the same time, Matthew heard a metal latch engage inside the house behind him, and he froze. She was back. His eyes darted to the window that he'd destroyed and the canvas that had been torn from it. There was no way to put it back. She would see it instantly.

Leaning all of his weight against the wall, he thrust one hand outside and opened it, palm up, as if it held food. He called the cat softly. Monty saw the hand, and in a moment rocked back and sprang lithely over the largest piece of glass. He continued forward, picking his way carefully until he was at the window, close enough to touch, purring loudly.

Matthew reached farther out. A jagged piece of glass cut the underside of his arm and left a thin line of blood. Monty sniffed the long bony fingers, and allowed himself to be stroked under the chin, his favorite spot.

A squeak of a floorboard in the next room made Matthew's blood run cold. His jailer was close to the door. A few more steps and the familiar drill would start: putting her ear to the door to listen; the slow twisting of the knob; the heavy wooden door opening just enough for her to see him in the bed. Except that this time he wouldn't be there.

With only seconds left, his hand continued to caress the cat's fur, his eyes never leaving the animal's. Eventually, Monty trusted the fingers and pushed against them strongly, and as soon as he did, Matthew closed his hand tightly on the loose folds of skin and held on.

Quickly, he reached under his waistband and found the long thin strip of fabric and paper he had hidden there ever since he had secretly made it. The muscles in his legs started to give way again by the time he reached out with the second hand and caught Monty around the top of his neck.

Swiftly, he maneuvered the cloth around both sides of the cat's head. He tied the two loose ends together once, then again to make a knot, and it was done.

"Go home," he commanded him. He turned

Monty and faced him in the opposite direction, then gave him a shove. "Monty. Go home now."

The cat jogged a few steps away, then stopped and looked back.

His strength gone, Matthew hoisted himself back out of the window and tried to make it to the bed.

Before he could get there, the door creaked loudly, the way it did when it was all the way open. He heard the crazy woman scream and saw that she was looking at the window. He saw her coming for him with something shiny in her hand and covered his head with his hands and turned away to the wall.

EIGHTY-TWO

F ava tried to shake off the chill that had been with her ever since Katlyn told her about the videotape. The call had come when she was still reeling from the discovery of Rosa Bogardis, Combs's probable partner.

On the spur of the moment she had decided to drive to Katlyn's. She knew she would be glad for the company, especially at the hardest time of the day, once it got dark.

She pressed the gas pedal to the floor and watched the speedometer creep higher. At the last of the level part of the road, she downshifted to second gear to give the Volvo's engine more muscle for the hill.

There was no reason to feel cold, but she did. Despite the unusual rain, the temperature outside was still in the upper seventies, and the Volvo's air conditioner was discharging only a tepid stream.

She drew a deep breath and settled more comfortably into the threadbare cloth seat. She did her best thinking while driving, and she concentrated on one of the questions that had now become even more difficult about Matthew's disappearance: how the person who abducted him had done it; how a man as strong as Matthew could be overcome. Especially if the abductor were Bogardis, she would have needed to take him completely off guard, probably someplace where he would never expect it. She would have needed a weapon to overcome his strength advantage.

What made it harder to understand was Matthew's presumed wariness at the time. He was on the way to the Trio party when the kidnapping happened, and because of Kate's impending broadcast he would have been especially on guard, suspicious of anything out of the ordinary.

It just didn't figure.

The vague feeling that someone was watching her made her suddenly feel creepy. Too many bad movies at three in the morning, too few men, she told herself, and tried to shake it off. She had already driven about half the distance to Katlyn's house and would be there in another fifteen minutes or so.

Climbing the hills that eventually led to Brentwood, she saw a dark stretch ahead where the streetlights ended and the road began to wind. The Volvo complained loudly as it hauled itself up the incline. If the engine failed at that time of night, she would be stranded.

In a short time the feeling came back more strongly. Just to be sure, she looked in the rearview mirror and saw a car about a quarter of a mile back that had not been there a short time earlier. She was sure of that. It was the only other car on the road. More ominously, only its parking lights were on.

She watched the car as much as she could without taking her eyes completely off the road. For a while it remained at the same distance, then all at once it sped up, only to decelerate again. The driver seemed to be playing a game, deliberately trying to frighten her.

She broke into a cold sweat and reminded herself that it was just her vivid imagination at work. Or maybe just a hotshot teenager showing off for his girlfriend. In case she was wrong, however, she needed a plan. Soon, the road would become steeper and more deserted, and her underpowered vehicle would become easier to overtake.

Ahead on her left, she saw an intersection, the first since she had noticed the other car. She held her breath as she came closer to it. She glanced at the rearview mirror and gasped. The trailing car was closing fast.

Without hesitating, she pushed the gas pedal to the floor and sped ahead. Just before the roads crossed, she slammed her foot on the brake, and cut the wheel sharply left. The screeching tires grabbed and pulled her onto a local unpaved road. She traveled another fifty yards in and finally came to a wrenching stop.

Panting, she watched the mirror for what seemed like an eternity until the other car hurtled past the intersection without trying to slow down. It was a Mercedes, a dark color, she noticed with surprise. Fava crossed herself and put her head on the steering wheel.

Her rest did not last for long. The sound of a powerful automobile engine whining in reverse came from the Mercedes, which shot backward into view. With its rear wheels spinning, it reversed direction and turned into the road with its high beams blinding her.

Fava made a quick decision. Instantly, she stomped on the gas and turned the wheel all the way to the left, spinning the Volvo completely around. She kept the pedal all the way down and aimed directly at the Mercedes. For a few seconds the two cars were on a collision course. About to crash, Fava closed her eyes and prayed. The Mercedes veered to the right, just missing her. In another few seconds, she turned back onto the main road and made a run for it.

Hoping against hope that her nearly suicidal stunt had ended the chase, she urged the car up the first of the upcoming hills. Almost immediately, the bright lights that appeared in the mirror signaled that the chase was not over. The slope steepened, and her engine sputtered unpromisingly. By the top of the first hill the Mercedes was almost on top of her. She could hear the more powerful engine straining as it easily overtook the Volvo. An icy current passed over the top of her shoulders, like a cool, clammy hand.

Behind her by only a few dozen yards, the Mercedes suddenly swerved to its left, into the passing lane. It was a dangerous move, Fava thought. If an oncoming car appeared, and was traveling fast, the big car would not be able to get out of the way in time.

A violent impact rocked her car along its left side. The collision made her car lurch to the right onto the narrow shoulder of the road. She managed to wrest control from the wheel when the car was only inches from the edge and, as she turned away, she caught a fleeting glimpse of the steep mountainside and the ravine far below.

The second strong shock lifted the wheels on one side of the Volvo off the ground. This time it went completely out of control, and the Mercedes hurtled past. With both of Fava's feet jammed on the brake, the Volvo went into a full sideways skid. Fava stopped breathing and watched the place where the mountain ended pass by the front windshield. This time she had gone too far to stop.

She reached for the door handle as the world went into slow motion.

EIGHTY-THREE

*S*ince the moment she heard of Arthur's capture on the news, she knew what the most likely outcome of his prolonged separation from her would be. Sorrowfully, there had been no way after that to communicate. Without her there to support his fragile mental state, his perilous descent into the vortex of his own childlike mind had been inevitable, and, in the end, the lure of not being had simply become the easier of his two choices.

What she had not been prepared for was her own reaction to his death—and the unabated fury which surfaced afterward. She knew then that justice for Katlyn could not be hurried, nor would the debt owed to Arthur be satisfied by her payment alone. The day Arthur sealed his own fate was the day the fates of the others had also been decided.

Getting rid of Katlyn's helper had turned out to be more of an entertainment than the chore it first appeared to be. Currently, Claire Fava could be found at the bottom of a canyon, once someone put the pieces together. Her unfortunate mishap would serve as a catalyst for Katlyn Rome to make one last careless decision—that and the message from the kitty, which had been intercepted quite by accident.

Katlyn's husband should have known better

than to try to escape. That point had been made painfully clear. Too bad he didn't have the number of lives his cat had.

Unfortunately, disposing of his body was a more difficult task than the single swift act that required it. At first, burning the corpse seemed like the best answer, but that would have required dismembering it and moving it outside to the fireplace. Also, the roast would extend the period of danger. And the meat would not smell like porterhouse.

The wooded area beyond the grounds had been a much more reasonable choice. Mercifully, hubby's weight loss and a wheelbarrow found in the garage made it easy to get him there. Providence, and an ancient-looking pulley and crank found on the ground not far away, had pointed the way to a well only two dozen yards into the forest, a made-to-order burial vault. A time-consuming search eventually led to the deep, covered-up hole over which a small section of mortar was all that was left of the original structure. The rest of it had long since crumbled and fallen in on itself, into the depths below.

Once a thick layer of vines and old branches were cleared away, the reward was an opening large enough to receive a body. The shaft was a dark, decaying tunnel that smelled of rot. The bottom was not visible, even with a flashlight, and a small rock took almost four seconds to land in the water. The splash was a catalyst for other noises—wet, slithering sounds of creatures for whom the old well was the known universe. In response to the disturbance, an insect, half-spider, half-beetle, crawled out of the opening to challenge the visitor with its spit. Soon after, the head of an iridescent snake appeared briefly from an unseen crevice, then disappeared back into its nest, which was only inches from a plunge to certain death. A sample of water from the bottom of the well was as cold as ice. At that depth, it probably stayed frigid year-round. The low temperature would retard the decaying process. But the body was wrapped well and weighted, perhaps continuing below the surface of the water until it found permanent lodging in the aquifer itself.

After the well had been fed, the opening was covered again with layers of creeping vines. In a short time the well, and its guest, would cease to exist.

It would not be long now before the ladybug came to call.

And as always, the spider would be invisible.

The web, a masterpiece of engineering.

EIGHTY-FOUR

The clouds had been gathering energy for most of the evening. Katlyn entered the house as the light rain started and went right to her message machine. There were no calls from Fava, who had been out of touch since the previous night. Her absence marked the first time in weeks they had not talked before retiring. There was always the chance, of course, that she had met someone and decided to spend a private and romantic night. Still, it wasn't like her not to call. If something bad had happened she would never forgive herself for involving Fava in this madness.

She could not even locate Monty, who'd been missing for almost as long as Fava. He hadn't been the same since Jarrett returned him after the fire.

In the absolute quiet of the house, the den offered the most physical comfort, owing to its relatively compact size and soft fabrics. Seated near one of its windows, she watched the silhouetted branches of the tallest trees moving back and forth in a macabre dance. It was getting darker every second, and the wind had picked up.

"Jarrett. Fava. For God's sake, someone call me!" she said aloud, looking at the phone.

A sharp clap of thunder jolted her out of her malaise and made her feel unusually vulnerable. The guards outside suddenly seemed very distant. Something was wrong. She could feel it.

The quiet was rent again, this time by a brilliant burst of lightning, which was accompanied by a sheet of water that splattered the windows once and then stopped, as if someone had turned a hose on them and taken it away quickly. The sound of pebbles clattering on the roof came quickly on its heels, and sounded like ice pellets mixed in with rain. From the window on the porch she could see only as far as the tree line. The long drought had ended in a summer whiteout caused by a thunderstorm.

Over the rain, Katlyn heard a familiar call from just outside the door, like a newborn cooing, or a pigeon. Once she recognized it she let out a sigh of relief. It was Monty, home at last. She had no idea where he'd been going all the time, only that he did eat the food she put in a saucer out back for him when he failed to show up.

The moment she opened the door the cat bounded into the house looking cold and miserable.

"Monty, where on earth have you been?" she said when she caught up to him.

His fur was wet, matted down from rain, and there were small dots of ice on his back. He rubbed up against her leg with a small pleading noise. No doubt he wanted fresh food as much as affection. Abruptly, with a change of mood, he took off past her, and settled onto the couch to groom himself. In a minute, she saw that the place where he sat was getting soaked, and she went for a towel.

After Monty was dry, he rose on his hind legs and arched his back against her. He pressed his pointed chin against the side of her arm, just as he used to do with Matthew.

Absently, she stroked Monty under his chin. At first she touched the object around his neck without thinking about it, but then she stopped what she was doing to examine it. It was a collar of some kind, something they were going to put on him in case he ever got lost but they never got around to. This collar was quite primitive, though.

Her first thought was that some of the neighborhood kids had made sport of him. She put her finger under it and lifted it. It was a homemade band of silver foil. She tried to pry it away, but it was on tight.

"What is it, Monty? What did they do to you?"

Monty tried to pull away when she tugged on it. "I'm not going to hurt you, you know that, don't you?" she said to soothe him.

She got a better hold and scratched the shiny paper to see what was underneath and then realized only the outside was made of foil. It was wrapped around a thin piece of cotton cloth that had some firmness to it, like a strip of denim.

Monty protested when she cradled his chin in both hands, but he stayed put when she tilted his head up. The fabric was tied together under his chin. The makeshift knot came apart easily. It was still dry.

The collar weighed almost nothing in her hand. When she separated the two parts, the foil was folded several times around itself and was serrated along one edge, like the paper used to wrap candy. *Or a stick of gum!*

Swiftly, she brought the paper to her nose and smelled the familiar scent of cinnamon. It was only when she held it away from her again and flattened it that she noticed there was writing scratched into the shiny side.

When she brought the wrapper to the lamp, her hands were shaking so much she could barely hold it. There were only a few words, etched with a sharp point. The paper was wet from the rain, and the impressions hard to read.

She was finally able to identify the words. The message read: *Hoffman cottage. Matt.*

EIGHTY-FIVE

Claire Fava opened her eyes too quickly, then narrowed them to slits. Only two places could be so blindingly white, she thought, heaven or a hospital. From the way her head felt, she figured she could rule out the former.

The vertical blinds on the window were shut, but it looked almost dark outside, either dawn or dusk. There was a blue hospital ID strip where her wristwatch had been, but for some reason there was only a number on it and no name.

Cautiously, she pressed the bandage that was wound tightly around her skull, and winced at a pain like you got from drinking a frozen piña colada—or twenty of them—too fast.

More gingerly, she traced the path of the bandage to where it wrapped around under her chin. Going over it inch by inch, she eventually determined that only the left side covered actual wounds.

When she tried to sit up, she realized there was something wrong with her left leg. It hurt from her knee to her toes, exactly where a hard plaster cast now covered her. Her ribs felt as though they'd been barbecued—a searing pain when she inhaled.

What happened came back in a flash. She'd jumped out of a speeding car right before it went over a cliff. Her Volvo went over the edge, and turned into a fiery ball when it hit the rocks far below. She had gotten out in time, but landed on the equivalent of a giant emery board.

The industrious, perky face that bobbed into view belonged to a young nurse with the name RITA on her hospital ID tag.

"I'm not dead," Fava announced when their eyes met.

"Welcome back," Rita said, turning with a chirpy smile. "How's the head?"

"Like a piñata after a birthday party. Where am I? How long have I been here?"

"St. Claire's Hospital. You were admitted late last night." Rita checked her chart. "Cleared emergency at ten thirty-two, not that there was any way you would be able to remember."

"Unconscious?"

"Like a walnut."

"What time is it now?"

"Eight-thirty, the next evening."

"Friday?"

"Very good."

Out for almost twenty-four hours, Fava thought. "My God." She closed her eyes. Her lids felt like ten-pound weights. In her mind she could still see the place in the guardrail where her car went through. After she jumped out she lay on the road until a truck driver with onion breath came and carried her to his rig and she passed out.

Katlyn, she remembered with a jolt. She'd forgotten that before the accident she had been on the way to see her, to talk about someone named Bo and a videotape. They had talked every night until now. Katlyn would be wild with worry.

The phone looked as if it were a mile away and weighed a thousand pounds. Just to round things out, the molten lava in her head sent out a new helix of fire.

"What do you have for pain?" she asked Rita.

"You're already on it."

"Thank goodness. For a minute I thought I was suffering needlessly."

Fava settled back into the stiff hospital pillow with a groan. "What's the damage, anyway?"

"One fractured leg, a moderate concussion, multiple lacerations of the left arm, generalized contusions on the upper torso and abdomen," Rita recited from the chart.

"Does any of that translate into a punctured lung?"

"No. But it could feel that way."

"Trust me, it does." She tried to get up on one elbow. "I need to make a call."

Rita reached over the bed and brought the phone down to the bed near Fava. She turned in

time to see a man suddenly appear in the doorway.

"Sorry, no visitors," Rita said sternly, taking a
small protective step between the bed and the
door.

The man flashed a badge pinned to the
inside of his wallet, but Fava had already recognized the bone-weary but greatly relieved face of
Capt. Dan Jarrett.

EIGHTY-SIX

*H*e's alive!

There was no doubt. The handwriting on the note was Matthew's.

Katlyn felt herself spinning out of control. Matthew was alive and had been right next door in the cottage all the time. She leaped to her feet. In an instant headlong flight to get to him, she ran all the way to the back door and started to twist the knob. But before she went outside a glimmer of reason brought her up short.

Don't be stupid. Someone is in the cottage with him. Bo!

She let go of the door and ducked down under window level. It was a certainty that his kidnapper would at least be close by—if not with him. Possibly she had sent the note herself and lay waiting in ambush.

But Bo wasn't the only one in the cottage. Rachel lived there. *What about Rachel?*

The phantom thought stung her sensibility. *Rachel is Bo!*

She hadn't seen or heard from Rachel since the note she sent with flowers to the hospital. She remembered the picture of Bo that Jarrett found in his search at Glenmora. Rachel's pleasant but inelegant face looked nothing like Bo's. Would makeup have been able to disguise the differences?

A new realization sent her into a spiral of dread. If Bo had held Matthew prisoner since she had been forced to flee to the safe house, that meant she had been at the cottage since then. There was a good chance she had murdered Rachel. Poor, fragile, innocent Rachel.

If Rachel were dead, it must have been Bo who sent her the flowers.

Katlyn recalled the exact words in the note that came with them: *We'll see each other before you know it.*

Another, more macabre, thought raced into her mind. Bo and Combs were living there together, a second home for him, the place where the two of them plotted the murders of their young women—and maybe even brought some of them back to the cottage for torture.

You can't go there alone. Need help.

Katlyn was still clutching the note Monty brought and looked at it again. She wondered again if Bo was treacherous enough to have written it, as a way to get her to come to the cottage.

But only Matthew would have thought of writing it on chewing gum paper, she decided, something he might have had in his pocket when he was captured that Bo would have never thought to look for.

Matthew must have written the note and found a way to get it on Monty.

Katlyn looked across the yard at the cottage. There were no lights on. Bo could be spying on her at that moment, as she probably had been all along from that perfect vantage point. She was angry at herself for having done exactly the wrong thing and raced to the window. It was nearly dark, and the porch was all lit up. She'd made herself an easy target.

Staying lower than the bottom of the window, she turned and crept back to the wall switch at the entrance to the room and quickly flicked off the light. The only remaining light in the room came from a chandelier in the middle of the hall-way.

Crawling on her hands and knees, she made her way to the living room phone. She had memorized the special phone number Jarrett had given her and called it. The number rang five, six, seven times before she hung up despairingly. No message machine. She had always assumed Jarrett would be there when she needed him.

Quickly, she agonized over whether or not to get Frazier. There was safety in numbers, but involving the guards brought its own risks. Frazier seemed cool under pressure, but probably hadn't had any experience in this kind of situation. He was a stalking investigator and bodyguard. Any mistake could cost Matthew or her their lives.

She fervently wished Jarrett were there.

She would go alone, she finally decided. But not helplessly.

Seconds later she raced up the stairs to the bedroom and returned to the porch, holding the pistol Matthew had insisted she keep. With luck, she might still have surprise on her side.

Returning to the window she peered out cautiously. Her thin cotton shirt was soaked with perspiration, and she felt as if she were suffocating.

It was maddening not being able to run to him.

So near. So far.

The rain had slackened to a drizzle since she let Monty in. It had turned foggy, making the two properties look eerie, obscuring the boundary between them. Behind the cottage, the Hoffmans' mansion stood on higher ground and dwarfed the smaller gardener's building, Matthew's prison.

Katlyn reached over her head and turned the doorknob until it unlocked.

She uttered a silent prayer, and slipped outside into the mist.

EIGHTY-SEVEN

"Can you talk?" Jarrett said, as he pulled a chair over to the bed and sat down.

Even though she was in pain Fava saw the humor in the question. No one had ever needed to ask her that before. "I didn't fall on my mouth," she said, then grimaced. It actually did hurt when she tried to smile. "Is Katlyn all right?"

"She told me you were missing and asked me to find you. You didn't leave much of a trail once you left your car."

"A truck driver got me here. That's all I remember."

"Yeah, I know that now. But he didn't stick around, and he didn't know your name, either. You were brought in unconscious."

"Does Katlyn know I'm here?"

Jarrett shook his head.

"I have to call her now," she insisted. She propped herself up to use the phone. After she dialed, she closed her eyes, counting the rings. The answering machine picked up after the fourth ring. "Shit."

Jarrett was agitated. "Leave a message that she's not to go out of the house—in case she's still there."

Fava agreed and did so. She also left the name of the hospital and the room number.

"What *did* happen to you?" Jarrett asked after she hung up.

"Someone ran me off the road. I think it was the woman who was involved with Combs."

"Katlyn told you about her?"

"Yes, about the records you found at Glenmora. Bogardis must have known I was helping Katlyn and knew where I lived. I'm sure she's the one who tried to kill me last night. She came up from behind and kept chasing me. I couldn't lose her. She crashed into me twice, and the second time my car went out of control."

"What kind of car was she driving?"

"A big Mercedes, dark blue or black. Maybe new. They all look alike, those Mercedes."

"I don't suppose you got a plate number."

"Yeah, right. In my spare time."

Jarrett seemed lost in thought.

A new pain halfway back on her head made Fava wince. She lay down on her pillow and was afraid to move. Even the bandage hurt.

"It's weird, you know, when I was lying there on the road? It was completely dark and I couldn't feel anything. All I could think about was how stupid I was not to realize I was being watched." She stared at Jarrett and realized he still wasn't listening. "What's the matter?"

Jarrett focused on her again. "I was thinking that if I were Combs, or Bo, and I wanted to take out Matthew, I could have done it at any number of places I knew he'd be."

"Because they knew his schedule."

Jarrett nodded. "We found notes about him at Combs's apartment. They knew all his moves."

"What's your point?"

"Just that it would have been a lot easier to ambush him when he was jogging, like early in the morning, when no one else was around. But they waited to take him somewhere between his house and the party he was headed for."

Fava let the thought sink in. Jarrett was ahead of her. Then, what he was getting at struck her all at once. "Which means they needed to be someplace where they could watch him."

Jarrett's eyes darted back and forth, then came to rest back on Fava's. "Jesus Christ!" he cried, and bolted to his feet.

Fava forced herself off the bed again. "Somewhere the police would never think of looking for her."

Jarrett's face paled. The muscles around his jawbone were pulsing from grinding his teeth. "Goddamn it, we checked the place," he snapped angrily, "but only once, in the beginning." He reached quickly for the phone. "We checked the whole damn neighborhood."

Fava watched him punch in the numbers. Her mind raced. "The Mercedes," she said all at once, breathless.

Jarrett turned to her, clutching the phone to his ear while it rang.

"I don't know why I didn't remember it before," she said. "They have one, a big new Mercedes. And it's dark blue." She shot an ominous glance at Jarrett. "I saw it a couple of times. In the Hoffmans' driveway."

EIGHTY-EIGHT

In a pounding rain, Dan Jarrett switched on his siren, downshifted into second gear, and jammed the gas pedal to the floor. After a slight hesitation, the heavy Land Cruiser hurtled a double-yellow median and muscled past the first of two vehicles ahead of it. Holding the wheel in place, Jarrett put his flasher on the dashboard and reached for the custom-installed police radio. When Frazier answered he checked the clock on the dashboard. It was 8:45, almost dark.

"We entered the house when she didn't come to the door for the last check," Frazier said anxiously. "We saw her when she came back home about two hours ago, but we didn't see her after that."

"Why in hell did you let her out in the first place?" Jarrett roared in disbelief.

After an embarrassed silence, Frazier's voice was vastly diminished. "That's just it. We didn't."

Jarrett cringed in his seat. A Chevy Caprice slowed down ahead of him and he leaned on his horn.

"Her car is still in the garage, if that's any help," Frazier added.

Jarrett slammed his fist into the dashboard hard enough to rattle the glove compartment door. He was certain that Bo wouldn't have made a move on Fava if she wasn't prepared to take out Katlyn soon after. A sickening image filtered into his mind, Katlyn lying battered on the grounds or in the forest behind her house. In a few seconds her face became the face of his dead wife and glared at him accusingly. He was swept by the same overwhelming sense of loss and failure he remembered from before.

"Did she have any visitors?" he said gravely.

"No. Quiet, as usual."

Jarrett agonized over whether to call in Stryker and his men. He quickly decided the situation was too delicate for a legion of uniforms to descend on the cottage, even the well-trained SWAT teams. Katlyn might already be inside the cottage, and outsiders knew nothing about who they were dealing with in Bo. It would take time to bring them up to speed.

With alarm, he thought about Rachel Prescott, the flower lady.

He turned his attention back to the immediate problem. Frazier and his rookie weren't an answer, he decided quickly. They were untrained in situations like this, and if a fast decision was called for their reactions would be unpredictable. Also, he was only minutes away from the house himself. He pressed down on the gas.

"Check the whole place, but don't do anything else until I get there," he barked into the microphone. "Don't leave the area."

"Okay," Frazier said. "Also, you got a message that was passed along from central. Dunellen said he wanted to speak to you. Said it was important and left his number at home."

As soon as he got the number, Jarrett cut off Frazier. But the next call went to his own house. If Katlyn needed him she would have called him there. When the phone kept ringing he cursed himself. He'd forgotten to turn on his answering machine.

He tried Dunellen. While he waited for Guano to pick up, he saw a line of cars ahead of him through the high-speed wipers. The traffic was stopped for a red light.

He cranked the siren as high as it would go, and hoped the bastards coming into the intersection would hear him coming. He got more than halfway through it when a BMW convertible came speeding in from the left. There was no way he could stop in time, so he pressed his foot all the way to the floor. Behind him he heard the sound of crunching metal and did not stop to look.

Dunellen's raspy voice was in the tinny speaker, barely audible until Jarrett turned off the siren. The forensic expert said something crude and laughed at his own joke.

"Cut the bullshit," Jarrett yelled. "Why did you call me?"

"Okay, tight ass—it's the videotape. The one with the couple going at it?"

"You get some prints?"

"Uh-uh. Just the ones from everyone who handled it. But there was something inside it when I took it apart. At first I thought it was some kind of mold spore, which was strange. I doubt it could have gotten in there where it was manufactured because those places are manic about dust and anything else that can screw up reproduction. So I figured it might have filtered in from where the tape was shot."

"So what if it did? What good would that do?"

"Hey, give me a chance for Christ's sake. When I put it under the electron microscope it was pollen, not mold. A cluster of pollen grains. See, mold spores don't look anything like them. They're a fungus with a stalklike structure, whereas pollen are fertilizing bodies that produce male sperm."

"What about it? I don't give a shit what they do."

"Okay, so once I knew it was pollen, I matched it against hundreds of varieties that are indigenous to this area. Turns out it's from the Malvaceae family, usually found in the East, New England mostly. No way that stuff grows here unless it's brought in specially, except I found out they got some growing at the L.A. Botanical Gardens. "

Jarrett felt a huge letdown, but he was quickly

distracted. The road veered sharply to the left and, still traveling at high speed, he spun the wheel a little too late. He felt the truck lurch onto two wheels, but it steadied again. "So what?" he said when he regained control.

"So I don't know so what. I thought you might do something with the information. That's your job, isn't it? Isn't that why you gave me the fucking tape?"

"Yeah," Jarrett said more quietly. "I guess so." He had no reason to be pissed at Dunellen. But the plant family Dunellen named didn't mean a damn thing.

"No shit, Danny boy. You really ought to chill a little."

"Wait a minute," Jarrett shouted. "Is there some other name for that plant you just mentioned? Something less technical?"

"Yeah, but I doubt you ever heard of it. To horticulturists it's more commonly known as Pavonia."

Jarrett stared at the road, which suddenly opened up ahead. *Pavonia.* The name lit up like a neon sign in his mind.

"Fuck!" he shouted.

"What's the matter?" Dunellen squawked in the speaker.

Jarrett didn't answer him.

Dunellen asked the question two more times before he realized that he'd been cut off.

EIGHTY-NINE

Katlyn leaned forward into the driving wind and rain. She was soaked to her skin and trying to keep the pistol from getting wet. The lawn was soggy, and one of her thin canvas sneakers sank up to its top in a pool of water. She pulled on it, and her foot came out without it. Not waiting to retrieve it, she made a wide circle toward the building on the left side, trying to stay out of the direct line of view from the cottage window. Eventually she reached a place where the footing was more solid.

Since the moment she read Matthew's note, the idea that Bo had dared to keep Matthew prisoner so close to their house filled her with an added sense of outrage.

It was hard to understand how the police had missed the obvious location. Why hadn't they thought about the possibility? Why hadn't Jarrett? Why hadn't she?

A loud clap of thunder directly overhead charged her body with fear. It initiated another round of ice pellets which stung her unprotected flesh like an army of hornets. Distantly, she thought she heard the phone ringing in her house, but there was no possibility of turning back.

The rain slackened a bit by the time she got to the side of the cottage, and she ducked under a narrow eave. For a moment she felt secure, with her back against a wall and a small amount of protection overhead.

Slowly. Everything depends on surprise.

Fifty yards or so away, she saw the mansion entombed in the mist, like a giant mausoleum. Bo had the run of the entire estate, she understood, not just the cottage. Since the Hoffmans left she also had access to everything they owned, their car, their jewelry, all of which she could turn into money—she might even have their gun, if they had one. A video camera.

She hesitated, all at once unsure of which way to go. Bo could be in the main house while she kept Matthew prisoner in the cottage. In case he was discovered it would give her more time to get away. It also meant she could be watching the cottage, ready to follow any visitor into the smaller building from which there was no other exit.

Katlyn scrutinized the line of the cottage to where it ended. There was one window on her side. She would have to pass it to get to the door.

A new and fantastic idea entered her mind. Maybe all of her caution, as well as her fear of discovery, was unnecessary. Her reunion with Matthew might be absurdly easy. Matthew might have sent the message at a time he knew he would be alone, when it was safe. He might be waiting for her now, praying she would hurry. All she had to do was get inside and free him, then take him home and call the police.

NINETY

Even before he pulled into the driveway Jarrett could see that the TMU car was empty and its front doors open. He hoped against hope that the men would have good news for him, that they had found Katlyn. He noticed that his hands were shaking. It wasn't like him to shake.

He jogged up the path that led to the front door and was unnerved to find it unlocked when he pushed on it. He stepped quickly inside and drew his revolver, then dropped to a crouch. Staying low he crept into the foyer, his ears pricked for the slightest sound. The lights were on, but the place still felt strangely deserted. Satisfied there was no one in his immediate vicinity, he ventured forward into the hall, keeping his body as tightly compressed as possible. Compact man, compact target.

He paused at the entrance to the living room to his right, listened for a moment, then continued down the hall. The sudden sound of someone breathing right behind him made him wheel around. When he turned completely around he was facing the barrel of a pistol aimed directly at his forehead. The hand holding it was shaking. Behind the cocked .38 police special was the face of the younger TMU officer assigned to protect Katlyn, Jim Jordan. Jordan was looking at him in horror.

"Jesus, Jarrett, you scared the shit out of me," he said breathlessly. "Why didn't you say something?"

Carefully, Jarrett used one finger to guide the shaking barrel away from his face. He breathed easier when it finally found its holster.

"Listen closely, Jordan. If you ever point that thing at me again you'd better shoot. Do you understand me?"

"Yes sir. I understand perfectly," Jordan said, taking a measured step away from him.

"What a goddamn genius!" Several small bones in Jarrett's upper back cracked back into position when he stood up and adjusted his neck. "Any sign of her?" he demanded.

"No sir, nothing. It doesn't figure."

"Did you check all the upstairs rooms? The basement?"

"The whole place."

The sound of a door slamming at the rear of the house made them both jump. Jarrett spun around, and in a moment Frazier trudged into view. His shoes were soaked and mud-splattered up to their laces. Dark footprints on the light carpet traced his path back to the porch.

"Looks like she went out the back door. There are tracks leading away from the house. One mother of a swamp out there." He lifted a shoe as proof.

"How far did you follow the footprints?"

"Only a dozen yards. You said to stick close to the house." Frazier looked at Jordan and saw him still trembling. "What the hell happened to you?"

Jordan's face turned a deep shade of crimson. He looked as if he was about to piss in his pants. He turned away toward Jarrett, but the man had already started down the hall to the back of the house and was gaining speed.

NINETY-ONE

THE GARDENER'S COTTAGE
9:00 P.M.

The downpour that had helped to cover her approach had ended in a fine drizzle. The humidity was oppressive. Katlyn would have given anything for one cool breath of fresh air.

She pressed her ear to the clapboard siding and listened for any sound coming from inside the gardener's cottage. So far there was nothing. Leaning out from the wall, she could see where the clapboard ended. The window was six or eight feet short of that.

Keeping one hand against the wall, she sneaked slowly forward. She heard moaning from inside the building as soon as she was near the window. She went numb when she recognized the voice. Paralyzed with fear.

Matthew was in terrible pain. She could not imagine what it had taken to make him sound like that. She hoped that whatever it was had happened before, that he was not still being tortured.

Commanding herself to try to stay calm, she leaned forward toward the window and saw that the glass was missing. A large section of canvas had been stretched over the opening in its place, and there was no way to see what was behind it. Matthew was in there somewhere, only a few yards from her. Every instinct urged her to call out to him, but she didn't dare.

Reaching the back door, she was again rooted in place by a new round of pitiful cries. At least he was still alive, she told herself again and again. Also, if Bo was there doing things to him, she would be too preoccupied to know someone was approaching.

The door was made of aged wooden planks encrusted with paint and rotted where they met the ground. She pressed on it with the heel of the gun, but it didn't budge.

Pushing harder on the next try, she was able to move the door back a small distance, but the price she paid was a loud scraping noise.

After another push it was open enough for her to fit through. She stepped inside feeling her heart was about to explode.

NINETY-TWO

When the cottage door scraped opened, Rosa Bogardis stepped back into a closet which was halfway into the front room. She pulled the door almost shut and pressed her ear against it to listen. Her entire body tingled with anticipation, the way it did when she told Arthur what to do and he left to do it.

Kitty had done his work well, she mused. It had taken only a few minutes after the cat went inside for Katlyn to read the message and panic to set in. She had been watching her when she realized her mistake and darkened the back room, and after that, when she slipped out to the backyard and approached the north side of the cottage by an indirect route. Now her husband's wailing was a siren song that lured Katlyn closer. Katlyn Rome was so inept as a stalker, so totally out of her element.

One more for the well.

The second scraping noise announced Katlyn shutting the door behind her. She would let her get to the bedroom before she came out of the closet, let her be drawn to Matthew's touching lullaby. Once she went inside her back would present an easy target.

Bo heard the floorboard creak directly in front of the closet door and bristled with delight.

Ever so slightly, she put her hand on the back of the door and waited.

This is how Arthur felt, she thought.

NINETY-THREE

The room was lower than the ground on two sides and felt like a tomb. The oppressively high humidity had left the floor moist and slick, easy to slip on. Matthew's heartbreaking lament echoed in the dark space around her, rising and falling.

In the pitch black, Katlyn had to use her hands and feet in order to navigate the obstacles between her and the next room. Before proceeding forward she moved all the way to the right, and reached a wall which she used for support. Her outstretched foot contacted something in front of her, a padded bench or hassock. She went around it, and took a few more steps before her knee bumped into another low piece of furniture and she lost her balance. Quickly breaking her fall with both hands, she let go of the gun, which fell to the floor with a clatter. She got to her hands and knees to search for it, but she couldn't find it.

The noise it made panicked her. There was no more time to lose. Katlyn got to her feet and moved forward again. It was like swimming in a dark sea at night, not knowing what was swimming with her.

A heightened moan from behind the door chilled her. She wished she still had the pistol. She was sure she would have been able to use it the right way this time.

The door to the next room became visible in detail only when she was right next to it. She could make out that it was arched at the top, medieval-looking. The wood was studded with black hardware. A metal latch that felt like ice was worn smooth. She pressed it and it gave easily, and she slipped in.

The moaning came from her right in the darkness, below her.

"Matthew?" she said in a hushed cry. "Is that you? Where are you?"

Another mournful cry cut through the blackness.

No reaction to me, she thought. Delirious.

She moved closer and felt the edge of a bed and reached for him. "Matthew?" Her hand slipped across the surface of a blanket that was taut on the mattress.

He wasn't there.

When she finally got to where the moaning sound was coming from, she touched a small rectangular object—metal, not flesh—and she began to sob. She picked it up and brought it to her ear. It was a tape recorder, the source of his cries.

"Don't do this," she yelled at the top of her voice. She sank to her knees and rested her head on the mattress. "Please don't do this."

"A little late for that," a pleased, thin voice behind her said suddenly.

Katlyn started to turn, but something heavy hit her full force on the back of her head.

NINETY-FOUR

Jarrett made his way through the sloppy ground and estimated that it would take a long minute to get to the cottage if he proceeded the cautious way, by a circuitous route. If he saw or heard anything suspicious on the way, he could sprint the distance in a straight line in a fraction of the time. Circling the cottage he was grateful for the darkness. He would have waited even longer if he could have.

He could barely see the fence when he came to it. It was low and decrepit, dividing the two properties more symbolically than physically. Several of the upright posts had settled at angles into the ground, causing their connecting rails to fail. The unlatched gate was hanging by a single hinge. As if beckoning him to go on, the gate swung open in a gust of wind.

When he was well into the next yard, he saw something sticking up from the ground and stopped. A canvas sneaker. He picked it up and remembered that it was the kind Katlyn wore. He flattened his fingers against the sole inside and felt that it was faintly warm. She had come this way, and not that long ago.

NINETY-FIVE

Katlyn lay on her back on a hard, narrow mattress. Her wrists were bound by a tight metal wire that cut into her skin. Another wire around her ankles was painful but not as tight. The room was dazzlingly bright. She remembered she had lost the gun.

She had difficulty focusing her eyes when a face loomed up and floated over her, upside down.

"Wake up, little sleepyhead. Rise and shine," the smooth, thin lips said mockingly.

When the haze finally cleared, the image righted itself and smiled at her provocatively. It was the face in the photo that Jarrett brought back from Glenmora. *Rosa Bogardis.* Bo had hardly changed at all from when the shot was taken, the same sharp-angled features, elegant high cheekbones, the mole over the lip.

She had been saying it was too late for Matthew when she struck her from behind.

"Where is he?" Katlyn demanded.

Without warning, Bo's hand shot forward and grabbed her chin roughly. Bo's dark green eyes darted back and forth, examining every part of her face, as if she had found a rare jewel and was excited by each new facet she discovered in its depth.

"Where's that million-dollar smile now?" Bo said, delivering a stinging slap to Katlyn's cheek.

The blow shook Katlyn out of her stupor. She raised her head and felt her hair catch on something sticky where it had been touching the floor.

"Where's my husband?" She tried to wrench her head free from the strong grip.

Bo's other hand came at her from nowhere, but it was a half-hearted effort that landed only an insulting blow.

"In the well, of course. Where do you think?"

"What well?" Katlyn screamed. She yanked her head free and thrashed furiously against the wires which only cut deeper into her skin, forcing her to stop.

"Don't worry, he didn't suffer. He was asleep at the time—*sound* asleep." Bo stroked Katlyn's hair as if she were a doll. "I'll take you to him soon. I promise."

The way she said it had the ring of finality. There was no doubt any more about what had happened to Matthew. Katlyn felt as if she didn't have enough energy to breathe.

"Why did you have to kill him?"

"A little late to ask, don't you think?"

Nothing left. All over.

"Where's Rachel?" she murmured.

Bo's head rocked back and forth sadly. "A shame, really. Nice girl, Rachel. Lovely flowers.

Unfortunately, not very good at swimming with her hands tied."

Katlyn closed her eyes and pictured the poor young woman who only wanted to be a good neighbor. *I'm so sorry, Rachel.*

"You've understood the rules all along, haven't you?" Bo said right away.

Her face came so close that Katlyn could feel her warm breath on her cheek.

"Someone like you understands that there are certain occupational hazards attached to your job. That *was* what all the fighting was about with your dear departed, am I right?"

Vacantly, Katlyn wondered how Bo had been able to get close enough to hear what she and Matthew fought over. But it didn't matter now.

"And can you see what happened?" Bo said, suddenly furious. "He was right. You killed him, didn't you? Just like you killed Arthur."

"Arthur killed himself. And you killed my husband," Katlyn shouted, the injustice of Bo's words rousing her. She could only think about getting loose and smashing that hateful face.

"You took something that belonged to me!" Bo cried.

Katlyn realized what she was saying. Bo not only controlled the monster known as Starman. As bizarre at it sounded, she must also have loved Arthur Combs.

Bo raised her hand quickly in front of Katlyn's eyes. She had a knife.

Katlyn drew back when she saw it.

Bo grabbed a handful of Katlyn's hair and twisted it into a tight cord. She put the sharp end of the blade next to it, next to her skull.

"Arthur would have liked this," she said. "He was a big fan of yours."

NINETY-SIX

Bo waved the knife casually in front of her eyes, as though it were an innocent toy. "It's a shame, really," she said with a mocking smile. "It would have made a great news story. Too bad you won't get to broadcast it. Show biz," she chanted gaily.

On the bed, Katlyn stared past her, hardly hearing her words. This was the way it was going to end, but only after Bo taunted her some more.

"Did I tell you that hubby was an absolute pleasure in bed? I don't know how he was with you, but he was a tiger with me."

Katlyn remembered the videotape and felt sick. She didn't give Bo the satisfaction of a reaction.

"Of course, he wasn't as good as he might have been with his hands. You can understand why, I'm sure."

The longer Bo talked, the longer she had to live, Katlyn thought. *Keep her talking.*

"I don't believe you. He was just afraid."

"He was a sweet little boy, a perfect, obedient little boy—just like Arthur." She went to another place in her mind, then returned. "He loved me, that's why he did what I told him . . . all those other pretty ones . . . Bradley, Spiegler, Warren, Dureau, Janedis. He chose me over all of them."

Katlyn did not recognize some of the names. There must have been a lot more than people knew about. She thought of Fava, but kept her eyes riveted on the madwoman.

Bo leaned closer. Her eyes were dancing, and a new emotion swept her face. Suddenly she was enraged. "Until you took him away from me!" she screamed.

Her hand tightened on the handle of the knife, and she raised it over her head. Katlyn drew in a deep breath and locked her eyes on its point.

She could try to twist out of the way just before it cut her, nothing more. In the end it would be futile anyway.

The room and everything in it seemed to explode all at once with a deafening crash. Taken off guard, Bo screamed and ducked to the floor. The instant she felt the concussion, Katlyn coiled protectively on the bed. The powerful shock from outside made it feel like the entire building had been picked up and dropped again. Bits of wood and plaster were shaken loose from the ceiling and showered down on the floor.

"What is it?" Bo shrieked. She shrank back from Katlyn and looked all around her, terrified.

A second shock, as mighty as an earthquake, rocked the cottage to its foundation. Two large rafters overhead separated from the mortar that held them in place and slammed to the ground near them. The whole building seemed about to collapse.

"Stop it," Bo cried out. She covered her ears with her hands, still holding the knife.

The third concussion made the lights go out momentarily and put a giant crack in the back wall. A large section of the stonework near the top of the wall collapsed in on the room and became a pile of rubble. Katlyn pressed her face into the mattress to shield it from the debris that came raining down.

"No!" Bo cried out again. She frantically scanned the room for a place to hide. She was afraid to move, afraid not to.

Katlyn fought the wires on her legs and managed to push herself back a few feet on the bed, nearer the wall and farther away from Bo. She held her breath and waited for the next impact that would surely bring the building down on both of them. At least it would not be Bo who killed her, she thought.

With the fourth concussion, the most violent by far, the cottage seemed to come apart at its seams. Bo covered her head with her arms and screamed until her voice became hoarse. Above her, Katlyn heard the canvas window suddenly tear open and saw a body hurtle through it, feet first. Two legs passed over her head and landed on the floor. A body rolled a half turn to soften its fall.

"Jarrett," Katlyn cried when she recognized him.

Jarrett got to his feet and saw Bogardis in a pile of debris. She was not moving. He waited a few more seconds to make sure, then turned back to Katlyn.

"She murdered Matthew, she's Bo!" Katlyn shouted. "She murdered him!" Her eyes were awash in tears. She put her face on the bed and moaned. "Matthew. And the woman who lived here," she said, her words muffled with her mouth pressed into the blanket.

"Are you all right?" Jarrett shouted.

She nodded and he moved closer to her. He unwound the wire around her wrists first, then switched to her ankles. He looked up in time to realize that Katlyn saw something behind him.

"Watch out," she shouted. With her untied hands she pushed his shoulder to try to turn him around.

By the time Jarrett faced Bogardis it was too late. He started to reach for his holster but saw the knife already aimed at his chest, about to slice into his heart. She came at him screaming, mad with rage. Lurching to one side, his angle on her arm was bad, but he threw an off-balance punch with his fist anyway. It missed and landed high up on her shoulder.

He jerked away in Katlyn's direction, and Bo's blade brushed his side on the way past. The knife continued forward and found the mattress at Katlyn's feet, sinking in all the way. Bo lay on her stomach on the edge of the bed, hanging on to the knife's handle with both hands. She looked up at Katlyn, who was lying on her back only a few feet away, cursed her, then became intent on the knife again. In a moment, when she looked up again, her eyes opened wide in horror. Katlyn had already drawn her knees all the way back to her chest. She was coiled, ready.

"No more!" she cried with a vengeful scream. "No more."

Both of Katlyn's feet shot forward, aimed at the center of Bo's face. Bo opened her mouth to cry out, but waited a fraction of a second too late to react. Katlyn felt the collision of bone on bone as her heels struck their target solidly. One of them collapsed the ridge of Bo's nose, the other cracking a section of cheekbone and traveling higher to split her brow wide open. Bo made a sound like a balloon deflating, and became a motionless heap on the floor.

Jarrett looked at Bo, then back at Katlyn, who was breathless and still full of fury.

"I love it when you get angry," he said.

NINETY-SEVEN

Laurel Canyon
Three Months Later

Dan Jarrett slowed his completely restored Land Cruiser, which had recently added a gardener's cottage to its list of kills. At the top of the driveway, the asphalt turned to crushed blue stone, and the big tires crunched to a stop in front of the enormous residence that once had been used as a safe house. It seemed like a hundred years ago.

From the close distance he could see that the building had withstood the fire in good condition, even though at the time every living thing around it had been turned to ash. Miraculously, there were already new sprouts on some of the tree limbs and shrubs, and since the fall rains had come, parts of the lawn had started to revive.

When he stepped out of the truck he could see into the house through the open front door. Katlyn Rome was standing in the hallway, looking into the huge, empty living room in front of her, waiting for him to go in.

Her call that morning asking him to join her there had sent him into a frenzy of emotion, and he had been shaky ever since. Now, as he approached her, he again felt an attack of nerves. It was their first private encounter since he and the Land Cruiser blew away Bo and the building—and since the bodies of her husband and Rachel Prescott had been pulled out of the well.

In a short time the two of them stood together in the desolate living room, the memory of the last time they were there a pervasive presence that for the time being stilled any exchange.

Eventually, Jarrett broke the silence.

"Feels like the end of the world happened here."

She nodded. "It did—of one world, at least."

Jarrett struggled for something more hopeful to say. "Things are growing again, around here. I noticed them outside."

"Yes, I saw them, too."

She turned to him with a soft smile that made something in his chest flutter. There were fewer little lines here and there on her face than the last time he was with her, and fewer signs of the fire. The healing had finally begun, in a number of ways, perhaps.

"I think we made the right choice," he said, pointing to one wall.

She saw how low the smoke had gotten. A chest-high line of carbon had painted a level ring all around the room. The house reeked of carbon. Above them, the heat had left huge cracks

in the ceiling, but, as advertised, the structure
hadn't burned.

"We couldn't have stayed," he added.

Their escape replayed in Katlyn's mind. The
end, especially. "If we had you wouldn't have
caught Starman."

"The thought occurred to me."

After an awkward silence, Jarrett asked,
"Why did you want me to come?"

His directness startled her. But she should
have been used to it by then.

"I needed to see you. I'm not sure why,
exactly." She turned to face him, perceptibly
closer than a simple conversation between
friends called for. "Maybe for a sense of completion—like the psychologists say."

He didn't know how to respond, only that he
was in deep trouble. For the first time in a long
while he felt like a schoolboy with the homecom-
ing queen. He could smell her subtle perfume,
which was heated by the warmth of her skin. It
reminded him of tangerines—someone else's
skin had smelled like that when it baked in the
sun on the beach.

"I also wanted to tell you I'll be leaving soon,"
she said.

He felt the walls of the house suddenly fall in
on him, and she could see the disappointment
that immediately etched his face.

"I'm going back north."

"Back to your college?"

"They've offered me a full professorship. Pick my subject. A minimum of politics. At least, that's what they're saying. I don't think I'll have as much trouble handling them now."

Jarrett struggled. His experience with colleges was limited to three semesters at U.S.C. "What are you going to teach?"

"I haven't got the slightest idea. The truth is, I don't even know if it's going to work. I just know I need to get away."

When she looked up at him from such a close distance he could feel the heat coming off her body. He felt clumsy. He was painfully aware that there was no comfortable place to put his hands.

"Do they have phones there yet?" he said. "In case somebody might want to keep in touch?"

She smiled. "Yeah, some small hints of civilization have made their way in."

"Turns out, I'm leaving town for a while, too," he announced matter-of-factly.

This time she registered alarm.

"Someone I know has a problem she needs help with."

"She?" Katlyn asked, too quickly to hide her disappointment.

"The daughter of a friend I once had," Jarrett finally offered.

After a few silent moments, Katlyn said, "When do you get back?"

"Depends on what happens, I guess. A few weeks, maybe."

"Well, maybe by then—" she started to say, but never got the chance to finish.

It had taken some time, but Jarrett finally figured out what to do, with his hands, and with his mouth.

EPILOGUE

CALIFORNIA INSTITUTION FOR WOMEN,
STATE PRISON AT FRONTERA
Five Months Later

*R*osa Bogardis listened to the sound of heels approaching on the cold cement floor. She didn't stir. A square-faced female guard reached her cell door, looked in at the prisoner, presumed she was sleeping, then moved on. The guards didn't come as often as they used to, Rosa thought. After a few months of incarceration, her celebrity status had waned considerably.

In the unaccustomed quiet of her isolation, Bo felt a curious sense of calm. In some ways, things had gone better since her capture than she could have hoped for. For the first few weeks she was inconsolable at her prospects and came close to taking Arthur's course of action. Like his, her initial anxiety was made all the more hellish by an enforced withdrawal from drugs.

There had been other potential terrors, more immediate. Reprisals by other female prisoners were likely, given her association with Starman.

However, the seriousness of the charges against her, and the continuing media spotlight, forced the authorities to isolate her. Ironically, after that, she *was actually safer in prison than she would have been walking the streets of Los Angeles.*

Not surprisingly, her case had attracted a top lawyer with something to prove, and he had actually become more hopeful about her eventual fate as time wore on. For one thing, the case against her and Combs was purely circumstantial. The prosecution would be forced to make it on their history at Glenmora and the coincidence of the first part of her last name. But she had done nothing wrong at the institution, according to the official record, at least. And two letters in a last name were not exactly compelling evidence. Beyond that there was no evidence that she had ever associated with Arthur Combs after leaving Glenmora. She had made sure of that.

What happened at the cottage was, of course, another matter. The law in California was clear on kidnapping and murder. Under normal circumstances, a jury could send her to an early death by injection, for murder in the first degree with special circumstances.

As it was turning out, though, there was nothing normal about her circumstances.

For one thing, her long history of drug abuse could now be used to show she was not in full possession of her mind during the murders, so a temporary insanity plea was a good possibility. Even though that would not get her off, it was something to bargain with.

Also, despite the seriousness of her crimes, there was still a great deal of discomfort over the state putting a woman to death. Only seven women in California state history had been executed, and none in the past thirty years. And there had been only one in the entire United States since the death penalty was reinstated in 1976. This by itself would no doubt help keep the penalty from being the extreme option allowed under the law, her lawyer said. And that didn't take into account the anti–death penalty groups who could be counted on to help.

But the real clincher was something no prosecutor, judge, or jury in the world could ever have imagined, not even something her own lawyer could have hoped for.

At first, the changes in her body had repulsed her, but the more she realized their implication, the more she reveled in it. Now, after almost five months, it was getting to be impossible to hide her parting gift from Matthew, the one he had never been able to give to his dear, sweet Katlyn—the gift of life now growing inside of her.

The baby was going to make for a very interesting trial, she thought. A defendant in her last trimester would be something unprecedented for the judge and jury to deal with—especially in a capital punishment case. And all she had to do was sit tight and get bigger.

She could feel it moving inside her now, the cutie pie.

Having a baby was a better feeling than she ever expected.

She just knew it was going to be a boy.

She would have to call him Arthur.

PROLOGUE

Near the summit of the mountain, the students stood in a silent knot taking comfort in the proximity of each other's shoulders. Their teacher was higher up on the narrow trail, separated from the class by more than the physical distance between them. She could feel in her bones something was about to happen. For the first time in thirty years she was afraid of the children.

There was no doubt in her mind that she'd shown patience with the little girl during the climb, but when they'd arrived at the peak and she called for Jessie to step forward, Jessie refused.

The response came instead from the biggest of her boys, the self-appointed leader. As if he'd been waiting for the moment, he threaded his way through the group with a purposeful stride, his head cocked and his jaw thrust out at an impertinent angle. He carried a walking stick fashioned from a branch taken along the route.

As he walked, he lifted it off the ground and it became something else.

Now, before it gets out of hand, she admonished herself. "Get back there. What do you think you're doing?" she shouted to him.

The young man stopped, but did not retreat. Emboldened by his example, two other boys swiftly left the group to join him. Tentative at first, their confidence increased as their own passage succeeded without incident. In a short time the three stood together with their eyes fixed intently on her.

A shiver of anxiousness spread down the teacher's rib cage. Her apprehension derived not only from the menacing challenge to her authority, but the time and location chosen for it. Somewhere behind her, the trees opened up onto a thick granite ledge which jutted out into space to form the highest point in state. Where it ended abruptly, the mountain plunged to a ravine of jagged rocks far below. Even the thought of the dizzying height gave her vertigo.

"You three get back with the others," she called out again, puffing herself up to full size. Again they didn't move. If anything, their expressions became more defiant. In the gap between two of them she could see Jessie, the one who'd been the catalyst for the insurrection. Jessie stood rooted in place, her little melodrama calculated to keep her fellow revolutionaries incited. *Evil, disobedient child.*

"Jessie! You come up here right now, young lady."

"Leave her alone," the leader of the boys shouted back angrily. For emphasis, he lifted is walking stick in the air and pointed it in her direction.

Reflexively, she took a step backwards, then another. It was a serious mistake. As soon as she retreated, the boys moved forward a greater amount. The choreography of fear, of advance and retreat, had been established.

Don't let them see it.

As imperceptibly as she could, the teacher craned for a glimpse of the returning park ranger. The ranger had remained at the last rest stop to attend to stragglers and was nowhere in view. The class mother, who'd come along as a proctor, was with him, her own daughter among the chief complaints. The only other adult had stayed near the bottom with those who didn't want to climb. The teacher was now completely alone.

In the confusion of the moment, she silently prayed for someone to help her, then quickly realized that she must have said it aloud without realizing it. The three boys looked at each other with a sense of discovery and started forward again, their intention now clear.

"Stay back," she challenged them at the top of her voice, then saw them increase their pace and not stop when she did. When she realized what was about to happen, she stepped off the path, turned away, and plunged ahead into the trees.

Hide. Wait for the ranger.

Deeper in, she fled over ground that was a tangle of roots and the tops of boulders. Behind her somewhere, they were chanting her name. *Wilkens. Wilkens. Wilkens.* Their taunting propelled her on faster. Her legs were growing weaker with each stride. She needed to rest but couldn't. Her throat constricted and she gagged on fear.

Run . . . run to live.

The trees thinned for a small space where the surface became a naked ledge. After a few steps she failed to spot the thick layer of moss that began to cover it and was slippery from recent rains. The toe of one walking shoe skidded out from under her, and she spilled to the ground with a yelp of pain. In full panic, she scrambled to her feet and bounded headlong into another dense area of underbrush. By then she'd lost her sense of direction.

A hundred stiff thorns clawed at her sweater as she fled into a thicket of brambles. A few tore deeper, into the flesh on her arm. She shut out the pain and kept going. *So afraid. Worse than anything, ever.*

She had no idea how far she'd come when it suddenly became lighter and the vegetation gave way to solid rock. It was flat here and much easier to run. Something she remembered about this place skipped in and out of her mind, something dangerous she didn't have time to think about.

She looked over her shoulder as she continued to flee. She couldn't see or hear them any longer but was certain they were still behind her, somewhere.

By the time she saw what was right in front of her it was too late to stop, and she let out a blood-curdling scream that pierced the quiet at the edge of the earth.